WHY WOULD I LIE?

Certificate of Excellence

Awarded to

Adriana North

in recognition of outstanding scholastic achievement

Weston Preparatory School

Valedictorian

WHY WOULD I LIE?

ADI RULE

Scholastic Inc.

ISBN 978-1-338-82990-7

12 11 10 9 8 7 6 5 4 3 2 1   22 23 24

Printed in the U.S.A.   37
First printing 2022

Book design by Stephanie Yang

1

My best friend Wren and I sit in the school cafeteria, waiting for the bell. Bleary students in light woolen coats shuffle through the double doors, their eyes puffy, while sunlight glows from translucent windows. Everything is warm and golden. This moment, this still, soft space in which Wren and I sit together before the first bell, is when I get myself sorted out for the day. It's the second week of our senior year. I close my eyes and press on my temples.

Economics quiz. Should be fine; I can go over my notes one more time in study hall. I should also reread the end of Murder in the Cathedral, *just in case there's a pop quiz.*

My hair is damp from my post-run shower. A mile every morning, the Scruton Back Road loop, like clockwork. That's me. Clockwork. Emphasis on the *work*. I'm finally in the home stretch; this is my year. I just have to stick to the plan—perfect grades, perfect extracurriculars, perfect recommendations. Then a perfect launch, an upward trajectory at last, into the life that's always felt out of reach. No distractions allowed. Almost there.

Muffled clangs emanate from the kitchen, the smell of bread and tomato sauce and just a hint of industrial cleaner. It's not unpleasant. Wren peers at their phone and scribbles in a glittery notebook while I find myself absentmindedly drawing long lunch tables in my sketchbook, their plastic seats occupied by large-mouthed creatures with googly eyes. I had a "how to draw the Muppets" book when I was a kid, and now they find their way into all my doodles.

Wren has a creative mind and a sparkling personality. Me? I draw Muppets a lot.

"You should try something new today, Viveca," Wren says. They never look puffy-eyed or damp or bleary. They're always put together. Even though we both thrift, Wren pulls it off like a runway model, while I tend to give off raccoon-that-raided-grandma's-closet vibes.

I squint at their notebook. "Are you doing my horoscope again?"

They hold up a finger. "*Anti*-horoscope."

"Right." This is Wren's new thing. It seems to involve an awful lot of calculating, despite the fact that, from what I can tell, it just means doing the opposite of whatever the official daily horoscope says.

Wren circles something in their notebook, then looks up with a crooked smile. "Yep, definitely a day to throw caution to the wind." They light up. "Let's overthrow the administration! Or get wasted! Or learn how to knit!"

A voice like a Disney prince's, deep and luxurious, cuts through my laughter. "What time's the revolution?"

My head jerks upward. Someone I've never seen before is standing over our table, blue eyes sparkling. There's a light scent hanging off him I can't even describe, like jasmine, or the moon, or Saturday. "You must be a Leo," he says to Wren.

"Virgo," Wren says. "I just live dangerously."

He laughs. "Flipping the universe a big old bird. I like it." He has shining blond hair, broad shoulders, and delicate ears. The fairy-king-slash-Greek-god extends a hand. "I'm Jamison Sharpe."

Wren laughs and shakes Jamison's hand. "Wren," they say. "Just Wren." Wren's last name is Beagle, but apparently they're being all mysterious right now. "Are you new?"

Jamison nods. "Yep. We just moved here from Paris." He says it casually. *Paris. No big deal.*

He turns to me for the first time, and I give a little start of surprise, like I've just won his attention in a lottery.

"I'm Jamison," he says.

"Viveca." Why am I grinning like a nitwit?

He leans in, delighted. "Viveca? Not Viveca North?"

". . . Yes?" The tips of my ears are getting hot. Crap. It's probably super obvious. "You've heard of me?"

Jamison winks and points to the bulletin board next to the lunchroom's double doors. At the top, bright cutout letters that look like they escaped from a kindergarten classroom spell out *Race to the Top!* My name crowns the short list posted below, the Senior Top Ten.

Viveca North. I can see it if I squint. My name has been destined for the top of that list since I was a freshman. Since eighth grade at West Bore Junior High, when I convinced Mrs. Halbert to let me do an independent Algebra I course a year early. Since fourth grade, when I won the county spelling bee—*obstreperous*, thank you very much.

"Looks like you're headed for that number one spot," Jamison says.

"I mean—I'm *in* the number one spot," I say. Wren gives me a look like *Really?* What, did that sound snooty? It's true, though. Why would Jamison say I was only "headed for" valedictorian? It's a little thing, but I can already tell he's the kind of person who means what he says. My skin prickles, and I feel the rosiness drain from my face. Who is this guy?

Jamison laughs. "Well done, Viveca North!" He adjusts his army-green messenger bag. "Looks like we have a lot in common. Back in Paris, *my* name was in that shiny number one spot."

Yeah, well, that spot's already taken here, I think. Okay, *that* was snooty.

"At my old school," Jamison goes on. "My old *lycée*, I should say."

Wren leans forward. "Wait, so that thing about Paris—is that really where you come from? It's just you don't have an accent."

"Oh! Sorry, no, not at all," Jamison says with an air of modesty, shaking his head. "I'm from LA. I've just been in Paris for the last year or so."

"Ah, okay." Wren's face is calm, but I know they're thinking about the half dozen French comic books in their backpack they're just dying to geek out with someone about. Too bad I took Russian.

Jamison grins and swivels his hips toward the door. "Well, it's great to meet you two. I hope you'll show me the ropes. I haven't made any friends yet." Then he makes eye contact with me. It's intense, but I'm not grinning anymore. To be honest, he's kind of creeping me out. "Although I know you're busy with academics, Viveca," Jamison says. "I know how much work it is to stay on top." His tone is gentle, but it rubs me the wrong way. He doesn't know anything about how hard I work.

Then, with a bright smile, he's gone. He breezes away through the double doors, the *Race to the Top!* list fluttering in his wake.

"So *this* year just got a little more interesting," Wren says. "Did you see that perfect hair?"

"Yeah. And perfect grades apparently." My words come out snarkier than I want to let them.

Wren snorts. "Wait, are you *jealous*? Of the charming new guy?"

"No, I just—he had to bring up the fact that *he* was valedictorian at his old school. Like he already earned it *there*, so now he deserves it *here*. Instead of me." I flop my head down onto the table as the homeroom bell rings. "It sounds petty when I say it, I guess."

"It's not petty," Wren says as we gather our stuff. "It's adorable. But I do think you're too stressed, Viveca. Are you worried about your Everett interview tomorrow? Because you're going to kill it, my friend. You're going to murder that interview in the first degree."

"Thanks." I hope they're right.

Wren wiggles their backpack on. "Besides, it's only October.

Nobody's been named valedictorian anywhere yet, not until the end of third quarter."

"Yeah," I say, but the moments replay in my mind, Jamison's words. *My name was in that shiny number one spot . . . I know how much work it is to stay on top.* Was that a challenge? What if he went to some fancy genius school—sorry, *lycée*—and finds all our classes super easy?

Wren skips beside me as we head through the lunchroom doors and turn left into the crowded hallway. "Maybe you should ask Jamison out. Defuse some of this angst or whatever."

"Maybe *you* should."

Wren smirks. "I mean, not gonna lie, I would ride that all the way to town."

I adjust my backpack. "You've never ridden anybody even half-way to town."

"Except Principal Washington."

Okay, I laugh. Wren knows how to crack me. Maybe I am starting to feel the stress of senior year. After school today, I'm tutoring a sophomore who's worried about geometry, then a freshman having trouble getting solid on his state capitals. Not to mention looming scholarship application deadlines and my online editing work. Oh, and, you know, my actual homework.

But I've got them covered. I've got it all covered. College is so close I can smell it—the fresh scent of three hundred miles between me and this town. The first North to escape. The first North to be valedictorian.

. . . Unless it's Jamison Sharpe.

6

2

Everett College is not famous. It's not Ivy League. Its mascot, the Fighting Wood Duck, isn't familiar to the average person; its campus isn't exciting or venerable. Even the Everett logo is slightly forgettable—two cranky lions cradling a stalk of wheat. But I know those lions well; I've been staring at them for four years. In my imagination, those lions are majestic, mighty beasts with roars like jet engines and the souls of poets.

Yeah, okay, I never claimed to be good with metaphors. But the point is, Everett College isn't just any old college to me. It's magical. It always has been. I know it's probably populated by the same stressed-out students and jaded professors as every college, but I can't help it—for my whole life there's been this glimmering Everett-shaped glow in my mind when I envision the impossible: life after West Bore.

I was over the moon when the glossy advertisement came,

addressed to me personally, crowned by those majestic, grumpy lions. It was separate from the information I'd already requested, meaning I was on a *list*. A legacy list, because of my mom.

Usually, that flyer is pinned to my bedroom wall, but now that my admissions interview is just a few minutes away, it adorns the front of the manila folder sitting next to me on a study table. There's also a nearly twenty-year-old photo paper-clipped there, and splashed across the front of the folder are the words *Everett College!* in hand-drawn glitter font made possible by Wren's impressive marker collection. Wren says glitter is good luck. At the very least, maybe some sparkle will rub off on my interview.

I'm in the Elton Prep School library, sketchbook open, doodling. It's how I think; therefore it's not a waste of time. I'm not worried, exactly—I've notched nearly flawless grades and curated my well-roundedness to become the glowiest of glowing candidates—but this interview is *important*, so I guess I'm feeling the weight of it. I'll be glad when it's over.

As my pencil scratches and smudges, I'm ticking boxes in my head: application, SATs, essays, letters of recommendation, video interview, financial aid forms. Now that my interview is imminent, I can mentally tick all but one of those boxes with big, fat permanent-marker Xs. The last box, the one with the dollar signs, I'm trying to think about and not think about at the same time. It's not going well. Mostly, I'm staring at the photo clipped to my folder.

In the picture, Mom and her friends are gathered in front of Everett's main dormitory in low-rise jeans and trucker hats. She's dead center, wearing messy braids with a forest-green Everett College sweatshirt hanging off her, her arms around people on either side. Freshmen, just starting out. They're pressed into one another, smiling, limbs entwined or thrown carelessly toward the sky, balanced and precarious, as though any moment the pose could collapse and all of them would tumble to the grass in a laughing heap. On the back of the picture, Mom wrote, *Everett. Where it begins!!*

It. Happiness? Success? Friendship? Life?

. . . Everything?

I want *it* to begin for me. I want it so badly it makes my teeth vibrate. My life in West Bore hasn't exactly been a raging river of success so far. I mean, yeah, academically I'm killing it. I got into prestigious Elton Prep after all. But that's also kind of the point. Grades are nothing more than a means to an end: Everett's sunny campus, a busload of friends, a clean slate, and all the possibility in the world. Everything Mom lost out on before she even became a college sophomore, when she died having me.

Now I'm left with this photograph, this frozen but incomplete moment, and the branded sweatshirt Mom is wearing in the picture. I don't wear it every day, or even often, but I'm wearing it today.

I flip the photo over and look at the writing. *Where it begins!!* It began for my mom at Everett College, and it's going to begin for me there, too. I know it.

"Something by Sharad Joshi," a voice twinkles over the soft thud of the library door closing. "Ooh, or Oscar Wilde."

I look up from my table. Jade Bowman, Min Park, and Dylan Boyle have bounced in, perky drama club energy swirling around them, rustling the pages of the magazines on a rack by the door. Wren's friends. Nothing to worry about, but not exactly people I'd call out to and wave at, either. Our spheres touch but don't overlap.

They don't acknowledge my presence, but I still pull my sketchbook toward me protectively like a raccoon guarding its trash. Dylan in particular makes me uncomfortable. We both went to West Bore Junior High, so although we weren't in the same class, there's a good chance he knows about my seventh-grade freak-out. If he were going to regale everyone with the story and humiliate me, he probably would have done it by now, but still. I try to avoid people from junior high here—there aren't that many of us, since admission to Elton Prep is so competitive, plus the town pays our tuition, so they can't afford to send more than one or two a year—but it's not like the school is enormous. Dylan's running his fingers over the spines of a row of paperbacks, looking around without aim as Jade and Min pile thin books on one of the study tables. For a fraction of a second, Dylan's blotchy face turns my way, and I suppress a shiver.

Nope. *No*, Viveca, we are not going down that road again. See? He's not even looking at you anymore.

I fix my eyes on my sketchbook. Back in seventh grade, I wasn't used to dealing with competition, and I didn't exactly handle it well. The mental itches from that time, the pinpricks of shame, are just about gone now. Just about. But I dream of a fresh place where I can erase them entirely—that Everett-shaped glimmer.

The drama kids settle around their table and start flipping through books. Hilarious books, judging by their reactions. I sink my neck farther into my hoodie and leaf through the documents in my folder. Wren has tried to persuade me to try out for plays, as though there's any universe in which that is a rational suggestion. I'm as comfortable on a stage as Wren would be in a corporate cubicle. Besides, plays don't look any better on a résumé than other arts stuff that doesn't suck up enormous amounts of time.

My phone chirps an alarm that makes my organs do backflips. *It's time.* I pull off my sweatshirt and grab the folder. At the back of the library is a pod of semiprivate cubbies with desktop computers, and I settle at one, smooth out the nice shirt I ironed this morning, and check my hair in my phone's camera. As usual, I won't be winning any beauty contests, but I'm clean, tidy, and pleasant— check. Then I fire up the library computer, hop on to the Everett College site, and wait in the virtual admissions lounge for my interviewer to admit me.

"Good afternoon, Viveca." She's punctual. Older than I'd imagined, with a friendly expression that indicates there's nothing she'd rather be doing than talking to me, right here, right now, which of course can't be true. People are always lying in small ways. "I'm Anne Gagnon," the interviewer says, "dean of admissions here at Everett."

Holy crap, the dean of admissions? I understand it's usually alums who do these interviews. But I stay composed. "Hello. Thank you for speaking with me."

"It's my pleasure," Ms. Gagnon says. Sure it is. I expect her to look down at a cheat sheet, but she doesn't. She leans forward, fingers woven. I *feel* like we're making eye contact, even though we're both just looking at our screens. "So tell me, what draws you to Everett College?"

And we're off. The questions are slight variations on a standard list I've studied and prepared for. I'm flying. She nods at my answers.

"You're thinking psychology?" she asks.

"Yes, I think so."

She nods. "That's a popular major."

Popular—is that good?

Ms. Gagnon smiles. "What do you love about psychology?"

Love? About psychology? I'm thrown. I don't love psychology. Do people love psychology? I don't know what to say, but I have to say *something.* "Uh . . ." I start, trailing off in a quiet panic. How important is this question?

"You don't have to answer," Ms. Gagnon says to the glassy-eyed, openmouthed grouper fish that is me right now. "And, of course, you don't have to choose a major as a freshman. I was just curious."

My confident grip on this interview is slipping a little. I blink, close my fish mouth, and inhale through my nostrils. "Psychology is my best class," I say, which is the truth. I took college prep psych last year and had over a one hundred average. Mathematically, that shouldn't even be possible. That's how much I killed it in psychology.

"I see," she says. Then there's a brief pause, like she's giving me room to keep talking. When I don't, she changes the subject. "Well, how about you tell me about volleyball?"

"Volleyball?" For the tiniest of moments, I'm stunned back into fish mode. But then I realize she's launching into my extra-curriculars. Good. I'm proud of that section of my application. One season managing the JV volleyball team, a stint as a science reporter for the school newspaper, an art class at the rec center—I am a well-rounded machine.

My responses sparkle as much as the cover of my Everett folder. I use buzzy words like *teamwork, integrity, responsibility, challenges*. I guess I talk about the art class a little too long, because now she looks really interested, leaning in with an inquisitive smile.

"Do you have any of your drawings with you?"

My eyebrows skyrocket. "My, uh, drawings?"

She waves. "Oh, it's not important. You just seem very authentic when you talk about your art."

Yeah, so I'm not going to be overanalyzing *that* comment for the next five hundred years. I clutch my sketchbook under the desk. "No, I don't have any drawings with me; I'm sorry."

It's true that I did actually enjoy that art class at the rec center; I wished I could go back the next semester, but there wasn't enough time. Never enough time. Still, the last thing I need is for the dean of admissions to be subjected to my amateur portfolio of creatures.

"That's fine." Ms. Gagnon looks down, and as I study her slightly frowning face, I feel like it's not fine. Not the drawing thing, but— something is wrong. With me, apparently.

What's going on? My brain zips. Did I give a disappointing response? Is psychology a bad pick for some reason? Do I not have enough extracurriculars? I've done so much research about the application process—this just isn't adding up.

"Well," the dean says, looking up. "It's been a pleasure speaking with you, Viveca. Do let me know if you have any questions, or if you'd like to add any information at any point." She says it in a final sort of way and again leaves a little room for me. But I'm an untethered astronaut, my grasp on this interview slipping away into space.

And with a twist in my guts, I realize why that is. I can see it in Ms. Gagnon's dulled eyes, the fakeness of her smile. It hits me all at once.

I am depressingly *average*. I didn't know that until this moment. I rehearsed my responses to all her questions—answers that, now that I think about it, I'm sure sounded just as cliché as her interview. Sure, my grades are exceptional, but they're all I am. I'm not a volleyball fan or a journalist or an artist or even *popular*; I'm a walking report card. What could I possibly bring to Everett College? Why would they want me? All my work, all that *time*, isn't enough after all. My application might have made me into something glossy in the corner of the dean's eye, but looking at me head-on? I'm just not memorable.

I feel sick. Ms. Gagnon lets the space close with another smile, saying, "Thank you for your time today, and for your interest in Everett."

"I should add," I begin, not knowing how to finish the sentence, just grasping at the air, pushing aside the little jab in my mind that I should have remembered to thank her before she thanked me. *I should add . . . I should add . . . What makes me special?*

"I'm the Elton Prep valedictorian," I say, a flood of warmth spreading over my skin.

"Oh?" Ms. Gagnon perks up at this. "That's quite impressive." She makes some kind of mark on a paper. "Yes, you definitely should have included that information. But I imagine it was too early to know when you filled out the application."

"Yes," I say, not adding that, technically, it is still too early to know. *Not that I have anything to worry about*, I tell myself. *If there's one thing I'm sure of, it's that I'm going to be valedictorian. Definitely.*

Then I remember that new guy, Jamison Sharpe.

. . . Probably.

"Again, let me know if you have any questions," Ms. Gagnon says, more chipper now. "You'll be hearing from us."

"Thank you," I say. "Thank you for your time."

Her window blips closed, and I collapse back against my chair. *Done.* Box ticked. This is the moment when my stress should be flowing away in blissful rivers of light from my shoulders and my forehead and the sore places where my jaw connects to my skull.

Except it's not. Most of the interview went as I'd hoped it would, but it has just made me feel hollow. And hungry. Will she question my line about being valedictorian? Probably not. It makes sense; my grades are where they should be. And why should I worry about it, anyway? My name is at the top of that top ten and it's going to stay there. The hollow, hungry animal inside me isn't going to give it up. Not when Everett College is so close.

I touch the old picture of my mom. Would she be proud of the interview I gave just now? Would she be impressed by my application? Would she tell me stories about Everett if she could?

Mom and Dad didn't meet in college. They knew each other before, in grade school. Mom tried to soar away from here, taking that first flight from Elton Prep—a smart kid from West Bore like me—and alighting for one brief year at Everett. But it didn't take. She made the mistake of coming home, just until she could get a job in the city to help with tuition, just to look after Grandpa during his chemo. It was supposed to be a pause, but West Bore had other plans; she never left here again. Got stuck with duty and debt and, eventually, Dad. See, West Bore is like that. It's a flypaper town.

But it's not going to stick me.

3

It's almost dusk when the late bus wheezes to a stop at the end of my driveway. Some days, I'm the only person on the late bus. The driver, Mr. G, has a melancholy smile and round shoulders. One time when I tripped up the steps, he called me *poulaki mou*, which I don't know the meaning of, or even what language it is, but the way he said it felt kind. I mean, life would be infinitely better if I had a car and a license, but I don't mind rides home on Mr. G's bus. He's one of those comfortable people. Someone your instinctual lizard brain tells you to run toward, not from, in a crisis. That doesn't mean he's not a serial killer. But you've got to trust some people, don't you? So I'm told. I'm working on it.

Our driveway is long, curving away from the road and up the hill. It's a nightmare to shovel. I shouldn't really do it alone, but ever since Wren's grandmother died of a snow-shoveling-induced heart attack two winters ago, I've taken over the responsibility. It's just

Dad and me at our house, and he's one of those Men™ who will push until he keels over rather than let nature win. I don't think I could haul his behind out of a snowbank. And I definitely couldn't pay the hospital bills.

This afternoon, though, it's autumn all the way up. I pull a little folding knife out of my bag, what Dad calls a jackknife, and cut some of the hardy Queen Anne's lace that still lines the driveway. My grandfather kept a jackknife in his side pocket, my aunts in their purses, my dad in his bulky, impractical wallet. I run my thumb over the two lopsided letters gouged into the side of the casing, *HP*, Hannah Pinchuk. Mom, before Dad.

Obviously, knives are banned at school. Not just banned like permanent markers and spaghetti straps—knives are *very* banned. *Spectacularly* banned. But my jackknife is one rule I break. It's useful. Besides, why would anyone ever have reason to search the backpack of the presumptive valedictorian?

As the driveway curves at the top of the hill, our house comes into view. Dad's truck is there. I never know if his truck is going to be there until I turn this curve.

Ruckus starts barking, dashing from one end of his muddy run to the other. "Rawp, rawp, rawp!" I bark back at him. He leaps and prances, his yellow tail a blur against the brown trees. I stoop to unlatch his collar and he's up, paws on my shoulders, tongue everywhere, still leaping. For a big dog, Ruckus is awfully good at getting airborne.

"Settle down, bud," I say, like that's going to do anything. People are Ruckus's absolute favorite thing, which was something Dad didn't count on when he bought him from that shady woman in the Market Basket parking lot. Dad thought he was getting a security guard, but Ruckus had other plans.

As soon as I open the screen door, Ruckus barrels into the house. He skids to a stop at his water bowl and slurps. I throw the flowers into a glass of water and grab a banana, then toss my bag onto the kitchen table and unzip the big pocket. In my *Everett College!* folder is a stack of forms, neatly paper-clipped and half filled out.

Financial aid. I printed it out at school, two copies, and meticulously completed all the "student" sections. The only thing left is for Dad to fill out the "parent" parts. That's the tricky bit, as Wren would say. For the last few weeks, this paperwork has lived in my bag. The moment to ask my father just hasn't seemed right yet. I don't know if it would have been easier or harder before he lost his good corporate job, but that ship has sailed, anyway.

I paw through the mail. Nothing for me. Nothing embossed with the grumpy lions of Everett College, not that I can expect anything for weeks yet. I scan out of habit, just in case they need me to do something else, or they've sent more information, or whatever. If I can only get in, if they'll only accept me, I'll find a way to get there, to pay for it, to flap away from West Bore—not like a baby bird, like a pterodactyl.

"Hey, princess," calls Dad's voice from the living room. "Come tell me about your day."

"Yep, just looking at the mail." I toss the junk mail and pause over a glossy postcard addressed to Mr. Leslie North. Nobody but bill collectors and the Elton Prep parent database calls my dad Leslie; even at the bank, he's Buck. *Don't forget to order your student's yearbook!* the postcard reminds him.

"How's the store?" I ask as I saunter into the living room and settle on the vinyl arm of the couch. He's in his favorite recliner as usual. After a day on his feet at the dollar store, it's all he can do to slouch home, squash down into that chair with his phone, and spend the evening fighting fruitless battles on social media.

"Visit from corporate," he says. "They're very impressed with our numbers. Told me I'm the top manager in the state."

"Nice." I nod like I believe him.

So here's what I haven't told Wren. Or anybody. Because it feels like something that people would end up making about me, when it's not about me at all.

My dad is a liar.

We're not talking about *Yes, I remembered to water your plant* lies. We're talking about *Yes, I own a water park* lies. Does he really think his underlings at Dollar Garden believe he pulls in $3K a month from online auctions? Or has a black belt in judo? Or went to Idris Elba's New Year's Eve party?

On some level, I always knew Dad was lying to me. He *had* to be—some of his lies didn't even line up with each other, much less reality. But it was around fifth or sixth grade when I started to realize that meant that the universe itself wasn't as solid as I thought. I spent a lot of time back then trying to make the world make sense, to home in on what wasn't *real* whenever Dad was speaking. Then, eventually, I started questioning everyone else's words, too.

My mind drifts in a bad direction, to seventh grade and the time I fractaled my way out from a shaky kernel of suspicion, forming an intricate spiral of increasing chaos that ended with one of my classmates, Jackie Boynton, changing schools. *Don't go there.*

I've learned to coexist with my dad's lies since then. They're largely harmless, just embarrassing. Inside, I hate it. I *hate* it. He lies about how much he makes, who he knows, what he had for *breakfast*, for god's sake. Mostly the lies just sparkle briefly to life and then dissipate, like tiny stupid fireworks. But sometimes they ignite—like when he claimed to be a certified accountant and actually got some clients two tax seasons ago. That's when I get stuck covering for him, telling people I don't know where he is, locking the door. Stomping out the flames.

"How was school?" Dad asks, staring at his phone.

"I disproved relativity," I say. "Everybody cheered."

"That's great," he says. A few years ago, I started telling my own lies back to him. Big, obvious ones that nobody in any universe would believe. It's like I decided that my dad and I do this thing where we tell each other outrageous falsehoods. Like a bonding ritual.

I hand him the postcard. "This came for you."

He looks up from his phone. "Oh." There's this minuscule moment where he notices I'm wearing my Everett sweatshirt, then sees me noticing him notice it, and we have this flash of a standoff about it. Dad's not a fan of college. I should have thought to take my sweatshirt off.

He looks down at the postcard. "You want a yearbook?"

I shrug. "I guess not. Or whatever."

Dad frowns. "Sixty dollars! Good lord." He slips the postcard into the catchall pocket on the side of his recliner.

And with that, I've missed my moment. Again. He'll be in no mood to fill out financial aid forms when his daughter is wearing a college sweatshirt and yearbooks cost sixty dollars. It doesn't make sense, but that's my dad.

"When I was a senior, I got an award for music," he says. "Did you know that?"

"Nope."

"Top music award in the school." His face mellows like he's reminiscing. There was a time in my life when I would have asked him what instrument he played. But he doesn't play any, and there was no award. Now I can figure that out on my own. "I was offered scholarships," he adds. The phone grabs his attention again. "This jackass," he mutters, and then he's furiously tapping.

I head to my room, grabbing my bag and the Everett folder on the way. Ruckus bumbles along with me and we settle at my desk, me in the broken rolly chair and him in a waggly pile on the floor. I try to focus on my to-do list and put the financial aid forms out of my mind until tomorrow. *Swoosh, swoosh, swoosh,* three edited term papers zip along back to paying clients from freelance sites. *Ding,*

I text schedule reminders to my real-life tutoring students; then I start to type up a summary of a *New York Times* article that's due Monday in economics.

An email chimes; a message from Ms. Racine, my English teacher: SCHOLARSHIP OPPORTUNITY! I open it even though I've already applied for an awful lot of local awards and a few highly specific national ones, with nothing too promising on the horizon. I'm hoping for a nice offer from Everett—maybe the Presidential Award Scholarship—but at this point, everything is up in the air.

Dear Students,
Please check out the Pinniped County Futurists' essay contest!
They only run this contest once every five years, and it's only
open to seniors. I think you all should give it a shot!
Ms. R

Ms. Racine has cc'ed a few other seniors, but not everyone, so I'm intrigued. It's not a long list, and it's mostly people I'd name as the best writers in the senior class, even though not all of them are in AP English. I do let a derisive snort escape when I notice j.sharpe@eltonprep.edu on the list of recipients. But I click the link.

It's a sleek website—almost too sleek for my outdated laptop to handle; subtle scroll effects jerk their way through the header, and polished photos ooze their way to visibility.

Pinniped County Futurists—Current Scholarship Contest
Open to all high school seniors.
Please respond, in no more than
1,000 words, to the following question:
How do you see the world?
All entries must be submitted by January 31.
First Prize: $20,000
Second Prize: Farsight the Futurist Walrus plush toy

"Oh my god," I say aloud, not meaning to.

Who are these Pinniped County Futurists? The website text is sparse and a bit opaque. They offer different prizes and things each year, but the high school scholarship is the biggest. It happens once every five years. They seem to be an exclusive but not very splashy organization of people who like to—think. They think about the future. Well, I'm certainly a pro at that.

I stare at the screen, unable to really understand the number twenty thousand. Still, it twangs a memory like a rusty guitar string. One day at the beach, when I was small, I heard an ex-girlfriend of Dad's mention something about ten thousand dollars in my college fund that had been left to me by Grandpa Pinchuk. To this day, I don't know if that money exists. I don't know if it was ever real, or if Dad spent it, or if it's waiting for me to turn eighteen. And for some reason, I don't dwell on it. More like I *can't*—there's a wall there in my brain. I definitely haven't talked to Dad about it. What would be the point? Sometimes the possibility is more comforting than the reality, like Wren dreaming of the big city.

I create a new document, *PinnipedCountyEssay*. At the top, I write *The World of Viveca North*. Wow, what a crappy title. Off to a good start.

I sit back and stare at the screen. A six-word prompt. A thousand-word limit. *It's just another essay*, I tell myself. I've written so many essays, term papers, critical summaries, what-I-did-on-my-summer-vacations. I'm good at them, even when I'm squashed under the most extreme pressure. Especially then.

A twenty-thousand-dollar prize. I can't envision that amount of money. It seems infinite. It's almost meaningless.

There's a soft knock at my door. "Hey, Dad," I call out.

He pokes his head in. "I'm gonna do the grocery shop tonight and fill up the tank," he says. "Restocking tomorrow, so not sure how late I'll be. Want to make sure it gets done."

"Oh, okay." I pull out my phone and send him a hundred dollars.

He responds to the buzz in his pocket like it's unexpected. "Hey, thanks!" he says with a smile. I hate this thing we're doing right now—this thing we do. I don't mind that he needs me to help pay for stuff; it's just this awkward exchange of silent words and weird, unacknowledged dynamics.

"Back soon, princess," he says. "Get that homework done." He shuts the door.

I tell myself it's not Dad's fault that the economy is garbage and not even Dollar Garden's manager makes a living wage. But part of me screams that there was no need for him to lose his good job at Elcorp in the first place; that it *is* his fault.

And that's why I have to be perfect. People like Jamison Sharpe can thrust themselves forward with confidence. They don't worry about failure because they don't *have* to—the failures of the powerful are just soft little missteps, and they'll soon be bounced back on track by their intelligence, their connections, their money. But every step I take has to be calculated. I think about those financial aid forms sitting naked in my folder. About how everything in my life is on a knife's edge—one poor application essay, one bad impression, one failing grade, and I'm in ribbons.

4

It's been eight days since my Everett interview, and I still haven't heard anything. Which is normal! Totally not a red flag! Still, I just keep turning my responses over in my head, analyzing and over-analyzing. Today, we're working on our group websites in economics and my page is already done, so I've got all the time in the world to sit here and percolate. Every once in a while, someone from my group glances back at me with a sour-apple look on their face, but I ignore them. They can be a whole barrel of sour apples for all I care. I'm apple-proof.

"Are you serious? Jamison is related to Ryan Reynolds?" A voice pricks my bubble of introspection. A conversation from a knot of slacking young economists has turned lively, and suddenly my focus is pulled.

"Yeah, that's what I heard."

I do a squirrel-cheek-puff exhale. I have two classes with Jamison

Sharpe—AP Calculus and Intro to Piano—yet here he is again. It's like I'm being followed around the school by a cloud of his jasmine-scented essence. People are practically falling over themselves to get close to him, as though he's the most fascinating person on the planet. My Tuesday English tutoree wouldn't stop going *on* about Jamison's deep thoughts about Nietzsche. Wren says his performance of some sappy monologue in drama club had everyone in tears. Oh, and of course the rumors are swirling. *Did you know Jamison has his pilot's license and his own airplane? Did you know he was a starting pitcher for the Little League World Series when he was a kid?*

"I heard that, too," floats an excited voice from the center of the classroom. "Ryan Reynolds is Jamison's mom's cousin or something."

Well, that's a new one to me, anyway. For some reason, I have this urge to write it down, to keep a list of everything that's so *amazing* about Jamison Sharpe, the way you might document a mole as it starts to discolor. But I don't. I just don't have time to care about any of it: the outlandish stories, his ridiculously good looks, his massive—if the rumors are true—brain. The only reason Jamison is even on my radar is because of the *Race to the Top!* list hanging in the cafeteria. I'm not intimidated; I've had my eyes on that prize for a long time and I know the game. I've worked hard to get here, and that's something I bet Jamison doesn't know anything about—everything seems so disgustingly easy for him. Well, it's not going to be easy to unseat Viveca North from that top spot. He can try if he wants.

My economics teacher speaks over the low din of groupwork in progress. "Viveca, would you take this laptop back to the equipment room?" I nod and get up. I always have to do this kind of stuff because I'm "not busy." Well, nobody else would be busy, either, if they just did their work on time.

I mosey down the second-floor hallway. The equipment room is just at the other end, so after only a minute or two, I'm headed back to class. That's when I hear a conversation from around the corner of the connecting hallway, where the science classrooms are. I recognize one of the voices. For some reason, I stop, creep up, and listen.

"That's an admirable accomplishment, Jamison," a man is saying. Maybe Mr. Valdez, the biology teacher; I'm not sure. "I know young people who fly, but I've never heard of someone your age being accepted into such a worthy program."

"It's an honor," Jamison says. "I caught the director's eye when I was flying flood relief missions in the Caribbean last year."

Mr. Valdez makes an impressed kind of noise. Relief missions in the Caribbean on top of a fancy Parisian school? Jamison had a busy year last year, apparently.

"Anyway," Jamison says, "the text I just got in class is from my liaison. I'm so sorry to have my phone on me. I wasn't even thinking about it."

"Please, don't worry," Mr. Valdez says. "It's fine. Go call your liaison. You can finish the quiz when you get back." There's a pause. "Actually, we're almost out of time—why don't you stop in during lunch and finish up?"

"That would be great," Jamison says. "Thank you so much. I really appreciate it. You know, not all teachers understand the way you do." Oh, what a *line*. And Mr. Valdez falls for it, I can tell. I'd probably fall for it, too, if Jamison's baby blues were pointed in my direction. People are so stupid.

I hear footsteps; someone is heading into this hallway from the science hall. I happen to be standing by a gap between banks of lockers, and without thinking, I flatten myself into it, against the wall.

What am I doing? Hiding from Jamison Sharpe? Spying on him? If he walks by, he'll see me creeping here like a weirdo.

But the footsteps don't get closer. I peek out. Jamison has turned the other direction. I watch his sky-blue T-shirt head away from me and turn the corner at the end of the hallway—going to make an emergency call to the liaison for his prestigious hero-pilot-whatever program. It sounds like a load of crap to me. What's he really doing?

Maybe I should follow him. The thought sends a little tingle over my skin. It's a good-bad feeling, like eating the last chocolate truffle you should have saved for someone else, shame mixed with delight. But if Jamison's really going to make an important phone call, what's the harm? And if he's not, if I catch him in a lie, I'll have the tiny, smug satisfaction that he's not as perfect as everyone thinks he is.

I step out and watch him disappear around the corner, then make my way down the hall as softly as I can. Unfortunately, Principal Washington appears.

Principal Washington is not a bad principal. By most standards, she's probably excellent. She's only been here a year and knows every student's name and one or two things about them; I have to imagine she's got a binder of notes somewhere that she studies. But she pays extra attention to the kids at the tops and bottoms of their classes. That means encountering her in person is guaranteed to throw my schedule off by at least a few minutes.

"Viveca North," Principal Washington says, looking up from a clipboard she's carrying. She extends her hand, and I shake it. "I'm hearing good things about you this year. Not that that's a surprise."

"Thank you," I say, hoping we're done.

She points her pencil at me. "Hardest-working student in the senior class, am I right?"

"Uh, sure." I try to be light. Cheerful. "Yep!" I'm going to lose Jamison.

"You had to make quite an effort to get here, didn't you?" she says. "That's an impressive commitment."

A ripple of tension stiffens the back of my neck. She means that most of the students here are from wealthy Elton families. To get in, I had to beat out who knows how many other kids from West Bore and Haverwood and all the other flypaper towns clustered at Elton's feet.

Principal Washington lowers her voice like she's getting real. "Tell me. What's your *least* favorite class so far?" She does this to make people feel like they've got some kind of special access to her ear.

"Economics." I say the first class that pops into my head. "I'm not big on group projects."

The principal nods knowingly. "I hear that. You're a pioneer."

"That's nice of you to say." Jamison could be out the front doors and halfway to the soccer field by now for all I know.

She gives me a wide grin. "Well, in any case, I'm sure you'll have a great year!"

"Thank you." I smile and give a little head bob in what I hope is a polite but final-looking gesture.

The principal shakes my hand again. "Keep it up, Viveca North." She clicks away down the hall. I wait a moment, then pad off in pursuit of Jamison. I probably have no chance of catching him now.

But as I turn the corner at the far end, I catch a glimpse of sky blue. I pull back, peeking. Vice Principal Reinhardt has Jamison cornered, chatting. Jamison's nodding, his back against a door, looking a bit guilty. Possibly looking a bit guilty. Okay, I'm not sure about the "guilty-looking"; maybe I'm projecting. I can hear bits of their conversation, but it's mundane, pulled from the same plan of attack Principal Washington uses. *How are you settling in? Are you enjoying your classes?* Do they just stalk the halls, looking for errant students to annoy?

"Oh, they didn't give you a school planner?" the vice principal says. "Come with me. I have extras in my office."

"That's so nice of you," Jamison says. Huh, his important phone call can't be *that* important. They leave through the double doors at the end of the hall, and I slump around the corner. Don't want to risk tailing Jamison while he's hanging out with Vice Principal

Reinhardt. At some point, someone might think to ask me why I'm not in class.

Speaking of, I actually should go back, even though the period's almost over. Oh well. There's still something about Jamison Sharpe that rubs me the wrong way, but my crack investigations will have to wait for another—

I realize I'm staring hazily at the door Jamison was leaning against. It's the teachers' lounge.

Was Jamison about to go into the teachers' lounge when Reinhardt found him? Is that why he looked so guilty? Things might just have gotten a little bit more interesting.

Don't get ahead of yourself, Viveca. Don't connect dots that aren't there. Remember what happened before. My brain is right, of course. Still, isn't there a *chance* Jamison was trying to sneak in there? For what?

I slink over and put my ear to the door. I don't hear anyone inside. Of course, there could just be quiet teachers in there, eating or grading papers. Should I risk a peek? Does *Sorry, wrong room* work when you're a senior?

I put my fingers on the handle. Still no sound from within. With a quick scan up and down the hall, I crack the door.

I peer inside. There's no one here. The room isn't very big, and the air reeks of cigarettes. There's a table with a few chairs, a couch, and a little kitchen area. Bookshelves line the far end and an ancient copy machine sits under the window. They've got a vending machine in here with real sour-cream-and-onion chips and peanut butter cups, not health-food bars and shrink-wrapped bananas. Lucky.

Huh. I step in. What could Jamison possibly want in here? Not that him standing by a door means anything, I remind myself. I take a quick look around. There's nothing particularly interesting or valuable. A few mugs sit on the kitchenette counter, a newspaper splays over an arm of the couch, and a stack of books sits on the table. A gap in the bookshelf indicates where they came from and stickers on their spines say *Teachers' Lounge.*

Footsteps outside freeze me like a rabbit. With a creak, the door handle starts to turn. I gasp, then dive behind the couch just as the door opens. Someone comes in.

I squish my back up against the baseboard heater and curl, just a shrink-wrapped banana peering suspiciously across the gross underspace of the couch with dust bunnies clinging to my face.

This . . . is not a good look for me.

A flash of white. *Sneakers. Teachers don't wear sneakers!* Wait, no, Mrs. Sherwood, the gym teacher, wears sneakers. And I'm pretty sure the nurse wears sneakers. I keep still, listening. Something rustles—books? Papers in someone's bag? All is quiet for what feels like a year but is probably just a couple of minutes. Then I hear the delicate *clink* of coins and the plasticky *thup* of a big button being pushed.

Someone is buying a snack from the teachers' secret vending machine. I worm my face a little deeper under the couch, but I can't see anything other than white sneakers. I'm not a shoe aficionado

34

like so many people here seem to be, so I can't even tell if they're expensive or cool or anything.

The sneakers head toward the door. If I pop out now, I might be able to see who it is while they're facing away from me, before they get away. I risk it, slowly uncurling and scooting along the carpet until I can stretch my neck enough to see into the room.

Too slow. The door is already closing. But I catch a blur of sky blue—the color of Jamison's shirt.

Aha! Jamison wouldn't have had time to make a phone call by now, so either his director's message really wasn't as important as he made it out to be . . . or he made the whole thing up just to get out of class and get a snack. *If that was even Jamison*, I remind myself. It could have been anyone wearing sneakers and sky.

I'm feeling undeservedly triumphant. It's only peanut butter cups after all. Wren's probably stealth-raided this secret vending machine a hundred times, knowing them. But I've caught—I mean, *if* it was *him*—I've caught Mr. Perfect Jamison Sharpe in a dumb little lie. Score one for Viveca.

My butt jostles the table as I extricate myself from behind the couch, and I notice the textbooks are no longer stacked. Was Jamison looking at them? A hefty volume lies to the side, separated from the others—*Amazing Biology: Teacher's Edition with Study Guides, Worksheets, Quizzes, and Tests.*

Quizzes and tests. Wasn't Jamison in the middle of a quiz in Mr. Valdez's biology class just now? Maybe he was after more than chocolate.

The thought makes me nervous. Because the dots that want so badly to connect themselves in my brain are bigger than snacks; they might be dots that matter. And it's a familiar, old feeling I don't want to revisit. It reminds me of seventh grade and the early days of my obsession with Jackie Boynton, when my marbles were just starting to rattle, before they all went rolling out of my head. And of how much I hurt her by connecting dots that had nothing to do with each other.

Academically, Jackie and I were neck and neck through all of sixth and seventh grade. We hated each other. Ms. Vargas, our teacher, said the problem was that we were too similar. I don't know. Maybe. We both wanted to get into Elton Prep, that was for sure. And we often did assignments in similar ways. I noticed that right off the bat. Then sometime around the beginning of seventh grade, it occurred to me that maybe Jackie was *copying* me. The logistics of that idea didn't fly, but the thought stuck with me like an itch in my brain. Then "copying" expanded into "sabotaging."

I stop myself before I can ruminate too much on what happened next. That's all behind me now. Honestly, the real miracle at the time was convincing my dad to get me to a therapist. Thank goodness for Ms. Vargas managing to convince him. I almost wonder if Dad thought he had a shot with her. Anyway, at this point, I'm pretty sure my name is more synonymous with "overachiever" than "conspiracy theorist," and I really want to keep it that way.

Here, now, I focus on the facts: someone in sneakers and a sky-blue shirt bought a snack from the teachers' lounge machine. *That's all you know, Viveca.* Maybe I'm remembering the position of the books wrong. It's possible.

I slip out, back into the hallway, just as the class period is ending. I have to return to the economics classroom and get my stuff, then get to English. I missed the entire rest of class, and I don't even have any real dirt on Jamison Sharpe to show for it. But for a minute, I just lean against the wall and watch as students and teachers mill by in endless opposing, eddying streams.

I'm scaring myself, just a little. Sure, I don't like Jamison. That doesn't mean I need to be suspicious of him.

You've been down this road before.

I try to tell myself it's different now, and it *is*. But I've indulged my curiosity, and from here on out, I need to leave Jamison alone. I can't have a repeat of the Jackie Boynton incident, not when I'm so close to getting what I've worked toward for so long.

The between-class flow of bodies starts to subside. I close my eyes and focus on sound: flapping footsteps, the metallic whine of doors, the rasp of the sturdy fabrics of jackets and backpacks, and the unbroken sea of voices. I try to quiet the part of my mind still churning away with thoughts of vending machines, airplanes, Paris. The voice that doesn't care about risks.

The part of me that just wants to catch Jamison Sharpe in another lie.

5

Tonight, the Elton Prep cafeteria is decorated with crepe paper, twinkle lights, and carnival-themed student artwork. Wren and I sip watery cocoa from mugs we brought from home.

Autumn Carnival used to take up two glorious weeks between late September and early October, starting with the fall coffeehouse and ending with homecoming. Each day in between had its own theme, classes were shortened, and we got to eat snacks all day long and practically anywhere on campus. It was the best time of the year, and I don't even like football.

So of course the parents had to slowly ruin it, starting with protesting "Halloween Day," which was obviously satanic, and continuing to chip away at everything good, until water balloon tag was the latest to fall (hypothermia risk). Now the coffeehouse is the only remnant of Autumn Carnival besides homecoming itself, and it's been renamed "Carnival Night," which is a pretty optimistic way of describing open mic night in the cafeteria. Apparently there were complaints about caffeine promotion. Did nobody think to mention that half the Elton Prep students show up to class every day sucking down lattes? I rarely defend my old school, West Bore Junior High, but at least we were allowed to talk about coffee.

Arts booster parents flit around a table laden with baked goods. One end of the cafeteria has been set up as a stage area with mics, an old spinet piano rolled out from the music room, and a couple of lighting trees. There's a sign-up sheet at the door. We're all waiting for our fellow students to wow us with torch songs and angsty guitar covers. I really shouldn't be here; I have a ton of work to do. But Wren was persuasive as always, so what could I do?

"Big night out for you!" Wren says. "I'm so proud. What could possibly be next? A full-back tattoo? Hitchhiking to California?"

I raise my eyebrows cheekily. "Well—I did find out something interesting about the new darling of Elton Prep, Jamison Sharpe."

Wren gasps theatrically. "Ooh! Do tell!"

"I did some secret surveillance the other day," I say, leaning in, "and I saw him sneak into the teachers' lounge, and . . ." I pause. Wren's so excited they're going to explode into stardust any second. I lower my voice to a whisper. *"He purchased a snack from the good vending machine."*

Wren screams with laughter. "Say it isn't so!" Now we're both laughing.

"Hey, you going to sing a song tonight?" I ask, wrapping my fingers around my mug. "I suggest 'Danny Boy.'"

They almost spit out their cocoa. "Only if you do an interpretive dance along with it."

"Okay. Just let me put on my go-go boots."

A booming voice flickers the flames of our table's decorative tea lights. "Should I come back later?" I turn to see Tyson LaRoche, his impressive fauxhawk making him seem even taller than his natural six feet four inches. He has one of those *look at me* voices.

Tyson seats himself at our table, blotting out the twinkle lights with his massive frame. I remember him at fourteen—he towered even then, waltzing into Elton Prep, already a football celebrity. But football was never the love of Tyson's life. It's drama. He took a stand halfway through sophomore year and quit sports to do *Guys and Dolls*. It was a school-wide scandal. Football season has been awkward for him ever since.

Between my rebellious college aspirations, Wren's life-off-the-beaten-path, and Tyson's short-lived sports career, we've got a whole barrel of parental disappointment seated around this table right now.

"When does this thing get going?" Tyson asks. He pats the paper tablecloth, *ba-dum-dum*. His brown eyes nervously scan the dim cafeteria.

"What's up, T?" Wren asks. "Looking for your secret admirer?"

Tyson gives a dry laugh. "Nope. Just my mom. She's definitely not a secret, and I'm fairly sure she's not even an admirer at this point."

"Did she say she was coming?" Wren asks.

Tyson shrugs. "Dad said he thought she would. But you know. Who knows?"

At that moment, Min Park and Jade Bowman saunter over and sit down, bubbling hellos. I know this is not technically the popular crowd, but our table looks pretty chic to me. Jade has this long, shiny braid that she keeps to the side, Min is wearing a black tie, and Wren—well, Wren always looks the best of all. This evening their long bangs are perfectly haphazard, their sleeves crisp, their shoes retro. Sheesh, I'm surrounded by four people who have clearly graduated from the prestigious Wren Beagle School of Style. And then there's me: Viveca "What Clothes Are Clean Today?" North. I'm slouching here in a pair of old jeans and a patriotic T-shirt from a thrift store.

"Why haven't they started yet?" Jade asks, whooshing her braid from one shoulder to the other. "Min, you signed us in, right?"

"Affirmative, Captain." Min cuts into a slice of apricot bread with the edge of a plastic fork. "We're fourth. Right after someone named Griffin Rodriguez."

"Freshman," Jade says. "He's supposed to be this amazing singer. Or something. Sucks we have to follow him."

"It's not a competition," Tyson says. He's doing a monologue from *The Tempest* later.

"He'll get the crowd warmed up for you," Wren says. Jade gives them a skeptical look. "I mean it." Wren rubs Jade's shoulder. "I heard you practicing yesterday—you sounded amazing!"

I peer down into my cocoa like I'm reading the future. I know

Wren has other friends. I mean, I *know* these people. They're nice! But it's still a little weird to witness Wren outside of our own quirky sphere of two. They're all so comfortable together. And I guess I envy that, but at the same time, it's just not me. Wren insists we're all one big, charismatic family, but I think what I have is actually a kind of frenetic anxiety that sometimes gets loud on the outside and can be mistaken for confidence. Or wit. Or something. But if Wren weren't here, I'd be sitting by myself, 100 percent. I'm not part of their solar system; I just orbit really close sometimes.

"What are you guys doing?" I ask Jade, gesturing to the make-shift stage.

"We're singing a duet from *Chess*," she says.

"It's *fantastic*," Min says.

"Do you know *Chess*?" Jade asks. I shake my head.

"It's *fantastic*," Min repeats.

Just then, a voice even more arresting than Tyson's rends the stale, non-coffee-scented air. "Are you talking about *Chess* over here?"

I turn, even though I know exactly what awaits me in the twinkly shadows of the cafeteria. He's not as loud as Tyson, or as glittering as Wren, or as shiny-haired as Jade, but Jamison Sharpe is a *presence*. The atmosphere right now is what I imagine a room full of starving screenwriters would feel like if Steven Spielberg walked in. All eyes drawn instantly, everyone with a pitch on their tongue. Only nobody's pitching screenplays to Jamison Sharpe. For some stupid, lizard reason, we're pitching ourselves.

"Do you love *Chess*?" Min asks.

"It's *fantastic*," Jamison says. He laughs. Everybody laughs except me.

"Hey, friends, this is Jamison," Wren says, scooching their chair over so Jamison can crouch down and lean into the table like an overly friendly waiter.

"I can't believe you're *Chess* fans, too," Jamison says. "My host family took me to see it in concert in London while I was studying abroad last year."

London? I thought it was France. I guess people can study abroad in more than one place, right? Or maybe Jamison visited London with his French host family. Between relief missions to the Caribbean . . .

Then everybody at the table is singing. I assume it's a musical. I assume it's *Chess*. All eyes are on us—I can tell, even in the low lighting. I try to suck my head back into my T-shirt to convey that I'm obviously not singing with them. But when you're at the drama table, you're going to get lumped in.

Some of the teachers and parents shoot us dirty looks. I become super interested in a poorly watercolored carousel taped to the wall by the windows. *Nope, I don't know any of these people. I don't even know how I got here. Cocoa? What's that?* I try to center myself and hang on to my senses—see, touch, smell, hear. Although "hear" is kind of the issue right now.

Mystifyingly, Jamison himself seems exempt from the stink eyes. He's smack in the middle, crooning tenor, looking into people's

43

eyes, seemingly mesmerized by his fellow performers. I guess it's only obnoxious to sing loudly if you're a run-of-the-mill Eltonion or, god forbid, from West Bore. Jamison Sharpe, of London and Paris and wherever else, can do whatever the heck he wants.

He looks over at me and I pretend I wasn't looking at him, but then I peek back and he's still looking at me and singing in this angelic voice, and for a second I feel a little tingly, though how much of it is Jamison-tingly versus how much is shame-because-seriously-*Jamison?*-tingly, I'm not sure. I'm annoyed at myself for enjoying his attention even a little.

By the time Principal Washington emerges and tells us to settle down, I feel like the world's reddest bug under a magnifying glass, one second from bursting into flames. But the coffeehouse begins, and people forget about our table and look to the performance area. First up is a junior doing a flute solo. It's nice, I guess.

After a flannel-clad junior growl-whispers his way through some indie band's sad ballad, he and his sticker-covered guitar rush outside to vape. Emcee Principal Washington checks her list and twitters delightedly into the microphone, "Jamison Sharpe."

"Wonderful," I say. "Is he going to sing some more?" All Jamison-related tingles have evaporated, and now I'm just embarrassed that he got to me. I could be imagining it, but the smattering of applause feels warmer than before as he glides to the front of the room.

"Maybe he'll tell jokes," Min says. "There haven't been any stand-up acts yet. I could use some good sardonic observations."

Wren swishes their cocoa with a plastic knife, digging up the settled powder at the bottom. "Nah, I'm sensing Billy Joel." A couple of students dressed in black roll the piano forward.

"Oh, *great*," I laugh, and it comes out more like a bark. The others are giving me confused looks, so I go on. "Jamison's in my piano class. Intro to Piano. We're . . . very beginner." I lean forward on my elbows, enjoying my evil little hope that Jamison will embarrass himself. "This should be delightful."

"What songs do you know?" Jade asks.

I picture the brightly colored songbooks that have lived in my backpack since the beginning of the year, emerging between tutoring sessions when I have time to rush to the music room and get some practicing in. "Well, I'm pretty sure everyone can play the heck out of 'Hot Cross Buns' at this point."

Tyson snorts. "Okay, now I'm invested."

Min's eyes sparkle devilishly in the candlelight. "What's the hardest one you've learned? Don't tell me it's 'Mary Had a Little Lamb.'"

I wrinkle my nose as I think. "The one that's due this week is the trickiest one so far. We have to have our hands in a different position, and there are eighth notes in it. I'd be surprised if anybody is really good at it yet, though."

"Okay, I hope he plays that one," Min says. "What's it called?"

I can barely keep from laughing. "'The Mysterious Wizard.'"

"Yes!" Min claps.

Jamison seats himself at the old spinet as tech students adjust the lighting.

Tyson cups his hands around his mouth, as though he could possibly make himself any louder. "Play 'The Mysterious Wizard'!"

Laughter ripples through the cafeteria, and I laugh, too. Jamison turns to the audience and grins, as though he and Tyson are best pals in on some joke together. Then he puts his hands on the keys and tinkles out a tune.

It's "The Mysterious Wizard." And it's perfect. Of *course* it is. There's polite applause when Jamison is done. But he doesn't stand up; instead, he turns back to the piano. And plays—

What?

Jamison's fingers cascade up and down the keyboard, hand over hand under hand. I recognize it after a minute—it's a new release, still at the top of the charts, and he's playing it like he's a member of the band.

"Close your mouth," Wren whispers.

I give them a shocked look. "Do you—"

They raise their eyebrows sternly. "Yeah, he can play the piano, whatever, just listen."

Jamison ends with a flourish, then stands for an infuriatingly modest bow. The crowd goes wild. He blushes.

I want to stick him with a plastic fork. "How can he *do* this?" I hiss to Wren.

They throw up their hands. "This? Do what? Play the piano? Uh, he probably takes lessons?"

I shake my head. "No, I mean—how can he take Intro to Piano when he *already knows how to play*?"

Wren's giving me this blank look.

Jade pipes up, "That song wasn't actually that hard, you know. It was just chords. He was arpeggioing all over the place so it sounded fancy, but I could teach you how to do that in about five seconds."

"It sounded hard," I say. "Harder than anything we'll learn."

Jade shrugs. "I doubt it. If that's the hardest thing he can play, a beginning class is probably fine. Maybe he's a little ahead, but whatever. I mean, he just switched schools."

"A little ahead?" My voice is getting squeaky. "Did you hear him blast through 'The Mysterious Wizard'? I can barely play it at half that speed." I can sense Jade, Tyson, and Min holding back laughs at my expense. At least they *are* holding them back, but I can feel my cheeks heating up in a sickeningly familiar way.

Wren leans back. "Okay, seriously though, why do you care? Who does this hurt? Who does nice piano music ever hurt in this tragic world of ours?"

"It's not the music." I look down, fascinated by cocoa dregs. "You know what he said about being valedictorian at his old school. What if he gets a better grade than me in Intro to Piano, when he shouldn't even be in that class? That wouldn't be fair. Not at all."

Jade, Min, and Tyson don't say anything. After a moment of awkward silence, they start chatting together. Wren is still looking at me, making this weird face. What is their problem?

I breathe in. "Look—"

"I'm out of cocoa," they interrupt, getting up. And then they're gone.

Jade watches Jamison glide back to his seat. He's over with Kasey Wheelwright, our quirky class president, and Miranda Nazarian, who's a minor internet celebrity. "I wonder if Jamison is talking to anybody?" Jade asks.

Great, *romance*. I recede from the candlelight, hoping the conversation doesn't even think about steering itself in my direction. I've embarrassed myself enough.

So, of course, Tyson says, "What about it, Viveca? Want to go shoot your shot?"

I can't tell if he's laughing with me or at me, but I'm definitely not laughing, so I suppose that's my answer. I respond without thinking, the words springing directly from the most sacred recesses of my soul. "I'd rather give myself a lobotomy with knitting needles."

Tyson laughs for real, and Min and Jade join him, and it does feel nice, like maybe I'm being clever rather than grumpy. I can't help the shadow of a smile. "I mean—he's not my type."

"What is your type?" Min says. "Asking for a friend." Tyson raises an eyebrow.

"You think Jamison has a date for homecoming?" Jade goes on when I don't respond. "I bet he dances as good as he smells."

"Hey, I thought *we* were going to homecoming," Min says. "I'm not going with Tyson again. He steps on my feet."

Tyson booms a laugh. "You wound me! Anyway, I have dibs on Wren this year. We're seniors now. This is the year style *counts*. There are votes riding on it!"

Jade tilts her head. "Tyson LaRoche, are you still chasing that dream of being homecoming king?"

"Of course I am!" He turns to me. "What do you think, Viveca? Can I beat the new guy? Do I have a shot?" They're all being nice to me even though I was weird about Jamison. Wren is lucky to have friends like this.

Jade winks at me. I look over to Jamison Sharpe's table and find myself wondering what they're talking about over there. It's like I'm at the plastic-laden kids' table at Thanksgiving, gazing across the dining room at the good china and silver serving dishes. But I compose myself.

"Tyson," I say, "if *you're* crowned homecoming king, I'll—"

"What?" Tyson grins. "Bake me a cake?"

I lean closer. "I'll bake you two!"

He laughs, and I sit back and sip my cocoa. But I'm not thinking about homecoming, which I've never been to and don't intend to start going to now. I'm thinking about Intro to Piano, about Paris and London. About what any of us really knows about the new guy.

6

"Hey, Viveca!"

It dawns on me that someone has been calling my name. I pull my nose out of a biography of Napoleon, noticing I'm now walking on the opposite side of the art room hallway from where I started. Luckily most people have gone home by now or I probably would have crashed into someone.

I turn around. And who's waving at me and hurrying to catch up but Mr. Phenomenal himself, Jamison Sharpe. Great.

"Hi, Jamison." I tuck my Napoleon biography under my arm. "What's up?" I keep my tone neutral. I'm not sure what his game is, but I'm not going to get sucked in this time. And if he's looking for more adoring fans, he can just walk right on by.

"I've been thinking about that essay contest Ms. Racine told us about—the Pinniped County Futurists." Jamison reaches me, stops, stands a little too close. I don't like it.

I don't know if I like it.

"You got that email, right?" he asks.

"Yeah." He knows I got it. He saw the recipients list, just like I did.

"Are you going to enter?"

I shrug. "Why not?" I'm acting casual, but there's this unpleasant shimmy behind my ribs, little jolts of resentment. Jamison Sharpe has alighted in the ritziest part of Elton, resting his gilded wings between flitting to Paris and London and LA. He practically has *Scholarship Material!* written across his forehead—baseball or piano or Shakespeare or anything else he cares to focus on for five minutes, apparently. Why on earth would he need the Pinniped County Futurists' money, which could be a lifeline to someone like me?

"That's great," he says, leaning against a locker like we're having a conversation. "Ms. Racine says you're the best writer in the senior class."

I can't help showing my surprise on my face. "She—really?"

He gives me a slanted smile. "Aw, come on, Viveca. You're a legend in this school. Even Howard let slip you're the smartest cookie in calculus."

"Mr. Howard said that?" The words come out before my brain can approve them. He smiles at me and his eyes glint like we're being a little mischievous together, and holy cow, Jamison is . . . *hot.* For a moment, I'm speechless.

But then reality kicks in. Rather—my insides kick me back to reality. You develop a survival mode, living with a compulsive liar.

A permanent cloud of static sparks that zap you right between the brain hemispheres when someone says something iffy, making you recoil, protecting all your important squishy parts from getting pierced. When someone lies to you, it's practically a fireworks show.

I want to believe my teachers said those things about me. I want to believe they see me as *talented*, not just a hard worker. But I see the lies in Jamison Sharpe. I see them when he's charming his fans in the halls between classes, or the center of attention in the courtyard before school. And I see them now, as he's complimenting me and making my lungs flutter.

"I've got to go," I say. "Wren's waiting for me."

He pushes himself off the locker, still smiling. "Don't let me stop you."

"I—won't." I let my book fall into my hands and hold it up like it's some kind of excuse. "Napoleon."

"Nice. I'll see you around, Viveca," Jamison says. "On my way to debate club. More fun than a barrel of lawyers." With that, he gives me a cheeky salute and moseys off down the hallway.

What was that smile? Those questions? What was any of that? My head is six kinds of mixed up as I scurry out the side door and skirt around to the patch of grass beneath the art room windows.

The lawns are still pretending they're growing even though there's nothing going on in those brittle leaves. I pull out my sketchbook as I wait for Wren to get out of comics club. One of the students I'm tutoring is going to meet me here in a little while, too. But right now, for these few minutes, I'm adrift with nothing to do but try to make sense of what just happened. I pull out my sketchbook without thinking about it. I'm not even good at drawing, but it's a habit, the way some people smoke just because they don't know what else to do with their hands.

How could I let Jamison get to me the way he did just now? Some measly secondhand flattery and I'm tongue-tied. He's so—*irritating*.

Was he lying when he said Ms. Racine thinks I'm the best writer in the senior class? Or about what Mr. Howard said about me in calculus? I . . . don't know. Would teachers really say that stuff to a student? Definitely not most students—but possibly Jamison, Mr. Charming. Or maybe he just made it up to get on my good side, whatever he thinks that will get him. Which is nothing.

I'm sketching the trees across the road, the tangled lines of their cold branches stark against the bleakness. I start to add Fozzie Bear poking his eager face from around the trunk of a big pine.

What I know is that when Jamison does lie, he's way better at it than my dad. My dad gets away with the little stuff, but when he comes out with a whopper, people who've bought his crap so far get this unmistakable look on their faces, this dawning realization. It's like a sad *Ohhhh.*

Ohhhh, this guy is actually a nutcase. It's disappointment in that moment they realize nothing Dad has ever said to them is trustworthy. It practically has its own depressing soundtrack. Every time I see that look on someone else's face, it scrapes away a little at my insides like sandpaper.

But Jamison never gets the *ohhhh* moment. He hasn't even been here a month, and he just gets more and more popular. So what has he lied about? Honestly, I couldn't say. Maybe nothing. *Probably* nothing. But my sparky shield says otherwise. Maybe he never went to the Little League World Series. Maybe he hasn't actually read *Ulysses*. Maybe his hair isn't naturally blond. Who knows? After all, whatever sins Jamison Sharpe committed at his last school are far away and forgotten on the other side of the Atlantic. He breezed into Elton Prep with the mystery of an unopened birthday present. Must be nice.

I shouldn't think stuff like that. I've been to enough therapy to know when I'm in danger of letting my imagination run away with me. After all, sometimes your own instincts are the biggest liars of all. Besides, what terrible person would be this suspicious of some random new classmate? Who even has time? It's just Jamison's confidence, speech pattern—the tone of it, the lilt. It's like he's my dad but leveled up. Only my dad exudes this microscopic subtext of desperation that makes you *almost* feel sorry for him. But Jamison's underpinnings are just . . . blank.

The sunlight on my sketchbook flickers as Wren plops down next to me. "The artist is creating!" They pull a pack of tarot cards out of their pocket and start arranging them on the grass.

"Do you think a high school senior would really enjoy *Ulysses*?" I ask without preamble.

"I can't imagine anybody really enjoying *Ulysses*," Wren says. "Hey, pick a card."

I run my hand over the cards. "Is this regular tarot or anti-tarot?" I ask.

They shrug. "I haven't decided yet."

"That covers a lot of bases, then." I flip over a card. "The sun. How cheerful."

"That's actually the moon." Wren leafs through a little book with an embossed cover.

"It's yellow and round and has spiky rays coming out of it," I say, squinting. "It's floating in a robin's-egg-blue sky. It's totally the sun."

"Look, who's the expert here?" Wren finds the page and reads, scrunching their mouth to one side.

"Definitely not me," I say. "Must be you, with that fancy book that looks like it came from an amazing-smelling boutique. And probably cost way too much."

They laugh. "Oh god, it did smell amazing in there." They look at my card again. "Well, apparently, the moon is all about deception."

"Huh. Weird." I sit back on my palms. "I was just thinking about deception."

Wren's eyes light up. "Ooh, really? I want in. Who are we scamming?"

"It's not who we're scamming. It's who's getting scammed already."

"Oh?" Wren asks. "Who's that?"

I run my thumb over the moon card. "Everyone."

Wren puts a hand on my shoulder. "Have we been spending too much time online? Is this a chemtrails thing?"

"Nah." I slide the moon card back into the deck. "It's nothing."

There's usually this lightness to Wren's face, like an exciting secret that's going to burst out at any second. But I have the unique talent—or anti-talent, I guess—of being able to squash that lightness right out. They know what I mean when I say it's nothing. That I'm thinking about *him*.

"Pink-whiskered Santa Claus, Viveca. I get it. You don't like the guy or something. That doesn't mean he's the Illuminati." Wren shuffles the cards absentmindedly. "Hey, you want to catch the ten o'clock *Pirates of Penzance* tomorrow night down at the rep?"

I snort. "See a play in the middle of the night? With a calc test next week and an English project due? Are you serious?"

Wren raises one eyebrow. "Are we playing the questions game?"

"Did I just win?"

They laugh. I do love Wren's laugh. It sounds like some kind of pushy barnyard bird and makes their dark eyes crinkle at the edges. "Look," they say, "since I can't convince you to go to homecoming—"

"I'm too busy," I say. "I can't waste a whole weekend on—"

They hold up a hand. "I understand. But you've been stuck in your own head lately. You need to be shaken up a little. So, obviously, poorly scheduled and poorly executed operetta is the only solution."

I pull at some brittle grass blades. "It's just that we're behind in calculus and Mr. Howard still has some new stuff to cover before the test next week. We only have a few real *test* tests, you know? So it's a huge deal. I mean, it could make the difference between . . ." I'm not sure how to finish that sentence.

"Between your passing and failing?" Wren offers.

"Well, no. Probably not."

"Between getting into your dream school and not getting into your dream school?"

Now they're messing with me. Before my interview, I would have said I killed it with my Everett application—solid essays, glowing recommendations. I would have said it'd take something gargantuan to foul it up, like if I stabbed someone on live TV or stole the whole jar of sick-orphan money from a fundraising ball.

But now, I feel like those essays and transcripts and recommendations don't mean as much as I thought they did. I feel like the only special thing about me is that I'm valedictorian. Which I'm not— not yet.

I have to tell Wren the truth, because they know, anyway. "It's just that AP Calc could really affect my GPA."

"You mean *everyone's* GPA," they say.

"Well, yeah."

"You mean *his* GPA."

"I didn't say that." But I'm thinking it. What if Jamison overtakes me in the senior top ten? That would mean I lied to the dean of admissions. And without the specialness of the title of valedictorian, who would I be? Viveca North, with the mediocre extracurriculars and the mediocre personality.

Wren squints across the lawn. "Your freshman algebra is here."

They slide the tarot deck back into its box, and we get to our feet. "I work until nine tomorrow. Then I'm picking you up. Tickets are fifteen."

Ugh, fifteen bucks. I don't complain, though. I have it. I don't have much left over after groceries, gas, and my meager savings, but it's enough to keep my nonexistent social life limping along.

I give Wren a half smile. There's no arguing with them when they're in you-must-have-fun mode. "All right."

"It's one night, Viveca," they say. "Calculus will still exist in the morning. And if it doesn't, well, that means we have bigger problems." They kiss their fingers and touch my forehead. "And I promise not to sing along with the show if you promise not to invite Jamison Sharpe. In the flesh, as a ghost, as your sexy rival fantasy—in *any* form. Okay?"

"Okay."

As Wren glides away around the corner of the building, I realize I missed my window to tell them about Jamison maybe flirting with me. It would be stupid to bring it up later. After all, there's probably nothing to tell.

And besides, I don't know if they'd believe me, anyway.

7

Genevieve comes over on Saturdays, my dad's day off. She's his lady-friend. She's . . . fine. Normal? Works for the state doing something boring. Wears clothes that match and don't have dog hair on them. Always smells clean. I don't really know what she sees in Dad, but I guess I'd say that I like Genevieve. Everything between us is fine. Tranquil. Beige.

Genevieve always talks like the two of them might do something—today it was "I wore my good boots in case we want to go for a hike." But they've spent the afternoon in the living room as usual, him in his armchair and her on the couch, the TV slogging through seasons of some random show while they both stare at their phones.

It's getting dusky. Only a few hours until Wren comes to collect me for *The Pirates of Penzance*, which I still can't believe I'm going to. But I know Wren, and if I'd refused this night of fun, I'd definitely get dragged to homecoming next week. And I'm not a big dance person, or a big football person, or a big social-life person. Sometimes I think about what it would be like, enjoying that stuff like everybody else. I'm even a bit wistful about it, really. But the stakes are too high right now. I can't afford distractions until I'm free and clear and starting my new life at Everett. All I want is to pack a bag and hop a bus, and the next step—the final step—is my financial aid paperwork. But Dad's going to take some buttering up.

"You guys want takeout? Lun Hing?" I stick my head through the living room doorway. I've been working on an English essay all day, but my growling stomach has finally forced me to take a break.

"Oh, Viveca! That's a great idea!" Genevieve looks up from her phone with this heartbreaking smile. Sheesh. She's desperate to win my approval; it saturates everything she does like a cloud of perfume. Every little thing I say or do that's decent she takes to mean she's one tiny step closer to the happy family of her dreams.

"Sounds good," Dad says. "Your treat." He and Genevieve chuckle like it's a joke, letting the kid treat the adults. I fake laugh along with them, but I know for a fact that if I don't pay for the food, it's not happening. Dad will make cutesy little hints as we all get hungrier and hungrier; he'll talk about picking something up at the market; he might even get up and put his shoes on—he might *even* walk to the door and grab his keys. But somehow Genevieve will end up buying and cooking something for them both, thinking spending her own money yet again was actually her idea, while I politely tell them I'll eat later and go to my room.

Not tonight. I've got to get Dad at ease before I hit him with the financial aid forms. Plus, I'm hungry.

"I think there's a menu in the drawer by the sink," Genevieve says, getting up. "What do you want, Viveca? Three bean delight?" She says this to let me know she remembers I'm a vegetarian.

"Yeah, probably." I follow her to the kitchen. We dig out the menu, make a list, remember the lettuce wraps. She calls the restaurant. Then, "Twenty minutes!" she chirps to my dad in the living room. No response.

"One of you will have to drive me," I say. "If that's okay."

"I'm happy to!" She gives me a big smile plastered over the neediness.

Genevieve's car feels like luxury to me as I settle in the passenger seat, but I think that's just because it's clean and smells like her shampoo rather than a convenience store air freshener. She puts on a Top 40 playlist; I'm not sure if it's for my benefit. We don't talk much. I don't know what to say to her. The obvious topic would be Dad, but I have no idea what kind of "Dad" she knows, and just the thought of trying to shore up whatever house of cards he's built with her is exhausting.

It only takes ten minutes to get to Lun Hing, West Bore's only restaurant if you don't count the sub shop–gas station combo on the main road where Wren works or the coffee place next to the laundromat. "You don't have to treat us," Genevieve says as we pull in. "It's very generous of you, but I'm happy to get dinner."

I unbuckle my seat belt and open the door. "No, it's fine." I try to look sincere. "Really. You always end up getting it."

"Oh, Viveca, you're such a kind soul." Now she looks like she's going to cry. Not from sadness or happiness, but fragility. Everything is precarious with her. I mean, I'm glad Dad will have someone after I leave. But the thing is, I feel like even *that* makes Genevieve sad, me being okay with her. If I were baking her cookies and calling her Mother, she'd be over the moon. But the next best thing would be if I were slamming my books down and calling her a witch who's not my real mom. It's like she just wants this intense connection, whatever it looks like. And I can't give it to her.

In the restaurant's entryway, a large fish tank stands luminous against the wood paneling. The lady at the register hands me a paper bag with handles, stapled together at the top. Our order smells incredible and costs almost fifty dollars. That's two tutoring sessions, kaput. But it's a small sacrificial move as part of my long game.

Back home, we sit in the living room to eat our Chinese food. I'm on the arm of the couch, forking noodles from a cardboard container and poking a ratty tufted footstool with my toe. Dad and Genevieve lean together next to me, the take-out boxes arranged haphazardly on folding TV tables. We watch an episode of some sitcom and laugh. Things are going pretty well, but I have to pick my moment carefully. I'm hoping Genevieve's presence will bring out supportive, in-favor-of-college Dad.

"Miss Mei never disappoints." Dad leans back. Miss Mei ran Lun Hing when Dad was a kid.

Genevieve pats his belly. "We needed a nice night in." I'm not sure when they've ever had a night out, but okay. Everyone seems relaxed.

I inhale as much enthusiasm as my body can house. "Genevieve, I don't know if Dad told you, but I'm applying to colleges." *College. One.*

"Viveca, that's wonderful!" She gasps and goggles at me with an openmouthed grin. I try to let it feel nice, someone being excited for me. But I don't know if she means it, or if she's just performing for my dad. I try not to hang too many feelings on what people say.

"Have you gotten in anywhere?" he asks coolly.

Ah, there's the six-million-dollar question right there. My throat gets tight. What I want to say is *Yes. Yes, OF COURSE I'm going to get in. How could I possibly not? Do you remember me being sequestered in this house for four years, crouched obsessively over my notebooks and rented laptop like a feasting spider? Have we even met?*

That sounds snobby, and I guess it is, especially since I don't even really mean it. I'm not sure I'm going to get in to Everett—not anymore. But I keep all that on the inside. Besides, my dad isn't really asking if I got in anywhere. He's asking if I'm really going, how he's going to make ends meet without me, how I could possibly do this to him.

"Should we have a cake?" Genevieve turns to my dad. "Hon, do you want to have a cake?"

"I thought you were still deciding what to do next year," Dad says. His phone vibrates, and he pulls it out of his pocket.

"I want to go to Everett," I say, keeping my tone even. I say it to both of them so it looks like I'm being informative, not argumentative. "Psychology."

"I'm sure you'll get in." Genevieve pats my knee affectionately, which I can tell is a big deal for her. I keep still in that careful way you do when you're trying to convince a cat it's okay to sit on you.

"Viveca's a smart cookie," Dad says. "Always has been."

"Thanks," I say, but Dad's comment doesn't buoy me. Sure, he's proud of me, but he'll use anything to puff himself up in front of other people and, right now, it's his daughter.

He points like he's giving a speech. "Knew she'd be valedictorian since her first day of kindergarten. 'That's one brilliant kid,' the teacher said. *Brilliant.*"

The word *valedictorian* knots my stomach, but I just smile modestly at Dad's false praise. I know he thinks I'm smart—he thinks *he's* a genius after all—but there's no way my kindergarten teacher called me brilliant. I don't remember a lot about her. She sent a note home about my chewing on crayons.

"I'm not brilliant," I say. "I just work hard, that's all."

Dad is undeterred. "Hardest worker at that high school." That's true, at least.

"So proud," Genevieve contributes.

Okay, so this is getting dumb. I have to hit Dad with the forms before things turn sour. "There's a long application process," I tell Genevieve. "Just one part left."

"Oh," she says, "what's that?"

Dad's phone buzzes again, and he's texting. There are always crises at the store. I hope he doesn't have to go in tonight.

I don't look at Dad; I focus on Genevieve. "I just have to apply for financial aid."

Dad is instantly alert. "You want a handout?" he says. "Not in this house."

And we're off, folks! My tongue burns with a hundred things I want to say to this, but I swallow all those words, the weight of a bowling ball in my stomach. Instead, as the blood in my face seethes, I just say, "It's not like that. Practically everybody applies for financial aid."

"Everybody from around here, you mean," he says. "Why don't you get a job? My generation, we paid our way by *working*."

This is bootstraps Dad, straight out of clumsy memes, here to impress ladies and manly men with his wherewithal. He's also totally implying that he himself went to college. I wonder if Genevieve has ever asked him what his major was.

"I'm going to work when I get there." I don't mention the jobs I already have, which just bought this Chinese food. "But college is expensive."

Genevieve nods. "I'm still paying off my loans."

Dad snuffle-snorts like a bulldog, then goes back to his phone. "Waste of time." His chin sinks into his chest as he swipes and taps.

This is not going well. We sit in silence. I know this is hard for him. I know change is hard, and that Everett in particular brings up memories of Mom, but shouldn't Dad want me to succeed? Doesn't he want to be able to talk about my accomplishments without having to make something up?

I give up waiting for him to come around and start clearing dinner away.

"Who's up for a movie?" Genevieve asks, trying to defuse the tension.

"I'm leaving pretty soon," I say, carting an armload of take-out boxes and dinner debris to the kitchen.

Dad's questions pop in through the doorway. "Where are you going to be?"

"Downtown. The theater. A—musical." I don't say *operetta*. Dad's hackles fluff out when I bring up subjects he thinks are snobby.

"Oh. Who are you going with?"

"Wren."

"All right." Like he's giving me permission. I close my eyes and lean back against the countertop.

"You want some help?" Genevieve comes in. I'm not really in the mood, but I don't object as she starts sorting through the dinner stuff, tossing the silverware into the sink. I turn on the water.

As I'm washing the silverware, she leans into my ear. "Where are the forms he has to fill out?"

It catches me off guard. "Uh," I falter. Then I glance over my shoulder. "On the table. I already did all the student parts."

66

Genevieve scoops up the papers and glances through them. She nods. "Don't worry," she says in a low voice, hidden from Dad's ears. "I'll make sure he fills this out. And I'll shadow him like a hawk as he sticks on the stamp and puts it in the mailbox."

I drop a fork; it clatters against the metal sink basin. I turn to Genevieve, hot water still running from the tap. "Really?"

She smiles. "Of course. I'll take care of it. I promise."

The words *I promise* cut my skin. They're not words I'm used to trusting. In fact, one of the only times those words have ever rung true in my entire life was freshman year when a skinny kid plopped down next to me in the cafeteria and said, "Hi, I'm Wren Beagle. I won't bite. I promise."

I don't know what to say to Genevieve or her promise. I want to believe it so badly. This right now, the two of us in the kitchen with the water running and the sound of the TV from the living room, feels so genuine.

"I know your dad is having a rough time with all this," she says. "Don't worry. I'll make sure he comes through." I can see fine wrinkles at the corners of her eyes, clumps of mascara, one tooth that isn't as white as the others. But in this moment, Genevieve is flawless.

"That would be amazing. Thank you, Genevieve. I mean it. You're really—nice."

She doesn't say anything, but she nods and starts to get weepy.

I've got to get out of this kitchen before it turns into a cry fest, I think, running the back of my hand over my eyes.

8

So here we are, Wren and me, in line at the box office downtown, waiting to pick up our tickets for *The Pirates of Penzance*. Wren shimmies with excitement while I'm still a bit off-kilter from my talk with Genevieve, when out of nowhere step two ghosts from my past: Alexis Kimura and Makayla Pierce. Girls I haven't seen since eighth grade. Jackie Boynton's former best friends. They were among the most vicious after what I did, not that they didn't have a reason to be.

I keep my eyes forward. My lungs start to do that vibratey breathing that promises to snowball into full-blown terror. I focus on a fixed point, try to inhale-exhale. Name three things I can hear: *voices, door closing, the zipper of a handbag.*

But I can still see them all in my mind, in my memory. Back then, I wanted to get into Elton Prep more than anything. I thought it would prove something about me, that I was smart or special, or that I deserved good things. Maybe I thought it would prove to my dad that I alone was worthy of being told the truth—about what, I'm not sure. Everything. Anything. I thought that getting into the swanky private school a town over might make me feel like I mattered.

So as Jackie pulled ahead of me in the grades department and I felt my shot at Elton slipping away, it was like a world-ending crisis. She had to be cheating somehow, I thought—trying to *steal* my spot at Elton. I clutched the idea, fostered it, protected it, and it wasn't long before it started to spiral out of control. If Jackie were cheating, she must be getting help. I started to suspect other people were involved—classmates, friends, even Ms. Vargas herself. My paranoia convinced me they were all conspiring to keep me out of Elton because they knew what I feared to be true—that I wasn't good enough. I wasn't worthy of Elton Prep.

On some level, I knew it didn't make sense, but all those brain itches, like little worms, had turned my mind into Swiss cheese. I became obsessed with finding the truth. And I wanted others to know I was on the case. I started leaving cryptic, anonymous notes around for various people to find—mostly Jackie, but not just Jackie. I created shadowy online personas to do my spying, collect my complex clues, make spiderwebs within spiderwebs of dubious connections. I remember Makayla's face as she looked at her phone to discover an insane rant I posted under one of her videos. I remember Alexis's face in the window of their shabby ranch house, horrified to catch me pulling shreds of papers out of their garbage can. And I remember them both, that day near the middle of fourth quarter in seventh grade, when in front of the whole class, all that mental cheese came glorping out of my mouth in a messy fondue explosion of wild accusations. No one was spared.

I accused my classmates, Jackie especially, of terrible things. It's not just that I was insecure to the point of absurdity—it was mean. It was mean to think Jackie wasn't smart enough to beat me on her own. It was mean to humiliate her in front of everyone, though of course once I calmed down my own humiliation was waiting for me. Not to mention Alexis and Makayla themselves, hidden in the curve of shortcut by the school where the teachers couldn't see.

After my outburst, the disdain of my classmates followed me everywhere, whispered and muttered and shouted across the parking lot. I couldn't turn around without someone telling me what was wrong with me. And the worst thing is, despite their terrible words, they were right, all of them. I was wrong about Jackie. I was mean and I was *wrong*, and it still knots my stomach.

Jackie didn't even end up applying to Elton Prep. She moved away halfway through eighth grade. I don't know for sure, but according to the rumor mill, she was just as haunted and harassed as I was, which is sometimes the strange way communities of rabid adolescents work.

And then I got into Elton Prep. It felt like a miracle, a fresh start that could save me. But to this day, I'm terrified of those old labels finding me again, of my secret getting out. Now Alexis and Makayla are right here, in this theater lobby, with the ammunition to tell Wren everything and ruin my life as much as I ruined Jackie's.

What could I say to them now? What would they say to me? I did the mandated apology thing—the four of us and our guardians crowded into the principal's tiny office, me, red-faced, staring at the floor, stammering out the paragraph I'd practiced. The principal said Jackie, Alexis, and Makayla didn't have to respond if they didn't want to, and they didn't. They just glared. And my apology, my changed behavior, none of it even helped. The principal said it would start the healing process, but all it did was make Jackie's friends bolder. Like it gave them armor and jet packs at the same time, and all they wanted was revenge.

I never took the hidden shortcut again, never ate a school lunch for fear of what someone might have slipped into it. I didn't reactivate my social media until last year. Yet our teachers were still inundated with complaints about me, all the way through eighth grade. My only protection against the mire of lies and misery I'd sunk into was to get even higher grades, win even more prizes, become even more perfect. Perfect enough for Elton Prep, where kids like Alexis and Makayla would never be welcome.

They haven't noticed me standing here in line yet. What will happen if they turn around? Will they talk to Wren? Will Wren believe them? Wren knows my side of the story, which was as truthful as I could make it without throwing up, but they're already more vigilant about me than I'd like. And I couldn't stand it if Wren thought less of me.

Alexis and Makayla are part of a bigger group having loud, bubbly conversations that roll their bodies like lily pads on the rippling surface of a lake. Then one raucous outburst propels one of the girls' friends right into my arm. Makayla looks over, and for a second, we lock eyes.

Her face changes. Stiffens. She looks older and harder as her eyes bore into mine. I thought just seeing Makayla and Alexis had brought everything back, but in this flash of a moment, there's so much more everything that floods me all at once. The whispers, the bruises, that awful sensation of having to pee when you know you can't go to the bathroom alone, and all the words: *bully, delusional, paranoid, crazy, crazy, crazy . . .*

I go rigid. It's that blink of time before fight or flight, when long-slumbering processes in your gray matter whir to life like a lightning strike. It's just like seventh grade.

Then, suddenly, I feel something else—the length of an arm pressing across my shoulders, a warm hand grasping my biceps with skinny but strong fingers. Wren escorts me out of line, away from Makayla's eyes and the boisterous group, over to the other side of the lobby where a little coffee bar still has a couple of seats open.

"Hey, I was just thinking," they say, pressing me onto a worn barstool. "Since it's the late show, we could probably use some caffeine. Why don't you get us a couple drinks while I grab our tickets?"

"Okay, sounds good," I say in a forced voice. I take some deep breaths, lay my palms flat on the surface of the bar. I concentrate on the feel of the smooth wood. With another shoulder squeeze, Wren flits away, back into line, as I collect myself in this safe barstool bubble. Wren couldn't have even known why I was starting to freak out, but they rescued me. They always do.

We enter the theater long after Alexis and Makayla have disappeared through the doors, and I get a glimpse of them near the front. They won't see me unless they twist around. Okay, that's fine. The house is about half full. As the lights go down, I try to let the electric silence that precedes live theater override the cacophony of worries in my head.

I've never seen *The Pirates of Penzance*, and for some reason, I'm surprised that it's actually about pirates. These pirates are decked out in bright colors, swooshing shiny swords. Their counterparts, beach-going maidens, are a mass of bows and ruffles. Wren is bright-eyed, leaning over to me with a stream of animated whispers, picking apart the performances, repeating the jokes.

I didn't remember to get the coffees. It's too bad because even with the lights and sound and Wren's running commentary, by the middle of act one, I could use a pick-me-up. At intermission, we duck out the door and jog to the convenience store across the street. "I need a Red Bull or something," I say. At least we won't have to hang out in the lobby.

"You'll be up all night," Wren says. "Philistine."

"The show is great." I mean it. "I just got up early today." I push open the door, and we step from sidewalk shadows into flickering fluorescent light. It's late, and for a moment, the guy behind the counter has this *oh god, TEENAGERS* look on his face, but as we head for the energy drinks, he puts his nose back into the guitar magazine he's reading.

Wren runs their fingers over the dusty tops of a line of mini cereal boxes as I look at the refrigerated rainbow of artificial flavors.

"Why are they doing the show this late, anyway?" I ask. "Is that normal?"

Wren laughs. "Oh, it's this *whole* thing. This season they're alternating shows each night—swapping the sets out and everything. And the other show is *Hair*, which does well with the late-night crowd, so now, through the magic of nobody giving in, we've ended up with ten o'clock Gilbert and Sullivan."

"Isn't *Hair* the naked people show? We should've gone to that one." I compare ounces, pricing. When did energy drinks get so expensive? Maybe I'll settle for stale convenience store coffee.

"I mean, yeah, but it's only one scene." Wren leans against the cooler door. "You know, I met a guy at a party one time, and he just seemed so familiar, but I couldn't remember where I'd seen him. Then, in the middle of a conversation, I blurt out, 'Oh! I saw you in *Hair*!'"

I laugh. A middle-aged man reeking of cigarettes wafts past us to grab a cheap six-pack from the cooler. As I turn to give him space, I see a figure on the other side of the store near the trail mix. Sunglasses and a knit cap, nondescript sweatshirt, body turned three-quarters from me—yet there's something familiar.

"Don't look," I whisper to Wren, pulling them behind the shelves of tiny travel medications.

"Don't look at what?" Wren hunches down. "The Preparation H?"

I point. "Over there. I think it's Jamison!"

Wren pops their head over the shelves like a meerkat. "Uh—you mean the hat-and-sunglasses who isn't even facing this direction?" They take my hands. "Viveca, is it time for an intervention? Or do you have psychic powers? Wait, *do* you have psychic powers? Because we should be taking way more advantage of that. Also, what did I say about you-know-who not being allowed anywhere near our operetta date?"

Now I pop up meerkat style. The guy behind the counter looks up from his magazine and the *oh god, TEENAGERS* look on his face has intensified so much his eyes are practically combusting. The figure is still mostly facing away, tall and straight with a jawline that could slice bread, hips forward and shoulders back with the hint of an insuppressible swagger. Still, it could be any confident stranger under those sunglasses. Am I seeing things?

The figure pulls some beef jerky from the rack, then turns our way to head to the counter. I duck down again.

"Is it him?" Wren whispers. "And, follow-up question, if it *isn't* him, why are we hiding? And, alternate follow-up question, if it *is* him, *why are we hiding?*"

"I'm not sure," I say. "Let's just be fascinated by this bottom shelf for a sec."

Wren gasps. "Ooh, nearly expired antacid!"

That makes me snort, which makes Wren snort. As the figure passes by on the other side of the shelves, we are shaking with nervous, repressed laughter. Then his wake brushes over my face, a disturbance of the store's cigarette–coffee–hot dog air—tinged with something else.

I peer through a crack between the shelving units. "That's so not even him." I'm trying to convince myself. The words come out as giggles.

"It so is," Wren whispers, but I know they can't even see him. "What's he doing? Is the cashier hitting on him? Is it awkward because of the sunglasses?"

I squint. "He's buying beef jerky."

"Gross."

"And—a gift card? I can't quite—no, I think it's one of those phone cards?"

Wren sits back, palms on the floor. "What, like a SIM card?" They knit their eyebrows. "That's weird."

The mysterious figure exits the store with the jingle of bells, and Wren and I get to our feet. "A SIM card. What even are those?" I grab a drink, and we make our way to the counter.

Wren shrugs. "I mean—I think they're for burner phones usually."

I clink my Red Bull onto the melamine countertop.

"Three ninety-nine," the guitar-aficionado cashier says.

"And these Good and Plentys." Wren slides the purple box across.

Labored sigh. "Four ninety-eight."

I bid adieu to my last five, and Wren and I jingle into the night. "Why would Jamison Sharpe need a burner phone? He has a phone."

Wren stops mid-candy-opening and gives me the *wait a minute* look I've come to recognize. "Okay, but that wasn't actually Jamison Sharpe in there. You do know that, right? We were just doing a thing."

"What do you mean? How do you know?"

They pause for a moment, as though they're not sure what to say. As though they're treading carefully. "Well, what would Jamison be doing downtown at this hour? Doesn't he live up on the hill somewhere?"

"*We're* downtown at this hour," I say. "Maybe he's at the show just like us. He's probably a Gilbert and Sullivan fan."

Wren nods. "Okay, but we didn't see him at the theater, and it's pretty small." The carefulness in their voice has increased.

I pop the tab of my drink. Now I've got to be careful, too. "Yeah, but—I *know* it was him. I don't know what he was doing here, but that was definitely him."

"Definitely him." Wren says it like a statement, but it's a question.

"Yes."

"Behind those sunglasses, under that hat, on the other side of that ass, which was the only thing we could really see. You *know* that was him."

". . . Yes." I know how it sounds, but I can't help myself. It's true.

Wren sighs. It's not theatrical like the cashier; they're not doing it to perform frustration. It's an unconscious display of the real disappointment I'm causing. "I just—how could you know, Viveca?"

I take a sip of carbonated sweetness. "Because I smelled him."

"Okay, what?" Wren can't help a cheeky smile. "I know Jamison's a fox, but please tell me you're not, like, stealing his gym socks."

"*Ugh.* No." Just the thought of coveting anything of Jamison Sharpe's makes me want to puke. "He's got this *smell*," I say. "I don't know if it's cologne or his laundry detergent or whatever he puts in his hair to make it do that thing it does, but it's very distinct. It's like jasmine, and Saturday, and the moon. And I smelled it just now in the store."

Wren doesn't say anything for a moment. Then they nod. "I don't know why you don't think you're a poet, Viveca. You are a poet."

"That's not really . . ."

They tilt their head. "All right, maybe it was him." They chew their licorice pills. "Maybe he slums it incognito in the theater district when he needs to get away."

We step into the dark street, then hop back as a line of cars just released from their light speeds by. "Yeah, I'm sure he really needs to get away from his fancy house and perfect life up on Snoot Hill."

"Perfect life?" Wren looks at me, shadowy and puzzled. "Where did you hear that?"

"Nowhere, I guess." I shake my head. "I just . . ."

"You know why his family moved here, right?" Wren asks. "I mean, you do know that?"

I give a dry laugh. "LA got boring?"

Wren frowns. I hate that. It makes me feel like I'm in trouble. "Mr. Sharpe has cancer," they say. "Mrs. Sharpe and Jamison are caring for him."

"Oh. Really?" I swallow. "That sucks." It starts to drizzle, shining on the blacktop.

"Yeah, it does." They close up the candy box and shove it into their pocket. "And Mrs. Sharpe has some kind of disease, like auto-immune or something, that means Jamison sometimes has to care for both of them."

"Oh. That's—terrible." It's ghoulish, but the first thing I wanted to say was *That's quite a coincidence.* But of course it's not a coincidence at all. Millions and millions of people are sick, and a lot of them must be married to each other.

"Yeah." Wren scans the empty street. They take my hand and hop down into the crosswalk. "Come on. We're going to miss the beginning of act two."

9

It's twenty minutes to first bell. I realized I could use *The Pirates of Penzance* as one of my senior "cultural event attendance" requirements, so I wrote up a review. But the vice principal needs to sign off on it before I can add it to my graduation portfolio, so I'm hoping to catch him before class. As I pass the lunchroom doors, I can't help glancing at the *Race to the Top!* list. There's my name in the number one spot, just as it has been since the list went up. Below it are Kasey Wheelwright and Gabe Ford and a bunch of other names I've known since freshman year. I know their strengths and weaknesses. I'm pretty sure about what classes they'll take next semester and how they'll do in them. Let's just say I've done my homework.

But I stop. I practically skid to a halt. Because today, for the first time, there's a new name on the list, one that has knocked the president of the robotics club out of tenth place—yeah, Jamison Sharpe.

I stand here, openmouthed in the hallway. I know he bragged

about being top of his class at his old school, but on some level, those were still just words. Like Buck North and his water park. But seeing Jamison's name on the top-ten list is a hypo of shattering reality. I stagger right here, my hand against the painted concrete wall. I almost fall over. It's like when I'm running Scruton Back Road in the predawn mist off the swamp and I can feel the exact moment I cross the town line from Elton back into West Bore. *Clomp.* Suddenly, that smooth *flap-flap-flap* of my sneakers becomes *crunch-hobble-twist-skid* on the crumbling road surface.

I grab hold of my senses and scurry away from the lunchroom doors, sinking onto the bench outside Vice Principal Reinhardt's closed office door.

How can someone who's been here only a few weeks already have infiltrated the senior top ten? How many homework assignments, tests, and quizzes can Jamison even have completed by now? Did they roll over his grades from his old school? How do grades work in France?

He's tenth, Viveca. You're fine, I tell myself. *Don't go nuts.* Flashes of seventh grade. Nip it in the bud.

"Viveca, good morning." Vice Principal Reinhardt blows in from the side door. He shakes off his long coat and unlocks his office, shooting me a friendly smile. "I assume you're here to answer for some heinous crime."

"Nope, just boring stuff," I say.

"Great." He pushes the door open. "Well, head on in."

I do, and take a seat in a cushioned chair. The vice principal hangs up his coat, slides his tablet and a few folders onto his desk, and whooshes back out the door.

"I'll be right back. I missed breakfast—just going to grab a muffin."

I should have told him I only needed a quick signature. Now I have to wait for him to go all the way across the building to the cafeteria. Oh well.

I tap my shoes against the old industrial carpeting. Maybe I should ask Vice Principal Reinhardt about Jamison Sharpe's grades when he comes back. Ha. He wouldn't tell me anything.

His tablet would, though.

Viveca, no. It's my head, but it's Wren's voice—Wren, who flouts rules and regulations like a boulder rolling down a staircase. Somehow I've had the spark of an idea that even they would chastise me for.

What's wrong with looking, though? It's not like it's a *secret* that Jamison is now in the top ten. Heck, he'd probably *give* me a detailed account of his grades so far if I asked—which I'd never do, because he'd know he was getting under my skin, but still. He'd be happy to.

I glance behind me. The office door is closed. Nobody's going to come in here until Reinhardt gets back, which won't be for a few minutes at least. I slide my chair over to the desk and spin the tablet around. I know the vice principal keeps track of the senior top ten; he must have a spreadsheet or something on there. I just want to know what *tenth* means, that's all. Is Jamison way behind, or is he practically ninth? I press the power button and crane my neck.

It's password protected. Of course it is. I spin the tablet back the other way and straighten up in my chair. *Get a grip.* Why do I want details on Jamison's academic record, anyway? What's it going to change?

I stretch my arms and go on a bored visual tour of the office, waiting. Then I notice the folders Vice Principal Reinhardt tossed onto his desk. In the top corner of one, I see a label: *Sharpe.*

Well, this is a development. How long has it been since Reinhardt left? Not long. I have time for the tiniest of peeks. Right?

I flip the folder open and look at the top paper. It's in French. Great. If only Jamison had studied abroad in Moscow, maybe I could get somewhere. The fancy logo at the top says *Lycée International, Paris.* "Lycée" means high school; at least, that's what Jamison said. It's some kind of official letter. Okay, nothing to see here, folks.

Only—I take a closer look at the fancy logo's lines and edges, until my nose is almost touching the paper. *That's weird.* It appears strangely—pixelated? I study the rest of the letter. Judging by the text itself, this isn't a photocopy. So why does the logo look like the printout of a low-resolution image, the kind you could just swipe from a website or something? It's definitely not the quality a fancy international school would use for their official stationery.

But it might be the quality you'd use if you were creating a fake letter and that image was all you could find.

"Hey, Viveca." The door clicks shut behind me.

I jump, flip the folder closed. Turn around.

Jamison is here, in Vice Principal Reinhardt's office, leaning casually against the beige wall. He definitely saw the paper, and there's no way he wouldn't recognize the logo. "Doing some investigating?"

He's smiling, but in this moment, I'm struck by his eyes. They're not cold. They're *roiling*. He knows exactly what I was doing. And suddenly his wide, affable grin is grotesque. Jamison Sharpe's rage smile is the most terrifying thing I've ever seen.

"Oh. Hey, Jamison." I try to be nonchalant. "I've got to get Reinhardt to sign my cultural event." I hold up my review as though I'm presenting evidence in court.

"That's fair," he says, and I'm not sure what he means. "I heard you went to *Pirates of Penzance* on Saturday."

Heard? From who?

"Yeah," I say. "It was good. Lot of pirates. Not too much Penzance."

"Fantastic," he says. Then he slides out some nasal, delicate words I don't recognize.

"What?" I say. I'm trying to keep my lungs under control.

He's still smiling, but his eyes are shrewd. They don't flick to the folder on the desk for even a nanosecond. "Oh, sorry. I thought you spoke French."

"Nope." I shake my head. "I took Russian. My mom's family was from Belarus."

"Is that right?" He crosses his arms, still leaning against the wall. For a moment, he just peers at me, grinning.

He's trying to decide if I actually speak French or not, I think. *He wants to know if I was able to read that letter.*

After a minute, Jamison drops his arms and lightly pushes himself off the wall. And . . . he's back to normal. "I've always thought Russian was a beautiful language," he says. His voice is warm and charming. There's not even a whisper of anger on his face.

"It is," I say.

At that moment, Vice Principal Reinhardt pops back into the office. He seems delighted to find Jamison there. "Good morning, Mr. Sharpe. Can I help you?"

"The secretary said to give this excused absence form to you," Jamison says, handing over a paper.

"Oh, certainly." Reinhardt glances at the paper, then slides open the drawer of a file cabinet.

"Thank you." Jamison turns to go, giving me a wave and a smile—a real, tingly, flirty smile. "See you later, Viveca."

Reinhardt turns to me. "Now, what can I do for you, Viveca?"

It's all I can do to slide my cultural event review across his desk. I'm still reeling. These last five minutes were so bizarre. Jamison was furious, then just . . . not. I mean, he obviously would have good reason to be irritated if he saw me looking at his personal files, but it seemed like so much more than irritation. Or was it just me, my own guilt and surprise coloring what I saw? Did I *imagine* that frightening, accusing Jamison?

Not to mention—was that letter a fake?

10

Wren has somehow convinced me to join them for comics club. I told them I don't have time. I told them I don't need any more extra-curricular credits. I told them I can't really draw.

Wren is impervious to logic. And apparently so am I, because today, when three o'clock rolled around, they swooped into the library, scooped up my backpack like an owl grabbing a rabbit, and flapped away down the hall with me scurrying behind and squeaking, "Hey!"

Now we're here in the art room. I'm not used to this color-splattered space that smells like paint and plaster. Intro to Piano is currently fulfilling my art-credit obligations, so there really hasn't been a reason for me to spend much time here. But it's pleasant. I like the racks of half-dry paintings, the shallow boxes of naked pottery waiting to be fired, the sanctioned unfinishedness of it all. Nothing is in a hurry to be *complete* here.

Tek, a local comics artist who advises the club, stands over Wren and me as we sketch inside our respective rectangular boxes with thick black edges. Tek has a soft voice, round glasses, and long hair. I was nervous about joining a club when everybody else already knew one another, but he didn't make a big deal about it. Most of the beginning of the meeting was him showing us a new project he's working on about a clam with a magic act in Las Vegas. It's hilarious.

"I'm not good at coming up with stuff," I tell him.

"Why don't you start with your world?" Tek offers. There's that question again, like the Pinniped County Futurists—*How do you see the world?* "Does your story take place in school? On a farm? In space? On the mean streets of a gritty urban hellscape?"

"I guess . . ." I start. "Well, I guess it could take place in, uh, the woods."

"Great," he says, moving to another table. He may talk softly and fumble with his glasses a lot, but I guess Tek is the same as all the other teachers here, checking me off the list. He moves on to two sophomores deep in conversation about their new superhero, Butt Man. He uses his butt to squash people or something. Part of me is trying really hard not to just jump onto the table and start declaiming what a waste of time this whole thing is, but the truth is, I'm kind of relaxed right now. And I want to do well for Wren.

They look over at my work in progress. "I'm very proud of you, Viveca. Look at you, shattering your cubicle, taking a risk! Tapping into the creative—aaaaaaand those woods are filled with Muppets, aren't they?"

"I can't draw anything else."

Wren pats my arm. "We'll get there."

"Screw you," I say.

They laugh. "Hey, we're going to Fort Kearsarge later to be delinquents. Wanna come?"

I don't know who "we" are in this scenario. Maybe drama kids. Maybe people from Wren's neighborhood, Eltonians I don't know. Or a pod of community college students who stumbled into the sub shop where Wren works one night and befriended them. It could be anyone. Just imagining it makes the paper in front of me start to go a little squishy, half good and half bad.

I want friends. I do. It's just been so long since I've had a real friend other than Wren, I wouldn't know where to begin, and I'm too old to start learning. I want to *be* friends with people, but I'm terrified of *making* friends with people. In my fantasy, it would be like Wren's drama friends—effortless and relaxed and stylish. But what if my hypothetical new friends just end up being more Alexises and Makaylas or, god forbid, Jamisons?

Everything will be easier once I get away from here, get a new start at Everett. *That* Viveca will be like Mom, not at all anxious about new people.

Just keep telling yourself that.

"Nah, I can't tonight." My fingers are shaky now; luckily trees don't care how messy their branches are. *Pirates of Penzance* was enough excitement to last me a little while. I need to build up my reserves of courage again. Besides, it's one thing for the safe and sterile Viveca-and-Wren bubble to roll out into the world; it's another to insert myself into a group situation where Wren's attention will be divided. Wren knows this and doesn't push.

"Maybe next time," I say, and I mean it. I'll try. I want to.

The World of Viveca North. The title of my nonexistent essay stares at me from the screen.

I've got my laptop set up at a table in West Bore Coffee & Donuts. This isn't a quaint artist hangout with soft jazz and overpriced lattes; it's a grab-and-go caffeine and sugar supplier with fluorescent lighting, old linoleum, and dead flies wedged in the windowsills. That means there's almost always a table open, and I'm definitely not going to run into anybody from school. I love it here.

I'm not a procrastinator—if there's such a thing as someone who is so completely the opposite of a procrastinator that that person touching an actual procrastinator would trigger the formation of a black hole, I'm that person—but I am a work-arounder. I prepare for my work by doing other work, setting all the pieces in place. That's what I tell myself. Reading guidelines, making sure materials are in order, strategizing, double-checking dates—let's just say I have a series of very impressive bullet journals. But sometimes, the work-around-the-work snowballs and becomes its own sort of anti-procrastination. Sometimes you just have to do the thing itself.

I'm not doing the thing. I've spent the last hour going over the fine print on the Pinniped County Futurists' site, and all I've learned is that the essays have to be snail-mailed by our teacher and they can't include any identifying information. That means I can't even use my terrible title, which is the only part of the essay that currently exists. So yeah, that's the progress I've made so far.

How do you see the world? It felt like a softball question when I first saw it. No hidden corners like "a challenge you've overcome" or "someone you look up to," subjects that make you think you're talking about yourself when you're really talking about something else. But now that I'm sitting here staring at glowing whiteness, it's not so easy.

"Top-up, dear?" One of the middle-aged employees buzzes out with a carafe like this is a real restaurant. Despite the regular in-and-out of customers, I'm the only one at a table this afternoon. I don't think they're technically supposed to give refills, but someone usually does, maybe just to check on me. I probably give off a running-away-from-home vibe sometimes.

"Thank you." I hold out my cardboard cup, and the woman tips in a wide splash of dark roast. I wonder if I've been here too long, if she's thinking of calling somebody. She gives me a smile that I warily return.

Is that how I see the world—from behind a wary smile? Do I see everything as conditional, precarious, corrupt? Or am I fooling myself, not recognizing the deceitful people and ideas I've already allowed in—do I not even realize it when my walls have been breached?

That's the problem with the Pinniped County Futurists' essay prompt. There's no concrete event to describe, no other person's philosophies or merits to discuss; the only thing that question wants is . . . me.

11

Calculus exam tomorrow. I'm in bed, but I've got this itchy little what-if voice keeping me awake.

My math teacher, Mr. Howard, is not what you'd call charismatic, but he has this weird energy. It's a lot. You feel like he's either going to playfully toss you up in the air like his beloved infant or wing a chair at your head, and neither of those actions would be related to an actual emotion he is feeling. He loves math, but he's also one of those teachers who have been lording over their tiny square of academia since the dawn of time. Entrenched. For Mr. Howard, every school year, every class period, goes exactly the same way down to the minute. He hasn't created an exam in decades; he just switches the questions around, because everything must always proceed according to the syllabus. Surprise fire drill? Snow day? Alien invasion? Too bad. If the syllabus dictates an exam is to be held on *this* date with *these* questions on it, it doesn't matter if you've actually learned that stuff beforehand or if that particular class period got nuked. You're on your own. The syllabus cannot be stopped.

So although we've learned a lot so far this year, frantically and loudly—I've got calculus spiked through my DNA at this point—I don't quite trust that there won't be some random crap we've never seen before on the exam tomorrow.

AP Calculus is Jamison Sharpe's only tough class. It's not fair, people being able to coast to the top ten on fluff courses, but Elton Prep doesn't weigh GPAs—affluent parents have made sure of that. After all, it's only the *name* of the school that matters to so many of them. But I'm not about to cheapen my record. I've always pushed myself.

I hate myself for knowing Jamison's schedule, but here we are. He's got AP Calc and a bunch of softballs, including Intro to Piano, and don't even get me started on that. I, on the other hand, have two other AP classes, English Lit and European History, as well as college prep physics. I'm doing fine—great!—in all of them. But if, in some universe, I were to slip up in calculus and Jamison were to ace it, well, that might put him ahead, numbers-wise.

Get a grip, Viveca. There's no way Jamison can make you do worse in a math class than him. You can only do that yourself.

The only good thing about Mr. Howard's class is that he abandoned the textbook long ago. Oh, we still use it, but Howard's tests are his own. Too bad for anybody thinking they'll just be able to sneak into the teachers' lounge and take a picture of the answer keys. If that's Jamison's plan, he's out of luck.

But I can't worry about that, or gloat about it, or whatever. I have to stay focused. Since sleep doesn't seem to be on my horizon anytime soon, I lurch out of bed and flip open my laptop. There, floating on my meticulously organized desktop, is the *PinnipedCountyEssay* icon. I open it.

There's this tiny part of me that hopes that maybe today there will be more to this file than just a placeholder title followed by an expanse of white. But nope, it turns out that when you don't write your stuff, it doesn't get written. Who knew?

I put my fingers on the keyboard. At least it feels like Step One. The black letters of my crappy title sit alone on the page like a tray of skinny dead slugs. As time ticks away, I stare and stare. *The World of Viveca North.* Why do I have such a block about this essay? It shouldn't be any different from any other assignment.

Then it hits me—it *shouldn't* be any different from any other assignment. So why am I treating it like that? These futurists don't want my soul on a page; they want an essay done to their specs, following their rules. And that is my *specialty.*

Start by fixing the title. I delete *The World of Viveca North* and try to get into academic mode. What sort of title would look good to a panel of judges? Something active, forward-moving, intriguing. Like about how I'm making my own way through the world, plucky and bright-eyed and worthy of twenty grand.

Finding My Path, I type. Okay, that works. Now, what would an organization like this want to see in a teenager's worldview? I call up their page and go over it again. They wonder, talk about the past, look for patterns. They use a lot of metaphors. I jot down some words that come up frequently so I can incorporate them. I try to imagine a member of the PCF—how do *they* see the world? It's a technique that's been useful to me over the years, imagining my audience. I want there to be no question that Viveca North is worthy of their time.

I get to work. I draft and redraft, tweak, rearrange. I'm flying. By the time I'm done, I have a perfect thousand-word gem that would fit seamlessly into the Pinniped County Futurists' database.

Check the box.

It's after midnight when I flop back into bed. As I lie there, I try to focus on Viveca. My studies. My future. My grades. I see the Everett campus bursting with autumn, and me wearing Mom's forest-green sweatshirt, surrounded by laughing people who actually like me for me.

But as I drift off, my visions morph into colorful pirates and beribboned maidens singing in beautiful, indecipherable French. Every one of them looks like Jamison Sharpe.

———

My phone buzzes me awake earlier than usual. *Ugh.* I can feel the wrong slant of sunlight even before I open my eyes. It's not my alarm, so who's messaging me at this hour? I flop my hand over to my desk and swipe my phone on. A text pops up.

EHS ALERT: All Elton Prep classes and activities are canceled for today.

I sit up. *What?* I tap open the official Elton Prep profile on every social media platform I can think of. They have all been active this morning, but there's no further information, just the same cryptic message: *canceled for today.* A few comments underneath mention police and fire trucks at the school, but nobody seems to know what's going on.

I hesitate before texting Wren. They're never up this early. Just the idea of Wren going for a morning run makes me snort. But if I run before I find out what's happening, I'm going to be so caught up in my own mind I'll probably veer off into the woods, never to be seen again. So I send a message off.

> hey, did you get the school
> alert? what's going on?

I stare at my phone screen, waiting for the "response in progress" dots. Does Wren turn their phone off when they sleep?

Are they okay?

There, see, that's my mind starting to froth with ridiculous little worries. Why wouldn't Wren be okay? It's not like they'd be at school at this hour experiencing whatever the heck is happening. After a couple of minutes, I make myself get up, get dressed, and cinch up my sneakers. Dad's truck is already gone. Ruckus is antsy, so I hook his leash and we head out.

The Scruton Back loop is misty this morning, that early moisture that burns off by breakfast. Ruckus lopes happily beside me, jerking to a halt every so often to investigate roadside earth or trees where other dogs have left interesting urine. As my legs brush against the tall grass around the edges of the bog, frogs jump into the water and kick-swim away. Thankfully, more often than not, Ruckus doesn't notice them.

I keep feeling phantom buzzing from the phone in my pocket, but I know there's no signal back here. I'm not sure why I think Wren will know anything, anyway. Maybe it's because they're connected; they do have an actual circle of friends, unlike me. Sometimes I think it might have been possible to make more than just one friend after I escaped West Bore Junior High, but in reality I could never have pulled it off even if I tried. Another sacrifice that will have been for nothing if I fail.

When Ruckus and I come around the other side of the bog, there's a genuine buzz from my pocket. I stop to look; it's Wren.

Tyson says it's a bomb threat. What is this, 1985??

wtf? Is there an actual bomb?

Not sure. T's mom is one of the officers at the scene. They're checking it out. I think there usually isn't a bomb, right, but they have to check.

This is gonna screw up the calc test.

You're predictable even for a Cancer.

You're crabby for a Virgo.

Ha!

Ruckus tugs at his leash, and I don't argue. It feels good to run, and all of a sudden, I'm itching to get home. I felt prepared for this exam yesterday, but now I have to sit on that confidence for a whole extra twenty-four hours. Some more review has to do me good, right? It's just that hiccups in the schedule throw me. In some ways, I'm a bit like the human version of Mr. Howard's class. Everything must go according to the syllabus—run, breakfast, exam, A-plus. A-plus. A-plus.

I'm going flat out now, and my dog is confused, delighted, and all over the place as we speed toward home. The cancellation didn't feel quite real until this moment; maybe my heart rate wasn't elevated enough to get my brain online, or maybe my reality has to be filtered through Wren.

I unhook Ruckus's leash when we reach the driveway, and he's off like a shot, disappearing around the corner at the top of the hill. He's waiting for me at the door when I stamp to a halt. Dad always leaves him out on his run, but Ruckus knows Viveca means "inside."

At my desk, I check my school email. I can only get it on my laptop, because my phone doesn't like the website for some reason. There's a message from Mr. Howard. It takes a year to download since he's attached twelve large somethings that turn out to be unnecessarily high-resolution images of math problems. And I can't even print out these museum-quality worksheets because we don't have a printer.

The room starts to get a little squishy, that underwater feeling that precedes the black sparkles in my vision, which in turn precede me falling over. I realize I haven't even grabbed a banana or juice. *You're hungry*, I tell myself, because it's true, and also because if I start to worry about whether or not the squishy room is because I'm *worrying*, I just worry more.

Banana. Juice. Shower. Put on your music. Then you have all day to study. An extra study day! This is a good thing!

A half hour later, I'm potassium rich, squeaky clean, and dropping the needle on *Abbey Road*. I sit cross-legged on my faded rug and open *Adventures in Calculus*, whose title makes it sound a lot more like the fantasy novel I wish it were. When my phone buzzes again, I grab it unconsciously, without even taking my eyes off the page. After a moment, I glance down at the message. It's from a number I don't know.

Hey Viveca, what's up?

> Not much. Who is this?

Jamison

My head twitches. Excuse me?

> Hi. What's up?

This is a scintillating conversation so far, but seriously—*excuse me?*

> That's wild about the bomb threat, right?

So Jamison knows about the bomb threat, too. My thoughts zip to that uncomfortable place where my brain starts to feel like it's taking over. *How does Jamison know about the bomb threat?*

I make myself take a redirecting breath before I can continue the thought. He'd know about it if he talked to Tyson, or to anyone Tyson has told, or to anybody who has any connection to the police or fire department or school administration or—or—or . . . Just because it hasn't been on the news yet—as far as I know, and I might even be wrong about that—doesn't mean there aren't possibly hundreds of people who know about the bomb threat.

> Yeah, what is this, 1985?

I roll my eyes at myself. Ripping off Wren—who am I trying to impress? *Jamison Sharpe?*

> Haha. Anyway I'm a bit concerned about the test. How are you feeling about it?

I should puff out. Say I can kick these functions in their y-axes any day of the week. What business is it of his? But instead I reply,

Fine I guess

Wanna be study buddies?
Can I come over?

Okay, and I can't stress this enough—EXCUSE ME?

12

He's at my house.

He's *at* my *house*.

How did this happen? Why didn't I say no? On the other hand, why *would* I say no? Because I feel like he looked at me angrily when he might have caught me peeking at his private documents? What specifically about that interaction paints him in a bad light and me in a good one? Nothing.

This whole thing is giving me a headache. In any case, I guess Jamison coming here is better than me going to his house, lurching my proletarian way around Snob Estates. But if you had asked me yesterday to name the person I'd be the least likely to find sitting on my bed leafing through my sketchbook, it probably would have been a tie between Jamison Sharpe and the pope. And honestly, I can come up with way more plausible scenarios in which the pope shows up. Like maybe my dad has been spamming the official papal

Twitter account with wingnut theories about how the Vatican is really a secret underground smuggling ring, and the pope just up and decides to fly his popejet over here and give Dad a stern look and a prescription for three hundred Hail Marys. Until ten minutes ago, that would have seemed more believable than Jamison hanging out in my room.

"You draw a lot of . . . creatures," he says in an easy voice.

I lean back in my chair. "That is a true thing." He doesn't know what Muppets are, apparently. Or I'm that much of a crap artist. That might be it.

There's no sign of the angry Jamison I saw in Vice Principal Reinhardt's office. This Jamison just seems comfortable and, honestly, pretty nice. Still, I'm regretting letting him in here. His room probably has six-foot windows and pristine white carpeting, with a floor-to-ceiling bookshelf full of trophies. My room is low and dark except for one poorly insulated window and a globe light from the 1990s. It's littered with the sort of battered, burdensome furniture that moves from house to house, generation to generation, that nobody in memory ever actually purchased.

I'm also regretting letting Jamison look at my sketchbook. But when he asked permission, the words I would have needed to deny him didn't seem to exist. Now his stupid pretty eyes are all over my clumsy drawings. I don't even know what I'm feeling.

I clear my throat. "Anyway, do you want to do these problems together, or just compare work?"

He's peering at a page in my sketchbook. "Hey, thanks again

for having me over," he says. "It's hard to study at home sometimes."

I notice, for the first time, his red-rimmed eyes. I remember what Wren said about Mr. Sharpe's cancer, Mrs. Sharpe's illness. Has he been crying? There's something un-Jamison about the way his body is arranged. At school, I mostly see him standing— looming large—and when he sits in class, it's ramrod straight. Now he's slouched, cross-legged, on my bed in his sock feet. He looks almost human. Beautiful and tragic like a Renaissance painting.

"You know, you're very good at whatever this is. Portraiture," he says, flipping the sketchbook around to show me a pencil drawing of Gonzo on a surfboard. "It's quite charming."

"Huh." I'm not sure if my response is a laugh or a scoff, but I'm suddenly desperate to change the subject. I hold up *Adventures in Calculus* like it's a cross warding off a vampire. "Look, do you want to study? I have no desire to fail this exam."

He smiles. Prince Charming. "No, I bet you don't. Everett, isn't it? I've heard that's a good school."

"I—" I falter. And then I realize how much I've let my guard down. How does Jamison know I applied to Everett? How much information does he have about me, and why has he been collecting it?

"Hey, you don't have to look so freaked out." Jamison closes the sketchbook and sets it next to himself on the bed. "I'm on the year-book committee. Remember the 'Hopes and Dreams' things?"

"Oh. Right." All the seniors had to fill out those sappy question-naires. But why would Jamison even be on the yearbook committee? Is he that invested in his new classmates' lives already?

I open the math book and flip to the correct page, keeping my eyes on the equations.

Jamison leans forward. "Or maybe I've been watching you, Viveca."

I look up and freeze. His gaze is strange and intense, his teeth bared in what might pass for a smile from a distance but feels almost primal up close.

Then he laughs. "Oh god, Viveca, I'm sorry. Wren said you were tied up in knots over this stupid valedictorian thing. I didn't quite believe it."

Wren? When does Jamison talk to Wren? And why would they tell him that?

Is the universe collapsing in on itself, or is it just me?

I look at him, but all I can say is "Wren?"

He lights up. "Oh yeah! Wren said you were best friends. Honestly, I'm not sure who to be more jealous of." *Sheesh, he's down-right endearing. Or at least he appears that way.* "Anyway, sorry I freaked you out," he says. "No more dumb jokes, I promise. You're right, let's get to work."

A cool gust of air through my cracked-open window fills the room with the captivating scents of pine trees and Jamison Sharpe. The chilling, toothy creature of thirty seconds ago seems like a weird hallucination. How much of that reality existed here in my shabby room, and how much just formed in my own head? It's impossible to know. I feel like I'm having flashes of clarity, but if that clarity is when Jamison seems like a calculating devil or when he seems like a likable study buddy, I'm not sure.

To an observer, Jamison and I would simply look like two mismatched classmates thinking about math together. I imagine what Wren would say if they were here, ogling the sharp-jawed Adonis lounging in my bed.

On. On my bed.

I guess I can ask them next time I see them, since apparently Wren and Jamison are super best friends. Or at least pally enough to talk about *me*. I take a breath and push a whole bunch of weird feelings down to the bottoms of my feet.

Right now, the only discussion I care about is math. "Okay, well, let's start with the first page."

For a while, we're intent on our studies. Jamison radiates confidence. I can practically see beams of it shining out of his skin. He speaks a little too loudly for the space, talks over the ends of my sentences. He nods and agrees with me and repeats phrases I've said or terms from the text. He talks about the teacher he had in Paris and teaches me some math words in French whose sounds I don't retain. But, strangely, I feel like I'm teaching him more than we're learning together. It's almost like one of my tutoring sessions.

"Hey, are you thirsty?" he says. "I don't want to impose, but I didn't bring my water bottle."

I'm in the middle of sketching a graph, but I put my pencil down. "Oh. Sure. Do you want tap water? We also have OJ. Well, like, that fake fruit drink stuff. And probably some ginger ale." *God, Viveca, could your refrigerator be more lower middle class?*

He grins. "I haven't had ginger ale since I was a kid! Would you mind?"

I shake my head and go to the kitchen. For a fleeting moment, I have the ludicrous idea that there might be ice cubes in the freezer, but of course, since I'm the only person who would think to fill it, the tray is just cold, empty plastic.

When I come back bearing a can of generic ginger ale, I'm surprised to see Jamison in my desk chair looking at my laptop screen. He nonchalantly turns to face me as I enter the room. A little too nonchalantly? Or just the right amount? I'm not sure.

"Are you done with your Pinniped County essay already?" he asks. I realize the file icon is sitting prominently on the screen. He goes on in an easy voice. "I feel like the fact that Ms. Racine doesn't want them until the day of the deadline is making me procrastinate, you know? I mean, that's a *me* problem, but I still feel like she put a bit of a psychological twist on the whole thing."

I'm not sure how to feel right now. Was Jamison looking at my stuff? There's nothing open that I can see. "I, uh," I say, "I'm pretty sure she just doesn't want to lose them. She's kind of disorganized. She does that with term papers, too, collects them all at once on the due date."

Jamison grins. "And you would know, Viveca, wouldn't you? How many other people have actually tried to hand in term papers early?" I can't seem to do anything but turn red right now, which is stupid. But Jamison doesn't seem bothered. Instead, he asks, "Hey, can I read it?"

"Huh?"

He points to the screen. "Can I read your essay?"

It's just like when he asked to see my sketchbook. My guts feel like *no*, but my brain can't come up with a reason. I shrug. "I guess."

He double-clicks the icon and leans forward. His lips move a tiny bit as he reads. There's something wriggly in my chest as I watch him—am I hoping for his approval?

Jamison sits back in my chair and exhales. "Wow," he says. "Wow, Viveca, I know Ms. Racine said you were a good writer, but *that . . .*" He pauses and nods. "That's a winning essay right there."

I'm flushing again. Or still? "Thanks," I say. "That's nice of you to—"

At the sound of barking, Jamison looks out the window. "That your dog out there? He's adorable."

"Um, yeah. That's Ruckus. Not much of a guard dog. Too friendly." I guess we're done talking about my essay. *What do you want, Viveca? You want Jamison Sharpe, of all people, to keep gushing about your work?* I have to admit it felt good.

He nods. "He reminds me of my dog, Checkers. He's the best boy. One hundred percent butt wiggles, like an electric eel." He laughs, and I laugh, too. I'm loosening up.

"Yep, that's Ruckus."

"I wish people were more like dogs, you know?" He tilts his head back, studying my water-stained ceiling. "Just . . . made of love."

I don't know what to say to that. What do you say to that? "Yeah," I murmur.

Jamison looks at me, and this time there's a murkiness there, like a sadness just below the skin. "You and I, Viveca—we're much more interesting than that. We're beasts of ambition."

I look back at him. After a moment, I realize my mouth is open as though I'm going to say something, but my mouth is wrong. There are no words on deck in my brain.

Jamison laughs. "And we're beasts with a math test tomorrow. Am I right?"

I inhale. "Yeah. We should probably keep going." It's like his every move is calculated to make me even more curious about him. But I don't want him to know it's working.

I pull another notebook out of my bag, and my jackknife tumbles onto the rug.

Jamison eyes it with an amused look. "Expecting trouble?"

"Oh. No." I scoop the knife back into my bag. "Just my jackknife. It's useful. Lives in my bag."

"Sounds handy. What's in the notebook?"

I show him some of the problems I've completed, and we move on. At midday, we're tired and overstuffed with math. Dad probably won't come home for lunch, but I don't want to take the chance of him finding a strange boy in my room, even a boy as not my type—not to mention out of my league—as Jamison Sharpe. It's never happened before, so I have no idea if Dad would be angry or delighted, but I don't want to deal with either of those things. I hurry through the last problem and wind the session down.

"Thanks so much, Viveca." Jamison gets to his feet and stretches his long arms to the ceiling, laying his palms flat against the plaster. He could take up almost my entire room if he wanted to. "You're a good friend."

He reaches into his bag and pulls out a hoodie to head home in. As he slides it over his head, I read the word emblazoned across the front: HARVARD.

Freaking Harvard. Yeah, okay. I hadn't really thought about where Jamison might be going next year, but *of course* it's freaking Harvard because he's so freaking perfect. He is an absolute *cartoon character.*

He smirks. "It's not really fair, me wearing this when I haven't gotten in yet. I don't even know where I really *want* to go, you know? But I've got some good options."

"That's great." My words come out flat despite my best efforts.

"Well, I had great recommendations. Glowing. From some very influential voices." Now his face lights up. "Ever hear of *Teen Vibe Magazine*?"

"Sure." Duh. Where is this going?

He blushes a little. "Well, I was fortunate to be chosen for a cover of theirs a couple of years ago."

I blink. "You. Were on the cover of *Teen Vibe*." It's so outlandish. And so easily verifiable. I . . . what?

"It was the Taiwanese version, actually. We were there on vacation. Wonderful place." He gets animated, like he's going to sell me a car. "Anyway, I scored a sweet letter of recommendation from the editor. She's a lovely woman, passionate, very influential. She really *got* me, took me under her wing. Her letter's going to put me over the top in a lot of Ivy League situations, know what I mean?"

But I don't know. He knows I don't know, somehow. My letters of recommendation were excellent. First-rate. Sterile. But not heartfelt, not like his. How could anyone speak of me from their heart when I'm not in there?

"That's the thing, Viveca." Jamison points at me, raising an eyebrow. "Grades are important, but the most important thing? It's people. Without people to speak for you, to lift you up, you're nothing more than a spreadsheet. Numbers. Rubrics. You're *paper*, Viveca, not a *person*. That's why this"—he gestures vaguely at the room, me, whatever—"is so important. Why people like us are going to make it."

People like us. My voice sticks. I'm not like Jamison. Does he know that—is that why he said that stuff about just being numbers on a sheet of paper? Was it a dig?

Or does he really think we're alike, that I'm the sort of person who has an impact on people? That I'm memorable?

"Anyway." Jamison slides his notebook into his bag and slings it over his shoulder. "Today was great. I hope we both do well."

He flashes that million-dollar smile, and it feels dirty, like payment for my efforts. The air seeps from my lungs. Nothing he said was mean, so why do I feel so taken down? Why do I feel like some scout-camp macaroni necklace trying to smile at the Hope diamond?

I walk him to the front door, and he's gone. Through the window, I watch his black SUV crunch down the driveway as Ruckus barks and pulls at his leash.

I sink into a kitchen chair. *Ivy League situations?* Teen Vibe *Taiwan?* I've lived with a liar so long my alarm is on a hair trigger. But—people *do* appear on magazines and go to Harvard. And Jamison certainly seems like someone who might be "discovered" for modeling gigs, if that's what happened. Still—

The textbook in the teachers' lounge, the possibly fake letter from some French school, and the heaps of unbelievable accomplishments . . . I know there are extraordinary people out there. Jamison is definitely one of them. But I'm just feeling more and more like the stories everyone has heard about him aren't the reasons he's unique—that his uniqueness is something much darker.

If I thought I was going to get clarity about Jamison Sharpe through spending hours alone with him in a small room, I was wrong in a big way. The only thing that became clear today makes me even more confused than before: Despite all his confidence and fancy education, Jamison was not prepared for the math test that we would have had today. In fact, the only reason he has a shot at passing now is because the best student in the class gave him a crash course in calculus.

And the only reason that was possible was because of the bomb threat.

13

It's five minutes to first bell, and things seem back to normal at school. I mindlessly scroll through the Taiwanese *Teen Vibe* website, even though I can't read anything it says and it seems like you have to subscribe to do any searches or look at pictures. The bomb threat turned out to be a hoax, so aside from some frayed nerves, everything is fine. Still, I got to school extra early today, as though I could beat any more disasters to the punch. *Too bad I'm already here with my number two pencil. Guess all you bomb threats or burst pipes or lice infestations will just have to wait.*

Wren and I sit on the bench outside Mr. Howard's classroom. "I feel like you're not telling me something," they say. "You've got this secretive air today. It's cool, I mean. But my curiosity is piqued."

"What about *your* secrets?" I ask. Wren hasn't mentioned Jamison Sharpe to me once, but apparently they're buddy-buddy enough to be having conversations about my anxieties when I'm not around. What is that? Is Wren having a laugh at Jamison's expense, or could Jamison possibly have them fooled just like everybody else?

It's not a big deal, I tell myself. Wren is friends with everybody; that's their charm. Jamison's never *done* anything to them. He's never done anything to me! Getting all jealous right now is just going to make me look bad. Besides, I'm probably just freaking out about the fact that Jamison is now third in our class. That's right. *Third*.

I'm starting to wish the *Race to the Top!* list were posted in the basement or a storage closet someplace instead of where I have to look at it every day.

"My secrets?" Wren says. "I have no secrets, Viveca. You know that." They don't seem to have picked up on my angst, which is good. "Now please tell me what delicious tidbits you're hiding before I drop all my petals and wither on my stalk."

Now they're looking at me with these big, gleaming eyes, staring into my depths. I have to tell them. I study my lap and inhale, which is stupid, because it makes it seem like I'm about to drop some earth-shattering truth when the only thing I have to say is . . . is . . .

"Jamison came over yesterday. We studied for the exam, that's it. That's *it*. I don't know why, and yes, it was weird, and to answer your next question, he was the one to message me. I definitely didn't send him an invitation. That's all."

I look up. Wren's eyebrows are practically on the ceiling. Their mouth is doing this half up–half down thing, like there are several wires crossed between lips and brain. They tilt their head. "I'm sorry, *what*?"

"Yeah, I know. I know! I said it was weird."

"Jamison. Jamison Sharpe. Mr. Shiny Popular. Wanted to hang out at your house."

My air slides out and doesn't seem to come back; my lungs are just wrinkled balloons hanging there in my chest. "Jeez, is it that unthinkable?"

They roll their eyes. "That's not what I meant. Come on, Viveca. Cut me some slack here. This is a strange turn of events, and I don't even have my cards on me."

Yeah. What a strange turn of events. How absolutely topsy-turvy that golden boy Jamison Sharpe would want to hang out with annoying overachiever Viveca North. Well, I don't care what Wren thinks.

"It's almost time for the exam. I gotta go in," I say. "Have fun in drama. Don't get, like, hug poisoning or anything." Wren slid through geometry last year and decided they were done with math. Now, in addition to drama club, they spend first block in theater class, playing improv games and being loud in the hallways.

Wren gets up. "I won't." There's an edge there, and I realize it was chipped from my own edge. Crap. Now we're being edgy with each other, and I hate that.

I sigh. "Look, I'm sorry, I didn't mean anything like—"

"I'll see you at lunch. Good luck on your test." They're gone.

What is wrong with me? AP Calc is hard, but I'm sure drama is hard, too. That's Buck North, right there—judging people for liking stuff he doesn't.

I set up halfway back. It's only a minute before other people start dragging in. Jamison and his Harvard sweatshirt glide through the doorway with Kasey Wheelwright, who has her pierced nose in a stack of index cards. Today the ends of her beach-sand ponytail are vibrant purple, neon green, and red. She's got on a professionally distressed patchwork jacket and long Alice in Wonderland stockings. Kasey Wheelwright has the money to be alternative. I dyed half my hair blue one time. It lasted a week, then turned this sickly shade of dead, bleached grass. Plus my shower looked like I'd murdered a Smurf. What a pain. Never again.

But Kasey's freedom to express herself through style doesn't matter right now. Neither do Jamison and his stupid sweatshirt. Because Mr. Howard is passing out the tests, and it's time to do what I do best. Get in the zone. Focus on the work.

The exam isn't bad; it's mostly limits. *And I know my limits!* I think. Ba-dum-tss. I come up with more clever things I could say in case I'm ever part of a witty, math-themed conversation. But that only makes me think about Wren, so I try to concentrate on the problems on my paper. The hiccup in my schedule is over, we're back on track, and I'm going to ace this test. If I can stop getting distracted.

I glance at Jamison, two desks in front of me, head bowed studiously. He's going to do fine, too. Part of me wishes I'd never agreed to help him—I could have had an edge today. That's such a gross thing to think. Still, school getting canceled yesterday was the best thing that could have happened to him.

Halfway through the final problem, I remember the SIM card. If that *was* Jamison in the convenience store the night of *Pirates of Penzance*, and if he *does* have a burner phone, what does he do with it?

Does he anonymously call in bomb threats?

I try to shake it off, focus on finishing up the last problem. When it's over, I leave class feeling confident.

At lunch, I can't find Wren in the cafeteria. They're probably out in the courtyard with their drama friends. And it's *probably* not a statement about our on-the-verge-of-strained friendship. Still, I shiver through about a half second of anxiety before I grab a bagel and orange juice and head outside.

I push open the exterior doors. The courtyard is busy. Students wallow in the cloud-diffused sunlight. The autumn air is pleasantly cold, whispering about crackling leaves and haunted forests. The courtyard benches are mostly full; small groups lounge against concrete planters and iron light posts, the swirly flagstones peppered with notebooks, sub wrappers, and bottles.

I see Wren and their friends at the far end, draped decoratively around a red bench. Wren's sitting on the ground with their back to me, but that blue paisley shirt is unmistakable. They're looking put together as usual.

A burst of laughter ripples through the drama kids as I

approach. They don't notice me standing there awkwardly.

"How can you sit there, calmly eating muffins?" Jade Bowman is saying. Her red vinyl jacket squeaks as she gesticulates. "It's heartless!" This cracks them all up for some reason.

As Wren tips their head back, they notice me. "Hey, how was your test?" They pat the ground next to them. People scooch over to make room.

"Fine," I say. "I hope I reviewed enough yesterday."

Jade laughs. "Don't tell me you came to school on bomb-threat day. That would be *so Viveca.*"

Tyson LaRoche raises his pointer finger. "I *might* get exploded," he says in his best Viveca North voice, which isn't very good, "but at least I won't be *late!*"

It feels good to laugh with them. I'm pretty sure they aren't really making fun of me. "I think a perfect attendance joke would have been sharper," I say.

"Dammit!" Tyson slaps the flagstones. "Jade, feed me the line again."

"The moment has passed." Jade pulls a scrunchie off her wrist and loops her hair into a messy knot. The wind has picked up a little, and a few random wrappers start scooting around the courtyard like bugs.

Min looks up from a script she's highlighting. "Wait, you didn't really come to school yesterday, did you?"

I bend my knees and pull my legs to the side. "Nope, I just lounged on the couch and ate ice cream."

Wren gives me a playful punch on the arm. "And I'm sure you did fine on your math test, brainiac. Besides, with such a scintillating study partner, how could you lose?"

My body tenses up at that. Okay, it's fine. This is apparently how we're working out our snippiness from this morning—Wren's publicly poking at my weird place, and I'm going to have to endure the drama club's outsized reaction. "Good point," I say. There's still a chance Wren's remark will die unnoticed.

"What scintillating study partner?" Min asks. Tyson repeats the phrase, trying it out with a commanding stage voice. A few heads around the courtyard turn briefly in our direction.

My cheeks heat up. If I deflect, everyone will just prod harder. So I shrug. "Jamison Sharpe." And there we go. Scandalized looks from the audience. One or two gasps of shock and delight. Is Wren happy now?

Jade laughs but then processes my embarrassed expression. "Really? Jamison Sharpe? He's a *fox*."

"Study buddies!" Tyson says.

I let my head drop backward. "Why is that so unbelievable? I'm a good study buddy."

"She so is," Wren says, putting an arm around my shoulders. "We just love a mystery, Viveca. That's all."

There's so much and so little I want to say about yesterday, all at the same time. And for some awful reason, with all of them looking at me, I decide to get chatty. "Yeah, well, I'll tell you the biggest mystery." The words tumble out. "It's the mystery of how Jamison sucks at calculus."

Wren snorts. "Wow, that's harsh. Maybe he's good under pressure?"

"I bet he is," Jade says with a smirk.

"No, you don't get it." I hear my voice getting more energized. There's something rising inside me. "He doesn't understand it. He can't tell a . . . a . . ."

"A calculus from a cactus?" Tyson booms.

"Right!"

"'A calculus' isn't a thing," Min says.

"That's not the point." Now I'm gesticulating like I'm playing Hamlet. "He's been doing some weird stuff. So I'm pretty sure he went in the teachers' lounge"—I'm interrupted by sarcastic *oooohs*, but I'm on a roll—"*and* I think there might be something off about his supposed French school last year. I—" I stop myself. *Don't talk about the logo; don't let them know you looked at his file.* I redirect. "Okay, so that stuff aside, listen, Jamison was not prepared for the test yesterday. If I were him, I'd have done *anything* to get out of it. Give myself more time. You see?" I turn to Wren. "So think about it. Remember when we saw him downtown? It makes sense now. *A burner phone.* You said it yourself. He—"

Wren puts a hand on my arm. "Viveca, I think you should stop before you posit a theory, in front of people, that you can't unposit." They squeeze. Not hard, but pointedly.

"What?" Jade asks.

I look at the rapt faces of the drama clique, and my energy drips away into the ground. "I . . ." Wren is right. Why would Jamison call in the bomb threat? It would have been a huge risk, and for what? He didn't *know* I'd be willing to study with him—how could he bet everything on it?

Besides, if I say it, I know exactly what's going to go through everyone's heads.

"Yeah, I—I guess it's just a crazy thought." I look at Wren. "Is that what you think?"

They give me this look I can't read. "I don't know, Viveca. All I know is that I don't think about Jamison Sharpe half as much as you do."

14

By the time Wren and I met freshman year, we were already too old for trick-or-treating. According to my dad. But that was obviously complete nonsense. Why wouldn't we trick-or-treat as long as humanly possible? Why wouldn't everyone? Dressing up in a costume for free candy, plus getting to kind of see inside any house you want—what part of that isn't universally appealing? So the plan has always been that I tell Dad I'm going to a Halloween party, then just meet up with Wren to go door to door with their little sister, Poppy. She's good for justifying our presence to the teenage-averse households. You can always tell the ones—they'll be watching like owls, making sure you don't take too many fireballs from the bowl, scrutinizing your costume for telltale bulges of toilet paper rolls. But Poppy wins them over. If her drugstore puppy or zombie costume doesn't do the trick, she has an adorable way of turning her *r*'s into *w*'s that will melt even the crustiest adult.

This year, however, Poppy has declared she's too grown up for trick-or-treating. She's in middle school now and they're having a Halloween dance. On Saturday morning, Halloween, I tell Wren over video chat that we should just stay in, stuff our faces, and watch horror movies all night. But they blindside me with an invitation to a party.

A party.

Me.

"It's only Min's house," they say. "You know Min. She's delightful. She's your friend."

The bats in my belfry are rustling. "I'm not saying she isn't delightful, but she's *your* friend. I just don't think I'm up for a party."

"'Up for.'" Wren does air quotes. That's annoying. "What do you mean 'up for'? Is it social anxiety? Are you freaked out about potential illegal activities? Are you afraid of the intensity of the romance that might spark between you and Min's brother?"

"It's just—what?" I almost drop my phone. "Who the heck is Min's brother?"

Wren looks at me like I'm a talking stump. "He's a person who is part of the Park nuclear family, of the generation that includes Min, but that does not include Mr. and Mrs. Park." They waggle their eyebrows. "He doesn't go to Elton; he's in some kind of expensive academy somewhere. Or, like, *more* expensive academy. But I have met him, so he is very probably a real person, or an excellent fake, which is almost as good. And he thinks you're cute, according to Min. Apparently he noticed you when you came to our play last year."

"Is this some kind of—threat?" I stammer.

Wren shrugs. "I don't see how it could be. You have a costume, right?"

". . . I could throw something together."

"Great! You get a puffy sticker." They wiggle their fingers at the screen. "I'll pick you up at seven. Hey, you don't have to lie to your dad this year!"

"I'd rather watch horror movies," I grumble.

"We can do that, too. I promise."

———

Min lives in Elton, not on the fancy hill, but in a nice development along the Kearsarge River just past the neighborhood where kids play in green parks and the trendy storefronts and artsy apartments are barely recognizable as the bleak mill buildings they once were. As we navigate to the Halloween party, a few trick-or-treaters are still out roaming the dusk with their plastic pumpkins.

Wren, wrapped in fabric-store fur and sporting a long latex wolf nose, parks their beater crookedly on the cul-de-sac. We head for the house with the most pumpkins out front. I'm expecting the drama club, maybe a few outliers, but the Parks' spacious driveway is packed. Cars sprawl up and down the quiet street. Music and voices pour from the windows.

This is a *party*. What do I do? I start to get squishy, the good-bad kind. My torso wants to swoosh right around and march away into the night, but my face is stuck staring at the house, biting my lip, eyes wide with some combination of nerves and excitement.

"Do I look okay?" I ask Wren. I feel silly about asking, honestly, but I could use some shoring up.

Wren stops dead. They make fierce eye contact and point squarely at me. "Viveca. Listen to me. You are the sexiest freaking Kermit the Frog I have ever seen."

I adjust my Ping-Pong-ball-eyes headband modestly. "I don't know if I believe you, but I love that that sentence just happened."

We walk up the driveway and step onto the porch. Min opens the door wearing a metallic astronaut costume and carrying a bowl of full-sized candy bars. "Hey, it's Kermit the Frog and his friend the werewolf!" A cheer erupts from deeper within the house, where I can see colored lights flashing and bodies moving in the fluctuating shadows. There are a lot of people here. What would happen if I just frog-hopped back out the door and hid in the bushes? Or maybe there's a special bathroom in the house somewhere that nobody's supposed to use; I could totally hide out in there under the lily pads.

"Thanks for coming, earthlings," Min says. "Follow the noise."

The spacious, open-concept first floor is swarming with people in costumes. I recognize a lot of the unmasked faces—jeez, it seems like the whole senior class is here. A long dining table is set with a crystal punch bowl and an array of snacks. Wren ladles out drinks for us. They hand me a cup, my green woolen mitten slipping a little as I grasp it, and I take a cautious sip. It's just punch. I'm not sure where Min's parents are, if they're out at their own party or sequestered in another part of the house, but it seems their specters are still preventing the beverages from getting spiked, at least for now.

I get my bearings. There's a sunken section of the living room with a couple sofas around a tall fireplace. Every square inch of sofa has someone perched on it, and more people lounge on the shaggy cream rug between them. In the center of one of the sofas sits a long, familiar shape: Jamison Sharpe.

Of course Jamison is here. My stomach sinks. I don't want to deal with him—effervescence, gleaming teeth, wafting charisma. He's grinning broadly and waving his hands around like he's telling the most entertaining story ever. He's not even wearing a costume, just a tight-fitting black T-shirt that says *boo* in Courier like he's some edgy artist or something. And people are just hanging off him, hanging off his words, draped around his person, clustered at his feet.

"Viveca!" Wren's voice cuts through my annoyed stare, and I realize they've said my name a couple times now.

"Oh!" I turn to them. "Hey!" They laugh and shake their head.

"Now it's a party!" booms a voice from the far corner of the room near the thumping sound system. Wren raises their cup to Tyson, who's wearing some kind of boxy suit with LED pinstripes, and we slither through the crowd toward him. As we walk, twist, edge, excuse ourselves, I keep my eyes focused on the glowing green ghost decoration hanging just over Tyson's head. I've learned it's soothing to have something concrete to focus on in crowds.

"Braaaawwwrr!" Tyson roars as we reach him. "Don't suck my blood!"

I laugh and tweak Wren's plastic dog nose. "Werewolves don't suck blood."

Tyson puts a heavy arm around my shoulders, sliding the jagged felt collar I made to complement my green thrift-store sweatshirt. "I was *obviously* talking to *you*, Viveca," he says.

I bare my nonexistent fangs. "Vampire frogs are the most deadly!"

"Wren! Viveca!" It's Miranda Nazarian in pinup makeup and full 1950s sitcom mom attire. I don't know her very well, but apparently she does some kind of cosplay–lip sync combination thing and has a crapton of followers who throw money at her. Rumor has it she's gearing up to get her own apartment in the city.

Miranda holds up her phone, and Wren and Tyson automatically pose. I can't come up with a good "frog" attitude fast enough, so I just raise my arms and stick out my tongue and she snaps a picture of us.

"Ha, that's great," she says, looking at her screen. Then, "Oh, Danny, Danny! Get in there. I'll take another one."

Someone I've never seen before steps out from a knot of people with their backs to us. He's wearing a full-on clown suit, floppy shoes, rainbow wig, squashy red nose. His cheeks are circles of crimson. He has gentle, dark eyes that glint as he tilts his head. And from what I can see behind the wig and nose, he looks a lot like Min.

Min's brother. The one who goes to an expensive academy, which means he's smart. Who Wren seems to like, which means he's interesting. And who thinks I'm cute . . . Well, at least according to Wren, who was probably lying.

But what if they weren't lying?

I'm not sure what to do with my arms and legs right now.

"Hey, Danny!" Wren scoops him over with a long, furry arm. "Scooch over here next to Viveca."

"Oh. Okay," the hot clown says as Wren squishes him next to me. "Hi, Viveca."

"Hi," I say, dressed as Kermit the Frog.

"Ready?" Miranda holds up her phone. Everyone poses. All I can think to do is open my mouth and make my eyes really big, like a fish. "Great!" Miranda gives us the thumbs-up and flits away.

"Viveca, this is Danny Park," Wren says.

I unintentionally give Danny a look that I hope doesn't read *terrified.* "Um, hi," I say. "Again."

"Hi," Danny says, and everyone laughs. It's an awkward moment, but we're all in on it, so it's not so bad. I catch his eye but look away immediately; I don't even know why. After a moment, I look back, and he cracks this beautiful smile in my direction. My organs are doing somersaults.

"Min says you like *Sesame Street*," Danny says. His cheeks look a little pinker under his big red circles, but I can't be sure.

"I said Muppets." Min spacewalks her way into our circle. "She draws them."

I shoot Wren an accusing look. How does Min know that? But they've got their impish face on, and there's no shaming them when they're like that.

Besides, Danny Park is still looking at me with interest.

Interest? Maybe? I should think of something clever to say. "Yep," I croak. *Well, that wasn't it.*

"Hey," Min says, "why don't you draw us something right now? Look!" She reaches behind a bookcase full of board games and pulls out an easel with a giant drawing pad. "We use this for Pictionary," she says. "I have the markers somewhere. Oh, here." She pulls a cookie tin from a shelf and hands it to me.

I hold the tin out to Wren. "Wren's the artist. Maybe they'll draw us a comic."

A few other people are glancing our way, showing mild interest in the easel. To my immense relief, Wren takes the tin and pops the lid. At the top of the paper, they write *Moon Adventures!* Then, underneath, they outline a big black square.

"Your turn." Wren hands the tin of markers back to me. I try to give them my wide-eyed *rescue me* look, but they just twinkle and shake the box like it's a bag of cat treats.

I stare at the paper, immobile. A rainbow of light from a spinning mini disco ball dances over the white surface in time with the bass from the sound system. People are looking at me. Danny is looking at me. I know I've only known him for three minutes, and a lot of the feelings I'm having are probably because Wren planted that dumb seed in my head about him liking me, which couldn't possibly be true, but my god, he's just about as gorgeous a clown as I can imagine right now. I look at Wren's blocky writing: *Moon Adventures!*

I take off my green woolen mittens, stick them in my pocket, and start to draw. I'm not a good artist, but I have a lot of experience—a lot of *specific* experience. So I draw what I know, a little sideways. I draw Min in her astronaut costume planting a flag at the edge of a crater—only her arms are floppy, her torso shortened, and the flag has gone sailing off into the sky.

"That's pretty good," Tyson says. "Hey, put me in!" I draw him next to her, with a wide mouth that splits his whole head in half, the lights from his light-up suit flashing. Wren grabs a marker and adds a label, *SOS!* A couple of people giggle.

With my adrenaline starting to ramp up, I draw Wren as a googly-eyed werewolf marking their territory. This makes everyone crack up, including Wren.

"Do me!" Danny says. "Do me as a Muppet!" And I sort of realize that I *have* been drawing everyone in a silly, floppy-limbed, bulgy-eyed style. They're almost caricatures, and they're pretty good. Huh. I didn't know I could do that.

I add Danny, with his colorful hair and bulbous nose, juggling moon rocks. Then, with a ridiculous burst of confidence, I sketch my frog-like self next to him. Wren adds a speech bubble beside my flapping mouth: *Hey! NASA needs those rocks!*

The jokes aren't that funny, but it's a party and people are ready to be entertained. I realize about half the living room is now gathered around, a collection of creatures, monsters, knock-off celebrities, and cartoon characters, all pointing and chatting. Wren grabs the red marker and makes Danny's feet and nose even bigger, which gets a good reaction from the crowd. In a bold move, I look over at Danny. He's looking back at me and grinning, and my stomach flutters.

What's going on? Is something going on? I don't have a lot of experience with boys. Guys. Men. I don't even know what they are anymore. A little *What is this? Is this talking?* type texting here and there that never went anywhere, maybe a movie with Wren and some of their friends, but really, there was never enough time for that stuff. Now Danny Park is grinning at me and I'm smiling back at him. It's always seemed like everyone in the world is good at flirting except me, but maybe that's what we're doing right now.

"Hey, Viveca." A voice made of velvet. "Draw me."

I turn around to find Jamison has joined us. Because of that, people are focused on him now. Center stage has moved from the easel to him. He watches me with a slick smile that doesn't extend beyond the corners of his lips.

That cold, calculating Jamison is back—and I'm the only one who can see it. My confidence dribbles away. But I realize something about him: *He doesn't like it when other people are in the spotlight.* Even when he's complimenting you, it's only because it affects how you feel about *him.* That's why it irritates him that Wren and I are stealing his limelight.

The only person Jamison Sharpe cares about is himself.

"Okay, Jamison, I'll add you," I say. I draw a thin figure, sparkling, sharp-jawed, floating above the moonscape like a deity. Then I add a T-shirt, with the words *Hipster Costume* across the chest, and the figure's spidery arms clutching its throat. I color the face blue. *Too Cool for Oxygen* I label it.

Everyone loses it. They're cackling, taking photos, uploading. Jamison pretends he's in on the joke, but he's not. He's trying to spin it. But this party is laughing *at* him right now.

And he *hates* me for it.

I stare into his icy blue eyes, and he stares back without blinking. Holy crap—*he hates me.* Probably from the first day he came here. Probably from the first time he saw my name at the top of that list: *Viveca North. The one I need to take down.* That's why he's been in my space, at my house, scoping me out, messing with my brain. But I've got his number now. And I've scored my first victory against him.

I close my eyes for a moment. There's an unsettling old feeling in the pit of my guts. A tiny zap at the back of my brain. *You see what you want to, Viveca. Just like with Jackie Boynton.* Is it my conscience? The shreds of my sanity trying to poke through? What can anybody really tell just from looking at someone's expression?

"I need some more punch," Jamison announces, and suddenly half the party moves to the snack table.

Min examines Wren's and my masterpiece. "This is magnificent," she says. "I'm going to frame it."

Tyson carefully pulls the large self-sticking paper off its stack and presses it onto the wall. "Okay, now who wants to play Pictionary? Double points for Halloween words." Min and Wren are in, and so is Jade Bowman, who's a late arrival. A few other people saunter over as the game begins.

I feel a hand on my elbow and turn to find Danny Park a lot closer to me than I thought he was. "Hey, frog girl," he says. "We've got a lily pond out back. Wanna see it?"

15

There *is* a lily pond out back of the Parks' house. It's artificial, with curving brick sides and mounds of dark loam around the edges with the chilly remains of what must have been lush summer flowers. At one end, the metal supports of a long, cushioned swing glint in the weak light from the windows.

Danny Park and I sit on the swing. He pops off his red clown nose and slides the rainbow wig off his head. He has dark hair like Min, a little messy. Oh god, he's even more handsome now. Not that it's totally unexpected that someone would be more handsome without a big foam nose and clown wig, but *still.*

I am now hyperaware of my ill-fitting, piecemeal, homemade frog costume. I smooth the big puffs out of my green sweatshirt and fold my hands in my lap. Look on the bright side: Even though there are quite a few skimpily dressed cats and vampires inside, Danny is out here with me. I've probably already made it past the *Is an unflattering frog costume a dealbreaker?* stage.

Stage of what, I'm not sure. *Ribbit.*

"It's nice to meet you," Danny says. "I feel like I've met all of Min's friends except you."

"Oh," I say. *Min and I are friends?*

"I've seen you around at her events," Danny goes on. "And in pictures and stuff. You always seemed a little shy. But cool."

Don't overanalyze that, I warn myself, but I'm already glowing. "I'm kind of busy a lot, I guess." I swing my legs a little, flapping my felt-cutout shoe coverings. I realize I still don't know if Wren was lying about Danny saying I'm cute. Maybe this was all an elaborate setup on their part.

"Yeah, I hear that," he says. "What do you do that keeps you so busy?"

"I . . . Well, I do tutoring and editing and stuff. And running."

He nods. "You like running, huh?"

"I wouldn't say I like it. It's just how I center myself in the morning." That was kind of negative. I feel the energy of this conversation threatening to slip away. "I like mornings, though," I add. "Outside. I run around this swamp near my house, and it's really pretty in the morning. Lots of mist and, you know, light through the trees."

"Yeah." Danny looks up like he's picturing it. "I've never been much of an athlete. As you can probably tell." He laughs ruefully. I'm confused for a second, but then I notice he's sort of bony under his billowy costume. Small. He probably gets told he wouldn't be good at sports. I think about Tyson, with everybody assuming he *has* to be some kind of athletic star, and wonder which is worse.

"You're such a good artist," Danny says. "Is that what you're going to go to school for?"

It startles me. Compliments often do. I've learned not to believe a lot of the things that come out of people's mouths, especially when they're nice. But there's something about the way Danny is talking that makes me think he's being honest. That he's just saying what he thinks and not sizing up every comment based on how it makes him look.

"Oh, thanks," I say, rattled. "But I'm not really an artist. I just draw a lot."

"I think *draws a lot* is kind of synonymous with *artist*." He waits for me to respond, but I don't know what to say.

"What are you doing next year?" I ask. "Or—wait, are you a senior?" I haven't asked him one single thing about himself so far. Smooth.

"I'm a junior. At Salmon Brook Academy," he says. "I've got some ideas, though. I'm thinking English lit, maybe. Or philosophy."

I imagine Buck North's reaction to me announcing I was going to study English lit or philosophy. I'm pretty sure the only thing he'd give grudging approval to would be something like Business or Advanced Business or Super Prestige Money Stock Market CEO Business. Or maybe law.

Suddenly, sitting here with Danny Park feels excitingly rebellious. It's a chilly October night, but with the splashes of window light in the little pond surrounded by the shadows of old flower stalks, you could almost believe it was summer.

"So what do you philosophize about?" I ask in a tone I hope comes across as flirty, but who the heck knows?

He gets this devilish look on his face. "Well, maybe the ethics of crushing on someone you've never met?"

Wait. He means me. Right? Holy crap, here we go. "I don't know if that's possible," I say. *Just gonna scooch in a little closer.* Now our hips are touching.

"I know," Danny says. "I just—Min has told me so much about you. I think she thought we'd get along." His cheeks are definitely pinker under the red clown circles.

"I'm surprised," I say. "Wait, I don't mean it like that. It's just that I didn't really think Min even knew much about me, to be honest. She's more Wren's friend."

He shrugs. "You're part of that whole group, though. I get curious about her friends. We're sort of protective of each other that way."

Part of the group. Is it true? I think about Min and Jade and Tyson. As different from me as they are, I think I'd like to be part of that group. Not just Wren's friend who tags along sometimes. The idea makes my insides feel a little warmer.

Or is it the way Danny is looking at me?

I swallow. "I'm, uh, glad Wren dragged me here tonight. I'm not very social usually. But this is fun."

"I'm glad, too," he says. Our faces are close together. This is the kiss, I'm pretty sure. This is the kissing part. I hope. Should I go for it? Should he? What if I get clown rouge on my face? What if I'm actually wrong about all of this, and he recoils in disgust, and then everyone—

Danny Park kisses me. It's warm. And glittering. And so *easy*. It's just how I thought it would be, that tiny, ignored part of me that imagined things like this. And he keeps kissing me, and I'm kissing him back, and I know how to do it, and I don't know how I know. Everything evaporates except him; I can't sense anything in the world other than this sweet butterfly moment. Maybe I've exploded. Maybe all my DNA is hanging in shimmering wisps from the trees, swirling in the dark water, sparkling among the stars. I'm finally seeping my way seamlessly into the universe. Danny Park is kissing me in the artificial moonlight, next to the artificial pond, dressed as our artificial identities, and it's the most real I've ever felt.

We're out here for what seems like a long time and no time at all. I'm not thinking about this year, next year, or anything else, just him and warmth and the metallic fragrance of water.

Finally, a few people stagger out into the yard. They want to dip their feet in the pond for some stupid reason. They don't notice Danny and me right away. We split apart before they can be sure they saw anything.

"Hey," he says. "Uh. Do you want my number? Or—?"

"Are you going somewhere?" It's a joke. I hope he gets that.

He does and chuckles. "Not at the moment, no. I just wasn't

sure if you maybe wanted to only add me on your socials, you know, for now."

"Numbers are more real." I hand him my phone, and he smiles, and his smile blows Jamison Sharpe's absolutely out of the water. He puts himself in my contacts. *Danny.* I send him a *Hi!* and hear the notification buzz in his pocket.

"Thanks," he says. "I guess we should probably go in." There are a few hoots and whistles as we make our way back to the living room's sliding door.

Wren and the others are still over in the corner, their game of Pictionary having evolved into some kind of speed drawing challenge. Jade is at the easel now, sketching frantically, as people sitting on the floor harass and/or encourage her.

"Time!" Wren calls. "Fail!" Everyone erupts into laughter.

Jade collapses. She brandishes a slip of paper. "Who the heck put '300 Spartans' in the basket? That's like three Spartans a second!"

Danny and I slip in behind the group, leaning against a sofa that has its back to the games corner. Wren looks over at me with a twinkly expression, and I blush, even though I try to stop myself. They grin.

An obnoxious ringtone blares behind me. I glance over my shoulder to see Jamison seated on the couch opposite this one, tapping to answer. He starts talking loudly. I try to tune him out.

"Hey, clown, where's your nose?" someone calls over to Danny in a joking voice. I tense up.

"And your wig?" Wren asks, stoking the flames, because of course.

Danny's hand flies to his face. "You mean they're gone?"

Tyson snort-laughs. "Thief! Quick, everyone, empty your pockets!"

The focus leaves us, which is a relief, but then, suddenly, everyone is quieting down and tuning in to something else. I turn around.

"Okay. All right. I'm on my way." It's Jamison. His voice is broken, his face twisted in anguish. He's on the phone, pacing between the couches as everyone at the party gawks in silence. "No, please don't move. I'm coming . . . Are you sure? Okay, I'll stay here, if you're sure . . . I love you, too. Please call as soon as you know anything." As he taps off the call, he breathes an enormous sigh.

"Are you okay?" Miranda asks.

Jamison stops and looks up, as though he's only just now noticing the rest of us. "Yeah," he says shakily. "Yeah, it's—my dad's O_2 level just plummeted. Mom's not sure why. She's having a flare-up, so it's bad timing. But she called 911 already, so there's nothing else we can do at the moment." He addresses the room. "I think most of you know my dad is battling cancer right now. There's a problem with his oxygen levels. I'm . . ." He chokes up. "I'm sure it'll be fine. He has an amazing team at the hospital, and the ambulance is on its way. I'm sorry, everyone. I don't want to bring the mood down." Now his gaze falls on the wall behind me, and immediately he looks stricken. Everyone follows his stare. I turn around.

The huge *Moon Adventures!* scene is still stuck up on the wall. And there's cartoon, blue-faced Jamison floating in the sky. Underneath, in my handwriting, it says *Too Cool for Oxygen*.

It was funny at the time. Now it's ironic. No, it's mean. I can sense the indignation frothing in this room already. How was I supposed to know Mr. Sharpe was on oxygen, or that it would get screwed up tonight of all nights? Luckily, only a few people know who drew the picture. Too bad Danny is one of them. I give him some kind of a look; I'm not even sure what my expression is—half pleading, half denial, completely pathetic. He doesn't even notice. He's focused on Jamison, just like everyone else.

"Min," Jamison says hoarsely, "would you mind taking that down?"

Min leaps into action. "Oh, sure. Sorry. Yeah." She peels the picture off the wall as murmurs start rippling through the crowd of party guests.

"Thanks." Jamison turns to me. "Sorry, Viveca. It's a funny drawing. I'm just feeling a little sensitive right now." He takes a deep breath and closes his eyes.

I feel the spotlight shifting to me. I look from one face to the next, to the next. If they weren't paying attention before, now they know who drew the picture. Some people are staring at me, eyes like pins scraping my skin. Everyone's whispering or talking, probably about me. The room is a fishbowl filled with gelatin, translucent and smothering.

I could just crumple into a heap. And I do. The floor rises to meet me, knees first, palms, then a slump to the side. I pull my legs to my chest and evaporate in the shadow of the couch.

I can't imagine what it must be like to know your dad is struggling to breathe and then to look up and see that awful blue-faced caricature displayed on the wall. I shouldn't have drawn it. It wasn't meant to be cruel at the time, just poking fun, but that doesn't matter. Jamison hasn't done anything to deserve something like that.

As the party slowly wheels itself back to life, I feel a body sit next to me, pressing against my side. Then a head on my shoulder.

"How was I supposed . . . ?" I start.

"It's not your fault," Wren says. "Not my fault, either. It's bad timing. Should we go?"

I pull my hood over my frog-eye headband. "No. I don't want to shame-walk through the room right now. Can we stay a little while?"

"Sure." They butt their head against my arm. "You want a snack?"

"Nah."

We sit in silence for a little bit. I'm still except for my heart, which is doing the bad fluttering instead of the good fluttering. I don't know where Danny went. Not a lot of people are hanging out in this corner of the room. Jade, Min, Tyson, and a couple of others are still standing over by the easel, and they're not shooting us dirty looks or anything. I want to believe they're giving me space to get comfortable again. Maybe it's true.

The music isn't super loud, but the bass vibrates the floor. The carpet I'm sitting on feels like a giant speaker. After four songs, I sense someone standing over me and Wren. Then they sit on my other side.

"Punch?" It's Danny, holding a plastic cup.

I take it and set it on the floor. "Thanks." I muster the courage to look at him.

He flashes me a kind smile and blinks long eyelashes. The skin on my arms and across my shoulders buzzes. Danny's not mad at me.

Suddenly, things seem a little bit okay again.

Wren raises their head. "Hey, Danny. How's Fancy Pants Academy? Are you the best cricket player there?"

Danny rolls his eyes, but in an amused way. "I'm definitely the worst comics artist there. I was hoping you two might give me some tips."

Wren gently rocks into me. "I like the new artist Viveca. It's about time."

All of a sudden, the music starts blasting. I look up to see Jade with her fingers on the volume. "I love this song!" she yells at the universe. "Dance with me!"

To an outsider, Wren may seem a bit unpredictable. Which is true. But something you can *always* count on, one thousand percent of the time, is that, if invited, they will dance. They'll often dance without any invitation at all, too. They're like a jar of dance bees, always ready for someone to pop the lid.

So Wren jumps to their feet and starts tearing up the dance floor. Or, rather, the games corner of the Parks' open-concept first floor. Danny hops to his feet, too, flashing me a smile like he expects me to follow him. Him joining in the dancing surprises me a little bit, I guess because he seemed kind of reserved. But it's his house, and you're braver in your own house.

I'm not a dancer. I'm not good at it, and I'm not graceful or hot enough to fake being good at it. People talk about just letting go, but I can't. Part of me is always clutching. So as more people cram into the games corner, I creep away, slide around the side of the couch, and sit on the end cushion, making myself as tiny as possible. Nobody seems to notice me. The good news is it feels like everyone is actually not noticing me, rather than ignoring me because they're still horrified by my crappy Jamison caricature.

Good job, Viveca. My first party in so long, and I've managed to screw it up. But Danny Park isn't mad at me, and most people here probably won't care by tomorrow. Heck, it seems like most of them don't care now. Wren will make fun of me later in that cheeky way that they do, and it will feel nice and normal.

The only loose end is Jamison Sharpe. I scan the room, but he's nowhere to be seen. Should I apologize, or is it better to let it go? I'm not looking forward to interacting with him again. Maybe each of us can just pretend the other doesn't exist until graduation.

I've had such weird luck tonight. Maybe Wren and their tarot cards can shed some light on it. On the one hand—Danny Park. On the other, well, it's unbelievable that Jamison's dad had a crisis with his oxygen so soon after I drew that dumb caricature. It's—

It is *unbelievable*, my brain says.

Okay, stop this train of thought right now. Yank the emergency cord and screech that sucker to a halt.

I mean, it is quite a coincidence, though. Right? I finally realize what Jamison's really all about, that he hates me, and I—mostly accidentally—embarrass him in front of everyone, and then he *happens* to get a phone call that turns everything around and makes me look like a jerk.

I roll my head, shoulder to shoulder, to try to shake these thoughts loose and send them tumbling away. Even if Jamison faked that phone call—which is an order of magnitude more screwed up than drawing a stupid cartoon of someone—it doesn't matter. What am I going to do, call him out on it? I couldn't prove it. And, let's be real, if his dad has cancer, there is a good chance he is having a health crisis at any given time, and I am an actual certified jerk for even thinking about questioning it.

Then I notice it. Jamison's phone. Naked and alone on the coffee table. Two feet in front of me.

I keep my head low but raise my gaze, looking furtively around the room. The lights are low and the mini disco ball flashes disorienting multicolored light everywhere. It's getting late, and people are less vigilant. Nobody's arriving and checking out the room; most people have settled into groups to talk or are caught up in the dance party behind me.

It would be so easy to slide that phone off the coffee table and take a look at Jamison's recent calls. Part of me is horrified at myself. But part of me is certain he blared his own ringtone and then put on the performance of his life, with dead air in his earpiece.

I pull my hood farther around my face and tug my long sleeves down until they're covering my fingers, as though I can hide inside my sweatshirt. I peek out. Nobody is paying attention to me.

Holding my breath, I reach, slowly, toward the coffee table, eyes darting around the crowded room the whole time. I slip two fingers onto Jamison's phone. Then I *shloop*, pull it back into my sleeve and sit back on the couch.

I bring my knees up and sit folded, hiding the phone in my lap. Not that anybody would be able to tell it wasn't my actual phone. I tap the screen to life. It's unlocked.

My skin is tingling now. I should be quick. Check recent calls. Where's the icon?

The music stops. The lights come up. People stop dancing, confused, or look up grumpily from their conversations.

Oh, crap. What's going on? I tuck Jamison's phone into the front pocket of my sweatshirt.

A voice cuts through the irritated rumblings of the partygoers. "I'm so sorry, everyone, but it turns out I do have to go take care of my mom." It's Jamison, standing in the center of the room. Where did he come from? I swear he wasn't there five seconds ago.

Now, instead of being irritated, people are cooing their concerns and love and best wishes in Jamison's direction. He takes it all in for a moment, but then says, "I don't mean to spoil the atmosphere, but I can't find my phone. Has anyone seen it?"

I gasp. Audibly. I don't think anyone hears me. What do I do? Everybody's searching—ax murderers, fairies, a giant chocolate bar. The Parks' downstairs looks like the cast of some bizarre theme park doing a scavenger hunt. I reach into my front pocket and wrap my fingers around the phone. I have to get it back onto the coffee table. But now it will be a lot harder to make that move without being seen. Still, I have to risk it. I slide the phone out a couple of inches.

"Hey, everybody, stop." It's Miranda. "What are we thinking? Jamison, I'll just call it. Everyone, be quiet."

Oh, crap. I have to ditch this phone *now.* I coil my muscles for a brazen *wing* onto the coffee table, but as I look up, I see Jamison staring at me. I freeze.

A ringtone screams from my pocket. It takes a few seconds for everyone to pinpoint where the noise is coming from, but soon enough, they're all looking at me for the second time tonight. Even Min and Tyson. Even Wren.

My hood falls to my shoulders. I take the phone out of my pocket and place it on the coffee table. Jamison is still staring at me with this blank look. A nothingness. It's scarier than any of the Halloween costumes in this room.

And I understand.

He knew.

He planted the phone there and waited for me to grab it.

"Viveca?" Now the other Jamison is back, the caring, heart-on-his-sleeve Jamison everyone loves so freaking much. "Why do you have my phone?"

I don't owe this creep an answer. I won't play his game. I look away.

Jamison takes a step toward me. He glances nervously around the room, as though he really wants to speak to me in private but there's nothing he can do but talk right here and now. Of course, everyone else is rapt.

"Viveca," he says quietly, "this has to stop."

I blink. "What?"

"This has to stop, Viveca." Jamison sits next to me on the couch. "Look, I don't *care* who's valedictorian. Heck, I want you to get it! But I'm not going to stop trying my best just so you can, whatever, get better grades. Is that what you're after? Getting better grades than me?" He gestures. "Than all of us?"

"What are you talking about?"

Jamison touches my leg. "I know your home life is hard. I know it's tough to do well in school when you're struggling. I know . . . I know that's part of the reason you lashed out with that drawing earlier. And I know it's why you tried to steal my phone."

"I didn't try to steal your phone," I snap. "I just picked it up." There isn't a sound in the whole room except him and me.

"Listen, Viveca," Jamison says, "if you're in trouble, I can help you out. Maybe find you a job. But I need my phone, and you need to stop this. If you had a sick loved one at home, you'd understand."

My jaw is in my lap. "There's no 'this.' I don't need your charity, and I didn't try to steal your phone. I was just looking at it!"

I see Danny across the room. His expression is clear: He's

disgusted. With me. Just like everybody else here. Even Wren is looking at me dubiously. And maybe I am disgusting. Danny takes a step back, pulls his phone out of his pocket, and taps a couple times. Then he walks away. *That was my number*, I realize. That was the message I sent so he could add me. He deleted it.

Jamison touches my shoulder. "I forgive you."

I push his hand away.

16

It's been a pretty crappy week at school since the infamous Halloween party, but I'll survive. Jamison haunted the halls for a few days like a droopy flower, soaking up the outpouring of encouragement in his time of need, but apparently his parents are better now, because he's back to his old, vivacious self. Everybody knows about the caricature, which, surprisingly, seems to be a bigger deal than the phone thing. No one shooting me dirty looks seems to understand that I drew the picture *before* he got that call, and I'm sure Jamison's doing nothing to correct that idea. But it's not like I was popular to begin with, so I can't really tell if people are avoiding me in the same old boring way or in new and exciting ways.

I haven't seen much of Wren's friends, but they're Wren's friends, not mine. I don't know why I let myself imagine I was part of their group. Danny Park's influence, I guess.

I mean—Danny *who?*

To top everything off like a worm-ridden cherry on a curdled ice-cream sundae, as I'm sitting in the cafeteria this morning waiting for Wren, I glance at the bright, blocky letters, each as big as my hand, across the double doors: the updated *Race to the Top!* list. And underneath, for the first time since September, a new name crowns the short list.

Freaking Jamison Sharpe.

I bonk my head down onto the table. The top spot. Valedictorian. I close my eyes and breathe in plastic and disinfectant. But I don't let my thoughts sink all the way down to despair. I stop them at angry. Because I just *know* Jamison doesn't deserve the title. I have this intense gut feeling he's running on charm, lies, and manipulation, but I can't prove anything. Nobody would believe me.

Then I have a stupid idea. It's pointless and juvenile, but . . . it makes me feel, for the first time in a long while, a tiny bit powerful.

I tear out a piece of notebook paper and snap the cap off a black marker.

No. I shake my head, like actually shake it. *NO, Viveca.* I push the paper away, pushing the thought away with it, because I recognize this insane line of reasoning, this teeny, tingly feeling of power. I'm back in seventh grade, and all the pieces are falling into place, spelling out, *Let Jackie know you're onto her. Make her squirm.*

But the puzzle I thought I was putting together back then turned out to be a mishmash of dangerous nonsense. It was like a dream that seems to make so much sense until you wake up and try to describe it to someone else. And I haven't ever gone back into those dreams, that twisted way of thinking. I've been a perfect student. Unimpeachable.

It's just that I can't stop thinking about Jamison Sharpe. He started as a pinprick of light in my brain and has grown into a glare that continually distracts me. I think about the evidence, about what my guts are telling me—am I out of my mind? How could all those incredible rumors about Jamison be true? What was he doing in the teachers' lounge that day? What's in the folder labeled *Sharpe* on Vice Principal Reinhardt's desk?

How dare he steal the valedictorian spot from me with his allure and his absurd stories? How *dare* he?

I grab the notebook paper and press down hard with the marker. *Dear Jamison,* I scrawl, *you are a cheat and a liar. And I can prove it.*

I scan the cafeteria furtively, but there are only a couple of people here, and they're not paying attention to me. I fold the paper and put it in my pocket, jittery. Then I jump up, push open the double doors, and run upstairs to the senior hallway. I know which locker is Jamison's; there's a crowd of admirers there every morning. Luckily, no one is there yet. Making sure I'm not seen, I shove the anonymous note into the crack above the latch.

"I, uh, saw the top ten," Wren says diplomatically as we make our way to first period. They're the only person in school who talks to me now, but they're the only person I care about, anyway. Six more months and I'm history—and I *will* get my top spot back. I just need a plan.

"Yeah. Freaking Jamison," I say. "I knew it. I knew AP Calc would screw everything up." Wait until he finds my note. I hope he slinks around every day sick with worry, waiting for the other shoe to drop, for my "proof" to come out. I'm giddy with a mixture of triumph and anger.

Wren steers me down the hallway. "I thought it was Intro to Piano that was going to screw everything up."

"That, too."

"Meaning the only two classes you actually have with Jamison Sharpe." Wren nods. "*That's* where he's carrying out his nefarious schemes."

"I don't know! But look at the evidence!" I hear my voice getting reedy. "Jamison just *has* to take Intro to Piano instead of literally any other arts credit because *reasons*, even though he can already play? Holy easy A, Batman! And—*and*—we get a convenient anonymous bomb threat that screws up that AP Calc test? And remember how he *looked* at me at the Halloween party? Don't you see the connections?" A chunk of hair chooses that exact moment to slip loose from my already messy bun, splaying across the left side of my face.

Wren looks at me and raises an eyebrow at the whole picture—my white eyes; squeaky, frantic voice; mad-scientist and/or crazy-cat-lady hair. "Uh-huh," they say. "Well, here's what I think. You have"—they check their watch—"five minutes before piano class starts, which you don't actually give a crap about and just think of as one more check mark in your 'well-rounded' column, which makes one wonder why on earth you would care if other people are better piano players than you."

"I just think—"

"*And*," they snap, "you have not drunk any of your coffee this morning, which is a problem."

"But—"

They point at my full extra-large. "A-*hem*."

"Fine," I say, and take a defiant sip.

"Good job." They pat my head like a puppy. "I'll see you at lunch. Try not to burn the school down before then."

I slog into the classroom, coffee in hand, and slump into a chair at one of the tables set up with little plastic Casio keyboards. Normally I'd take this time to go over the song I practiced, but it's all I can do to slide the glossy lesson book out of my bag and flip it open. It's not like I'll ever be able to play—what is it this week? I squint. "Pep Rally Polka"—it's not like I'll ever be able to play "Pep Rally Polka" as well as Jamison.

Other early arrivals are already clicking on the preset backing tracks we're not allowed to use, probably because they're super annoying. Or maybe it's just me. Being subjected to "Hot Cross Buns" plunked out ironically against a cheesy salsa beat at eight in the morning wasn't charming at the beginning of the semester, and it hasn't gotten any more charming since.

Then *he* comes in, and it's like static electricity, everyone's crackling and clingy. I glare. That's right, I've sunk to glaring now. I'm some kind of hostile amphibian staring daggers out from under a rotten log.

"Hey, valedictorian!" Kasey Wheelwright says in her stupid perky voice. Then everybody's congratulating the new head of the class, like he's the recently crowned prince of Elton Prep or something. Oh, wait, I heard he was already crowned homecoming king. Well, now he's got another crown. He could hang one off each ear. It's like the heartwarming ending of a made-for-TV movie.

"Now, hang on a minute," Jamison says, raising a hand. A hush falls over the music room. "I have an announcement."

I tap my phone and check the time. Where's Ms. Pillay? She's nearly late.

Jamison keeps talking. "I know some of you saw my name at the top of the list out there, knocking Viveca into salutatorian." A couple people throw mocking glances at me. I don't look at them, but I can tell, anyway. "But it's all a mistake."

Gasps. Theatrics. Probably a few hands placed on foreheads in distress. I do look up now, just to see where this is going.

"No," Jamison says somberly, "I should not be lauded as your valedictorian, friends. I've got to come clean. You see, I'm a fraud. I'm a fraud and a liar, and I cheated my way to the top."

I blink. *Okay . . .*

And he holds up a piece of paper. My note. That anonymous little poison thorn I jabbed into his locker. "See?" Jamison says.

"It says so right here." There's a moment of silence. I hold my breath.

Then everybody laughs. *Laughs.* The idea of Jamison Sharpe being a fraud is the most ridiculous thing they've ever heard. Har-dee-har-har.

"What are we laughing about?" Ms. Pillay floats through the door in a delicate cloud of cotton printed fabric.

"Sorry, ma'am," Jamison says. Nobody says *ma'am* around here except him. "I was just joking around." He takes his seat.

Ms. Pillay takes a marker and begins drawing rhythms on the whiteboard. "From the sound of it, you're ready for your comedy career."

Kasey pipes up. "He's a cheat and a liar." The piano class laughs again. As I look at Jamison, I see something like triumph on his face. And I realize—*this is his strategy.* If he *were* a cheat and a liar, the best thing to do would be to announce it. Beat his accusers to the punch and make it look like the silliest idea in the world. Because then, if someone like me were to call him out, I would be the one looking ridiculous. You can't be tried twice for the same crime—something like that.

But that also means he's afraid. At least a tiny bit.

He looks over, and I make eye contact, giving him my own triumphant look. And he just—looks back. Suddenly, there's that chilling blankness. I don't know which Jamison is worse, the one filled with boiling rage, or this one. The Nothing Jamison that emerges every so often, like a creature from another world, calculating and devoid of emotion, staring out from behind glass.

———

My big plans this afternoon were to slog home and curl into a ball, fixate on the *Race to the Top!* list, then feel guilty about slacking, then go over the homework assignments for tomorrow that I've already done. But instead, I let Wren convince me to come back to comics club—despite it being a waste of time now that it's too late to put it on my applications.

We're drawing in silence, focused on our creations. Only I'm not focused. My pencil is on autopilot, and my brain is spiraling.

Okay, fine, I shouldn't have left that nasty note for Jamison. It didn't even accomplish anything, just like the venomous little scribbles I left for Jackie and her friends. The thing is, part of me still feels victorious, like I got to him. After all, my suspicions of Jackie were wrong. This isn't the same thing. Jamison is a *fraud*, and I know it. But what does that mean? What does that change? What is wrong with me?

"Ooh, she's fierce!" Tek says, pointing to my drawing. "What's her name?"

"Oh, uh, Miss P—" I pause. Think for a second. What could her name be? I erase the pig nose and draw in some curving horns that poke out from the figure's long, beautiful hair. "She's Lola the Gorgeous Minotaur."

Tek laughs. "I love her! She's so gorgeous!" He moves on, settling at the other end of the conference table to talk with the Butt Man sophomores.

I feel eyes on me and turn my head. Wren is giving me an amused look.

"What?" I ask.

They shake their head, grinning. "Lola the Gorgeous Minotaur. You made a character, Viveca! Look at you!"

I give them a soft punch on the arm. "I'm capable of being creative, you know. I'm not just a computer that eats textbooks and spits out test scores." *Or am I?*

They turn their paper my way. "This is a thing I've been working on. It's an invisible moon vigilante."

"An invisible main character? That makes things easy," I joke. I look at the page they're working on. The lines are skewed but not confusing, and the characters seem as though they're really jumping, jabbing, flying. "Hey, wow, that's so good."

"Thanks. I got the idea for it at the Halloween party."

"Oh." I think they meant that to be an opening, but I'm not eager to take the bait. Still, I can't leave them hanging. "Well, at least something good came out of it, then."

"Yeah." They're silent for a long moment. I hear the sound of their pencil scratching, but I know it's really their brain that's moving, whirring, trying to decide how to approach the next thing. Finally, they say, "So . . . I wasn't going to ask. I really wasn't. I've tried so hard. And honestly, if you tell me Jamison's phone just sprouted wings and flew into your pocket against your will, I'll believe you, but—I need *something* from you, Viveca. I need this to make sense."

I didn't want to get into this. Energy bubbles off me and evaporates, like my skin is decaying with every second. I thought Wren might leave it alone, but Wren never leaves anything alone. Not forever.

But. If anyone will understand, it's Wren. I have to trust them. I must force myself to. The last thing I want is to be completely alone in this.

"The thing is . . ." I start, and hesitate. The room is filled with enough chatter that I'm not worried about being overheard. "The thing is, I'm not convinced he actually got a call from his mom that night." I wait, but Wren doesn't say anything. They just keep drawing. But I know they're listening. "Doesn't it seem a little too perfect that his dad suddenly had a crisis that was the exact thing I drew?" I ask. "And it made me look like a jerk?"

"Viveca—"

"And I'll tell you something else." I brandish my phone. "When Miranda called him and it rang in my pocket—that was a *different ringtone* than the one we all heard when he got that supposed emergency call."

Wren gives me a condescending look. "Welcome to Earth. A magical place where you can have different rings for different people." They take my phone and tap. Their phone starts chiming out some synthesized 1980s hit.

"Dance party!" Tek calls from the other end of the table.

"That's you," Wren says to me. "Your ring is Donna Summer. Everybody else is geese honking."

I look at them. "I—geese honking?" I'm speechless for a second, then blurt out a laugh. Wren laughs with me and tosses my phone back onto my lap.

They weave their fingers together under their chin. "All right, what else do you have?" they ask. "Lay it on me."

"Okay." I point at them, energy surging back into my fibers. "Okay, listen. Jamison turned the lights on, because he needed to find his phone *immediately* so he could go take care of his mom, right? But if his phone was missing, how did he know he had to leave? How did he get that message? Alien brain-wave communication?"

Wren shakes their head. "Impossible. He wasn't wearing a tin-foil hat." We giggle. It feels like the old us. Then they nod. "You know, that is weird, Viveca. I agree that is weird. Maybe he had a sudden urge or something. Or maybe someone called the Parks' house."

"Maybe." I give Lola the Gorgeous Minotaur a gleaming spear so she can defend herself from an onslaught of dumpy-looking bandits. "And, you know, there's something I never told you about."

"I'm listening."

I lower my voice. "I found a 'Jamison Sharpe' folder in the vice principal's office. I didn't have time to see everything that was in it, but there was a letter from his old school."

"Sinister!" Wren says. "What did it say?"

"I don't know. It was in French."

"The evidence is piling up!"

"All right, all right." I give them a conciliatory smile. "But listen—there was something really sketchy about the logo."

Wren weaves their fingers. "This I have to hear. The sketchy logo."

"I'm serious," I go on, conspiratorial. "The logo was low-res. Like, no preppy fancy-pants school would have official stationery like that."

Wren snorts. "Not exactly an M. Night Shyamalan plot, Viveca." They do a creepy voice. "The *logooooo* . . . was *crap*." We giggle again.

"Plus, you know, Jamison hates me," I say.

"I don't know about that," Wren says.

"He does." I pull over a box of colored pencils. "He has this side of himself, this inner face that he never shows anyone. But I've seen it. It's cold."

"He's dealing with a lot of stuff," Wren says. "Including you."

We laugh again, but I know they think it's true. When, actually, I'm the one having to deal with *him*. Also—how does Wren know so much about Jamison anyway? I think again about Jamison's calculated little remarks about Wren, trying to get me to believe they're best pals behind my back.

I put the thought out of my head. "I have to get into Everett," I say. "I want it more than anything, you know? But I'm not sure they'll take me if I'm not valedictorian. I'm not special enough." I can't believe I said that out loud.

Wren sighs. "Viveca—"

"Look, Jamison's been chasing valedictorian from day one,"

I say. "He just acts like it's no big deal, but he's as obsessed with it as I am."

"Nothing wrong with healthy competition," Wren says.

"Yeah. *Healthy* competition." I slide a brown pencil out of the box and start shading my bandits. "I *know* he's not cramming in the library before exams. Or giving up his weekends to do test prep, or skipping homecoming to study. He's too busy being charming. It's like it's all so *easy* for him."

"You've been watching him a lot."

I look up. "Of course I have. Healthy competition, remember?"

". . . Sure." Wren goes back to their invisible vigilante.

I lean closer. "But I got him today. I stuck a note in his locker calling him out. Letting him know that somebody *knows* he's a cheat and a liar."

I wait for Wren's reaction, but they just keep drawing. After a moment, they say, "What if he's just smart?"

"He is," I say, "but he's lazy. And the thing is, he has to get practically *perfect* grades to beat me. Just doing well won't cut it. So he's definitely cheating somehow, besides just getting out of doing work."

"Uh-huh." Their tone is noncommittal.

"And guess what?" I murmur. "Jamison's getting a quiz in US History tomorrow—they just found out at the end of class today. But if he thinks he's going to swipe the answers from the teachers' lounge, he's got another thing coming." My voice gets a little more energized. "See, the only time he'll have a chance to get in there is after debate club, which ends in half an hour. So I'm going to beat him. Hide the teacher's edition that's in there—I think he's been sneaking in to look at them."

Wren looks at me but doesn't say anything. Then Tek speaks up from the other side of the table. "Oops, we're over time, friends. I'm really digging all your comics!" He stands up. "Who's coming to the gallery today? Those of you who aren't driving, my van is in the visitor lot—make sure you turn your permission slips in to the office if you haven't done it. Mrs. B should still be there, I think."

"Let's go." Wren starts putting away their stuff. "You coming with me or riding in the teacher van?"

"Oh. I forgot."

Crap, Wren told me yesterday that the comics club was going to see Tek's new show at a little gallery downtown. I can't believe I forgot.

They look confused. "Okay. So you don't need a permission slip if you're riding with me."

"I know, but . . . Jamison's US History quiz . . ." I trail off.

I expect Wren to give me some sort of snappish comeback, but they don't. They just close their mouth, hoist their backpack over their shoulders and leave along with everybody else in comics club.

"It makes sense," I mutter to myself as I shove my half-finished drawings into my bag. "This is the only chance he'll get. And he has to get a perfect score on that quiz. On all of them."

Wren doesn't get it. They don't care about grades. Maybe they should. Maybe they should be focusing on getting into a school next year rather than making dreamy plans with no basis in reality.

I check the time: 4:42. Debate club doesn't get out until five. Golden. I half jog down the halls, through double doors, up rubberized stairs. A quick peek into the teachers' lounge shows me nobody's in there, so I slip in, bunny-quick.

There's the stack of teacher's editions. *History, history* . . . I scan the spines. Nothing. It must be over on the big bookshelf. I hurry over; the books are arranged by subject. Here are history and social studies, and—voilà!

I slide out the book, which feels like it weighs as much as a bowling ball: *The History of the United States until 1900.* This must be it. There aren't any other US history titles. I wedge it under my arm and appraise the room. It's a large book to hide somewhere. But he won't look under the couch, will he?

I snort-laugh to myself as I get down onto the floor and lift up the musty couch skirt.

"Stick 'em up!" a voice barks.

I jump practically out of my sneakers. The book tumbles. "Ack!"

"Got you, you little deviant," Wren cackles.

I collapse onto the stained carpet. "Well, there go five years of my life."

They step inside and turn the lock. I can't believe I never thought to do that.

"You're hiding it under the couch?" They click their tongue disapprovingly. "He'll find it there."

"Fine." I get up. "Where would you hide it?"

"I wouldn't," they say, "because Jamison Sharpe is *not* stealing quiz answers from an ancient teacher's edition, and you sound like an absolute lunatic suggesting it. But that aside . . ."

They cross the room and take the heavy book. Then, in seconds, they slide open the window and chuck *The History of the United States until 1900* out into the white sky.

For a moment, I just stare. "I— You threw it out the window."

"Yep." They put their hands on their hips. "Two floors. We're in the back here; nobody will be walking by." They peek down. "Ha. It's splayed over a bush like a dead bird."

"Okay!" I grin. "We've got to get out of here. Should we go to Tek's show?"

"Yeah," Wren says. "But first, I want to see this French letter."

———

We don't go in through Vice Principal Reinhardt's door. We use the first-floor window, which isn't very visible from anywhere on campus, tucked inside an inverted corner of the sprawling brick building that snakes its various halls and wings in a few different directions. Wren says we'll be less conspicuous this way. I'm not sure; you can always come up with some marginally believable excuse for using a door. Not so much when you're using a nail file to slide back a window latch.

Wren bites their nails; it's one of their few imperfections. So I'm not sure why they have a nail file in their bag, but hey, it's lucky. They get the window open, and we hoist ourselves through, leaving our shoes outside so we don't track telltale dirt across the carpet. It all feels very cinematic.

"Reinhardt's in a student council meeting," Wren says, glancing at the wall clock. "We've technically got no time, but they always run long. Especially if Kasey Wheelwright is going on about something."

Wren's nail file gets us inside the big bottom drawer of the vice principal's desk, too. They are surprisingly good at this. There are a ton of folders in there, but they're organized, and we find Jamison's pretty quickly.

I flip it open on Reinhardt's desk. The letter from the *Lycée International* is on top. Wren takes a look.

"See the logo?" I whisper.

They nod. "Yeah. You're not wrong." They start to read.

I lean over their shoulder. "What does it say?"

They raise a finger. "Jeez, hang on. Most of my vocabulary is less academic and more action-adventure oriented." After a minute, they put the letter down.

"Well?"

They shrug. "I mean, my French isn't that good, but it just seems like a letter saying how great a student Jamison is and recommending him for enrollment here."

"Sounds like a pretty important letter, though," I say. "Imagine superstar Jamison getting rejected by Elton Prep and forced to go to plain old Elton High."

"Yeah." They close the folder and stick it back in the vice

principal's file drawer, looking a little puzzled. There's a foot-step in the hall outside, and we both freeze. "We should go," Wren whispers. I hesitate, but they tug my sleeve and we each swing our legs over the sill and hop back out the wide window.

We crouch below the window, listening, but don't hear anyone enter the office. After a moment, we relax, sitting on the mulchy ground to put on our shoes.

"You're thinking about something," I say.

They squish their mouth to one side. "I can't really say. Like I said, my French is just passable. But . . . well, something just felt weird about that letter. A word here and there. A construction."

"What do you mean?"

They consider. "It's almost like—it's almost like someone wrote a letter in English and just ran it through an online robo-translator." They shake their head. "But to send something like that to the administration, assuming they wouldn't notice? Like assuming, I don't know, that whoever received it would just do the same thing in reverse, explaining away any errors? That's audacious. That would take *guts*."

"Yeah." I loop my shoelace, tighten. "But maybe that's Jamison's secret. Maybe the problem most people have with telling lies is that the lies just aren't big enough."

Wren gets to their feet. "Maybe so. Come on, let's get out of here before poor Tek thinks we've abandoned him."

But I'm thinking now. I stand up slowly as my brain steers me away from Wren's outstretched hand. "You know, I bet there's a *lot* more good stuff in that folder."

Wren glances up at the window, then out to the walkway. "Too late. There's activity happening; you can feel it. The meeting's out. People are moving."

My hand is on the windowsill. "Reinhardt's not back yet. I'm just going to grab the folder. It'll only take a second."

"Viveca, hey." Wren touches my back and does a nervous half laugh. "Like, I know you're not a seasoned veteran of the wrong side of the law, but there's kind of a big difference between having a peep at one letter and stealing someone's entire confidential file."

I shake them off. Wren just *admitted* there was something fishy about that letter. And aren't they always saying I should live a little more instead of studying all the time? Why aren't they supporting me here?

"If you don't want to come, fine," I say. "Just don't waste my time." Their raised eyebrows sting me, because I know I've stung them, but I've got Jamison's stupid face at the Halloween party on replay in my mind and I just want to smack it into space. And there's a potential gold mine of ammo sitting a few feet away.

I haul myself back through the window, leap over to the desk where the file drawer is ajar. Then *swoop*, the folder is up and away, and so am I, hips forward, legs up and over the windowsill. I can't wait to see what kind of dirt I can dig up on Jamison.

"Hey!" a deep voice calls out as I hit the ground.

Where did it come from? I crouch, looking frantically around for Wren, but they're nowhere to be seen.

"Miss North, answer me!"

I realize the voice is coming from the window above me. And it's angry.

17

Arms crossed, chin tucked, scowling, Vice Principal Reinhardt couldn't be more of a caricature if he tried. Only I'm not laughing. I'm up a creek. And I didn't even get to look in Jamison's folder.

"What on earth were you doing?" Reinhardt asks. He holds the folder up and shakes it, then tosses it onto his desk. "Did you break into my desk?"

"No, it was open," I lie with a soft voice. Maybe I can mitigate some of this. *What would Buck North do?* He wouldn't be sitting in this chair looking at his faded sneakers and weaving his guilty fingers together, that's for sure. He'd be puffing his chest out and raising his voice. Dad's lies get more confident when they're called out. But I can't think straight. Scrutiny sloshes my mind around; exposure makes me wither into brittle threads.

"So you just decided to have a look through confidential student files?" the vice principal asks.

I shrug. "It was a dare." Ugh, that was dumb. Dares require two people—he'll jump on that. And I'm not giving Wren away.

But he doesn't. "You expect me to believe that? *Someone* dared you to climb in my window and steal Jamison Sharpe's file?" He throws up his hands. It's the most animated I've ever seen him.

"I didn't even know it was Jamison's file. I just grabbed one."

"Do I look like an idiot?" Reinhardt turns away and puts his hands on his desk. Then he takes a breath and pulls up a chair across from me. "Look, Viveca, I've been hearing some concerning things about your fascination with Jamison."

Now I look up. "What?"

He sits back. His face isn't angry anymore, but for some reason, this veneer of compassion is far worse. "I know about the incident at the party."

"Oh." My stomach sinks.

He goes on. "I know you've been following Jamison around, making him uncomfortable."

"I— Wait, I have?"

"I know he had to tell you that you could no longer be friends."

"I'm sorry, he *what*?"

Vice Principal Reinhardt leans forward, forearms resting on his knees. "You're a good student, Viveca, and you've always kept out of trouble, but this is serious. Look, I'll let you off with a one-day ISS. But I don't want to hear one more *whisper* about issues between you and Jamison—is that understood?"

Oh, I understand. I understand that Jamison has been in here filling the actual *vice principal's* head with lies about me. Who else could have told Reinhardt about the Halloween party? And why not? Jamison has everybody else fooled. It makes sense that he'd start trying to turn teachers against me, too.

But all I do is nod.

———

It's not even third quarter yet. Plenty of time to knock Jamison down and get back into that top spot, I tell myself, as though I'm not currently the only student at Elton Prep with an in-school suspension. I sit at a desk in the ISS room, also known as a random unused office behind the gym. The desk has a dull blond surface scratched with a few unimaginative efforts at graffiti, and I keep banging my knees against the open metal storage pocket that hangs down; it smells like stale erasers, if that's a thing.

I think there's technically supposed to be a teacher in here, but maybe they figured they didn't need to bother since I'm flying solo. Vice Principal Reinhardt met me at the front door this morning and walked me to my locker to get my stuff, then escorted me to this vacant office. I wonder if he was impressed by how faithfully I seemed to stick to the "no interaction with other students" rule as we made our way through the halls. Little does he know, it wasn't even my choice.

So here I am, alone, ruminating, filling out my practice sheet for piano class. ISS would be a torturous punishment for someone like Wren, who needs banter to survive, but for me, a whole day just to study and do my work without distraction is positively refreshing. It's not a hiccup in my schedule; it's an enhancement.

I spread out my review materials as much as I can over the little desk, glancing at the round clock next to the room's one small window. Reinhardt spelled out my schedule for me in detail. At nine o'clock, I'll open the door and collect today's new work from the bin outside where my teachers will have left it. Lunch will be delivered; I don't see a Victorian asylum–style slot in the door, so I assume a human will actually have to come in here and hand food to me. I have two bathroom breaks, at ten thirty and twelve thirty, and the vice principal will collect me again at three. Other than that, it's me and my schoolwork and my guilty conscience. In theory.

The truth is, I don't have a guilty conscience. What I have is a glare in my brain, overpowering and distorting everything else. The hot, bright light that is Jamison Sharpe. But I harden that light into a searing beam of concentration, burning through integrals—zap!—the hero's journey—zap!—and Waterloo—*zap!*

At eight thirty, a gym class starts up, and the echoes of ball bounces and sneaker squeaks permeate my Refuge of Seething. I hunker down, bore my gaze into the fan of flash cards I've made to help me remember important historical dates. But then something else cuts through the gym noise, and I blink myself to the present.

It's *his voice*, just outside the door. *Great.* I can't even be punished by isolation without Jamison Sharpe unintentionally horning his way in on it. Still, I can't help but eavesdrop.

"I'm so sorry," he's saying. His voice is muffled through the door, but I can make it out. "I didn't realize they would call me during the school day."

"You shouldn't have your phone on you during class." It's Mrs. Sherwood, the gym teacher. She's probably the last person at Elton Prep who would fall for Jamison's charms. I subconsciously lean toward the door, ears pricked.

"I know," Jamison says sheepishly. "It was disruptive and unacceptable."

This seems to suck some of the wind out of her sails. Oh, he's *good*. Mrs. Sherwood clears her throat and says, "Yes, well—"

"I'll tell them to make a note," Jamison says. "They have to find someone else to take Mrs. Reed shopping when I'm in school."

"I don't care what the call was about," Mrs. Sherwood says. Even though I can't see her right now, I know exactly what she's doing—standing there with her strong arms folded and her head sucked just slightly back, giving her neck the shadow of a double chin, staring at Jamison with eyes glossed by the kind of refined jadedness that only comes from years of dealing with high school nonsense. I'm silently cheering. In my molded plastic chair, my butt wiggles with glee.

"I understand," Jamison says. "It's just—may I have permission to call the center and let them know I can't pick her up until after school? They'll make sure she understands—she gets confused sometimes, especially when her expectations are disrupted."

I roll my eyes. Who *talks* like that? And what is Jamison even on about? Does he expect everyone to believe he now, what, volunteers to take frail elders out on their errands? Forget Harvard, Jamison's practically ready to found his own religion.

But to my disappointment, Mrs. Sherwood says, "All right," and I hear Jamison make another one of his over-explanatory phone calls, speaking with a volume and clarity that would make Tyson raise his eyebrows.

"Thank you," Jamison says to the gym teacher after he's done. "It's all worked out. Mrs. Reed's going to take the center bus to meet me here after school. She's such a lovely woman. She'd do anything for me."

"Fantastic," Mrs. Sherwood says in a voice like a day-old pancake. I let out a snort-laugh I hope they don't hear. "Now put on your shorts and grab a red pinny from the box."

Just hearing another person who's not completely enamored with Jamison Sharpe lightens my mood, even if Mrs. Sherwood did let him make his (probably fake) phone call and didn't punish him for breaking the rules. I plod through the day's work feeling more centered. The glare of valedictorian Jamison subsides just enough for me to start feeding my own light again—I *can* overtake him. Midterms will be huge, especially AP Calculus, which is my chance to make up a lot of ground all at once. *Sorry, Jamison, you're on your own—no more study buddies.* Now is the time for every small assignment to count. Nothing but hundreds and As from here on out. I can do this, starting now, with seven entire hours to make all of today's little assignments pitch perfect.

I finish everything by two thirty and decide to get in some more flash card review. But I find myself pulling out my sketchbook instead. I'm done; what does it hurt? There's nothing sketchworthy in the ISS room, so I drag my chair over to the window and start drawing the parking lot. It's nothing I'd want to hang in my living room, but the different shapes and angles of the cars are good practice. *Practice for what?* I remind myself. Comics club must be getting to me.

Just before three, a minibus pulls in. It's not a yellow school vehicle, but pale lavender, with the words *Haverwood Senior Center* written on the side. This couldn't be Mrs. Reed's bus, could it? The lady Jamison is supposedly helping with her shopping this afternoon? Okay. I mean . . . it's perfectly plausible for someone to weasel his way into the valedictorian spot *and* volunteer to help the elderly, right?

Right?

I peer at the bus and scan the parking lot for Jamison, but the door handle clicks and Vice Principal Reinhardt steps in.

"How did it go today, Viveca?" he asks, giving me a bit of side-eye as I stand and pull my chair away from the window. "Getting some drawing in?"

What's that supposed to mean? Never mind; I know. It's that stupid rule about not drawing or listening to music or doing creative writing during ISS. But what was I supposed to do, stare at the wall? So I just scoop up my small pile of flawless assignments and hold them out. "All finished," I say. "It was very peaceful."

He chuckles, and for a moment, it feels like it used to, when

Viveca North was a model student any administrator would be delighted to see coming. And we'll get back there again. I'm on a mission.

"Great," Reinhardt says, flipping through the papers. As he shuffles, he's marking off what must be a checklist on his clipboard. I'm dying to peek out the window again and maybe get a glimpse of Mrs. Reed, but I don't, staying careful to appear attentive.

The vice principal makes a final tick on his paper, then reshuffles my stack of work. Then he shuffles it *again,* and looks up. "Just missing your English."

I frown. "My English?"

He checks his clipboard. "Uh—yep. Here. Read 'Goose Pond' by Thomas Williams and write a one-page reaction." He looks up. "Did you do that?" His eyes flick to my sketchbook, and I slide it to my side defensively.

"I did all the work that was in the bin," I say. *Don't argue. Just state facts.*

"It was in the bin," Reinhardt says.

My face is starting to warm. "It wasn't," I say. "I brought everything in at nine, as instructed."

He lowers his clipboard. "Could you have missed it? I'll take a look."

But I stop him before he can turn away. "The bin is empty. I took everything out, and I did it all."

"Then you took a break and did some drawing," he says.

"I didn't take a break," I say, the heat from my cheeks spilling over into hot words. "I was *done.*"

Reinhardt does one of those obnoxious half shrugs, freezing his shoulders at ear level and raising his eyebrows incredulously. "You weren't done. You didn't do your English assignment."

My tone officially crosses over into disrespectful territory. "It. Wasn't. There." My hands are shaking now. Does he think I somehow missed a whole short story in a small bin that I literally emptied? Does he think I'm trying to get out of an English assignment, when I had all day to do it, when *every assignment counts* for me at this point? I know he's mad about me going through his files, but does that just erase everything he's ever known about me? I'm owed more than that.

He shakes his head. "I checked with all your teachers this morning. Ms. Racine said she put your assignment in the bin before school."

"Then Ms. Racine is lying!"

Even as the words are vomiting out of my mouth, I know it's the exact wrong thing to say. All my pent-up anger evaporates into mortification. Ms. Racine is one of the most positive teachers at this school. She loves discussing literature with anybody and handles the drama kids with joy.

But she can be a scatterbrain. As the vice principal gapes at me, outraged, I jump into the silence. "I'm sorry," I say. "I didn't mean that. But sometimes Ms. Racine forgets when she does and doesn't do stuff, you know?"

He crosses his arms. Not a good sign. "I don't know what you're implying, Viveca, but when a veteran teacher assures me they did something, my default assumption is neither that they are lying nor that they are confused about it."

"I—I know, but—"

"I'll meet you at the front doors tomorrow at seven forty-five," the vice principal says. "Let's see if another day of ISS can get you back on track." He slides my work into a pocket folder and opens the door.

My gaze falls to the floor. Industrial tile with a speckled design that camouflages the grime.

"And Viveca," Reinhardt says, "I don't want to see that sketchbook tomorrow. Do you hear me?"

I nod. He pauses, like he's considering demanding a verbal acknowledgment, but after a moment, the door clicks shut.

Whatever. It's not like ISS is that bad, anyway. I'm telling myself this as I shove my things into my backpack with more force than necessary. But at the same time, I'm positive there was no English assignment in that bin this morning. I took everything in at nine o'clock and did every assignment in the pile. There's no way I could lose an entire short story between the door and the one desk in this room. Ms. Racine *must* have forgotten to put it there.

But Reinhardt is right—she wouldn't lie about it. And if she'd forgotten, she'd *remember* that she'd forgotten when he asked her about it and own up to it right away. *Oh, dratty rats, it completely slipped my mind!* I can practically hear her saying the words.

So the only explanation is that someone . . . took my English assignment out of the bin? Nobody even comes back this way, behind the gym. There's nothing here.

Suddenly, my backpack falls from my hands and thuds onto the floor. Someone did come back this way this morning—with the excuse of making a phone call.

Someone with a vendetta against me.

18

My November flies by in a whirlwind of perfect scores, and I hope each one is a mosquito bite on Jamison's backside. That missing English assignment in ISS was a wake-up call—I'm not going to let myself lose focus again. You can't take your eyes off perfection, not for one second.

I work harder than I ever have before, turning down Wren's requests to hang out no matter how skillfully they beg. Wolfing down ramen in my room while Dad and Genevieve talk endlessly about nothing night after night. I've learned my lesson, that sinking to Jamison's level won't get me anywhere. Only one thing will: hard work. With no distractions.

Now I'm killing the midterms. *Flip, flip, flip,* like dominoes—I am a GPA *monster.* My name still sits just below Jamison's on the *Race to the Top!* list, but I know it's only a matter of time before I unseat him and take my rightful place again. Today, finally, is the day of the AP

Calculus midterm. In terms of the race for valedictorian, it's the most important test this year, since the final will happen too late to count toward the class top ten.

Of course there was a weird-energy email from Mr. Howard in our inboxes this weekend. It looked like he just copypasted the syllabus, threw in some page numbers from the textbook, and added a bunch of all-caps thoughts that sometimes seemed calculus adjacent and sometimes sounded like vague threats. And stuff about areas of planes, which we've never studied in class.

I'm the first one in the classroom when the bell rings at eight o'clock. Mr. Howard is still finishing his breakfast. He gives me a tired look, but what am I going to do, sit alone in the hall? He should expect it by now, anyway. I am on time. I am a punctual person. Deal with it.

Kasey and Miranda arrive, and a few other people. Mr. Howard starts organizing some papers at his desk.

Second bell rings. It's 8:05 now, and Jamison hasn't shown up yet. *Huh, good luck trying to talk your way out of missing the freaking midterm.* I stop that train of thought, trying to concentrate on anything other than him.

I stick the eraser end of my pencil into my mouth, that flimsy metal band bending between my teeth like I'm still in third grade. Is that what I'm worried about—Jamison talking his way out of this? Okay, first of all, he's not even late yet. He'll probably just breeze in at the last minute like he always does. And second of all—which should actually be first of all—what I *should* be worried about is the exam itself. Eyes on your own derivatives, Viveca.

At 8:10, Mr. Howard hands out the first section of the test, multiple choice. I quickly flip through. *Of course* areas of planes are in there. Just look at all those curvy little jerks. I mean, I felt pretty solid on them last night, but I was sitting there in my comfort zone with a parade of internet tutorials holding my hand.

Kasey Wheelwright raises her hand. "Jamison isn't here."

"Then Jamison gets a zero," Mr. Howard says. It's a jolt. I start running numbers in my head—a zero on this midterm puts him so far out of contention for valedictorian, I could space Intro to Piano altogether and still beat him.

Those aren't the numbers you need to worry about right now, Viveca.

"You have an hour and a half for part one," Mr. Howard says. "We'll take a break at nine forty-five, then you'll have from ten until lunch for part two."

I'm off: Test Mode. I kind of enjoy it. Maybe *enjoy* is the wrong word—it's this weird relief-soaked focus, a final goodbye to my stacks of neatly written, color-coded note cards. No *future* to worry about for the next three hours, nothing *impending*; there is only the present. It's like floating in a pond. I'm busy pedaling my legs, keeping my head up, breathing, but the arduous swim out to the deep is over.

At the break, Jamison still hasn't shown up. I don't really want a break, but I stretch my legs anyway, take a stroll to the window.

It's overcast. Something about those high, flat clouds makes the sky seem to go on forever. I can hear Kasey Wheelwright and Miranda Nazarian conversing in grave tones: *Not answering. Hope he's okay. Do you really think Howard will give him a zero?* Et boo-hoo cetera.

I've received exactly one zero over the course of my academic career. Sixth grade, public speaking, a one-minute speech about a personal success. I was going to talk about winning the science fair. Practiced in the mirror the whole week before; that went fine. Then, the morning of the presentation, Dad found my notes on the sink. As he was handing them over, he said, "You already won the science fair. Your friends know that. Why are you rubbing it in?" And it threw me. As I faced the class that day, my whole speech just fell out of my head. I stood there like a fence post for a good thirty seconds until Mr. Fontaine took pity on me and handed me my notes. But even with the speech in front of me, all I could focus on were my classmates' faces. When it became clear I wasn't about to utter a single word, Mr. Fontaine told me to sit down. I wasn't upset with him. He had to give me a zero. I earned it.

The second half of the exam is harder, but I'm in the zone. Well, except for areas of planes. Ugh, I wish I were more solid. I hate guessing, half remembering, logicking around the long way when I should just be able to snatch the solution like an alphabetized file from a drawer. My only solace is that everyone else had to free climb that chapter this weekend, too. *Everyone.*

When Mr. Howard calls time at eleven thirty, I've already gone over my responses twice. *Leave time to check your work*—that would be my motto if I had one. Yeah, it's boring. My motto *would* be boring, if it existed.

Still no Jamison.

19

The night after the calculus midterm, I drift to sleep with scattered formulas rattling their way around my brain like chickens in a bathtub. But I don't dream about math. I don't dream about anything. When my alarm goes off in the morning, I'm yanked from perfect, deep blackness.

"Sorry, bud," I tell Ruckus, who stands by the door with his leash in his mouth, ever hopeful. "I've got tutoring at seven. No time for a run."

"Out!" my dad barks as he enters the kitchen. He says it like it's a reprimand, even though out is clearly where Ruckus wants to be.

Dad opens the door, and the dog bolts. When Ruckus hears the truck start, he'll come back and let Dad hook him to that god-awful run to spend the day zooming back and forth in his frozen groove.

"You didn't get the mail yesterday." Dad clips on his nametag: *Buck North, Manager.*

"Oh. Sorry, I forgot. I had a big test." He notices when I forget to get the mail. Doesn't ask about the test.

"Uh-huh." Dad grabs his enormous work keyring/Swiss Army knife/array of keytags off the hook by the door. "Well, something came from that school."

"Oh." *That school.* He never says its name. He only speaks of it as though Everett College itself is the manifestation of some act of defiance on my part.

I wait for him to close the door. I wait for the truck to rumble to life, for Ruckus's *rawp rawp* as he's tethered for the day, for the receding sound of tires crunching over the gravel. Only then do I turn to the kitchen table and the pile of yesterday's mail.

And then—there it is. *Holy crap, there it is.* Two lions and a stalk of wheat. *Ms. Viveca North.* Three and a half years, and this is all going to be over today, now, one way or another.

I stare at the envelope for a full minute. I've been so confident about everything—the SATs, my grades, my essays. But now that this letter is here, I have no idea what I'm expecting to find inside. My thoughts flit back to the interview. I was so fake, like a hollow person papier-mâchéd from scraps of rehearsed speeches and half-hearted extracurricular activities.

I slide a fingernail under the seal and carefully tear open the envelope. There are a few papers inside; I scan the first one, formatted like a letter, without even really reading it.

And then it's real. *Congratulations! We are happy to offer you a place . . .*

I'm *in.*

My skin zings, undiluted joy cascading downward from the top of my head. I read the letter for real, then flip through the attached checklist, the website information, the list of student resources. My heart is thumping like I'm tearing around the Scruton Back loop, but my body is utterly still. I don't think I could move if I tried.

Then I read it again. *Valedictorian of your class.* It's set in stone, then. My breath stops for a second. I *have* to be valedictorian. I can't let Jamison Sharpe take it from me.

I start putting numbers together in my head—tuition, fees, materials. Housing. Food. But I'll get some part-time, minimum-wage college-town job. I'm already going for all the local scholarships I can find. I'll have to see what they've given me for financial aid— or even scholarships. What if I get a full ride?

Plus, there's the money from Grandpa . . . I inhale, almost letting my brain go to that place I don't want it to. No. I don't have to think about *that* money, whether or not it exists. Not yet.

I message Wren.

> ACCEPTED

> VIVECA WHAT!!!!!!! YAYYYYYYY!!!!!

> Everett

> yep

> !!

> Aw shucks

> You have earned one free anti-horoscope divination and three free hugs. *not redeemable for cash

> ty lly

> you are a magnificent beast and I am so proud

As usual, when I think too hard about next year and setting off on a new adventure, I have a pang of guilt. Wren doesn't know what they're doing yet. Flying the coop at eighteen is pretty much a must for their sanity and safety; their mom is all right, but their father has never come to terms with having an artist for a kid instead of a future oil executive. Wren's talking gap year and travel. For their sake, I hope it doesn't end up being another year of scooping ice cream and making subs, unless it's in a town far from here.

Then there's the part of that pang that's my own dad. He'll be okay, I tell myself. He has Genevieve and Ruckus and a job that's not too bad. But I still don't want to hurt him by leaving him behind. Mom, though—she would probably be proud of me. That counts for something.

There's more to the packet from Everett, so I keep leafing. And

I'm surprised to find what looks like my financial aid letter, already included. But it's only a single page.

It takes me a half second to take in the gist of the letter, but I read it three times, every word. I let my hand drop to my side, tapping the paper against my leg as I look up at the ceiling. Then I read it again. The language is sparse and unemotional, but one word keeps shouting itself over and over, jabbing me in the guts like a hot poker.

Denied.

It's nestled between other words, things like *problems with your financial aid application* and *discrepancies* and *tax returns* and *we take this seriously.* All words that would be disturbing me more if it weren't for the deafening presence of *denied.*

No financial aid. And—I look once more, horrified and transfixed, like I'm rubbernecking at a murder scene—and no scholarship eligibility. Gone. Everything.

Gone.

I sink into a kitchen chair, half expecting to just dissolve, dribbling to the floor through the holes in the wicker seat. No matter how hard I work, how great my grades are, even if I was the most celebrated valedictorian in Elton Prep history, you can't go to college without money. Aid. Scholarships. Loans. A full-time job. *Something.* With hard-earned savings that barely allow me to live and a father who won't cosign anything, what are my options now? This form, this most *basic* of *basic hoops*, was my gateway to everything else. How could Dad—

But I can't even ask myself the question. It's obvious how this happened. It should have been obvious from the beginning. Did I think my father was capable of being honest about something so personal? Did I think he would own up to the fact that we don't have money, even on something as important as an official form that his daughter's future was dependent on? Genevieve promised she'd make sure he mailed it. But I'm such an idiot, I didn't even piece together the fact that Dad's ladyfriend must also have *watched him fill everything out.* Of course he would lie. Nothing is as important to him as inflating his own image, his own ego, with lies.

My hands are shaking as I dial the store. I'm—what? Angry? Not exactly. It's more like I'm one of those mad-scientist balls you can buy at the mall, where you touch the plastic sphere and arcs of colorful current jump to where your fingers are. There's a sparking core behind my ribs, and a million flashing, crackling tendrils of electricity shoot through my organs, rippling in waves under my skin. It's anger that's so new and raw, it doesn't even know how to be anger yet.

There's no use in my calling him. Besides, he might not even be there yet. But it's out of my control. I ask to speak to the manager. And after a moment, he picks up.

"Manager."

I open my mouth. The silence is too long. He's going to hang up. "Dad," I say finally.

"Hi, princess. What's the matter?"

I try to keep my voice even. "Dad, did you—did you lie on that financial aid application for my school? You have to tell me, okay?"

I don't think I've ever said the word *lie* aloud to my dad before. I can't picture what his face must look like now; I just don't have the data for a working model of his reaction. It's uncharted territory, and despite my anger, I'm suddenly really grateful we have most of West Bore separating us for this historic moment.

"That thing I had to fill out? Of course not."

I squeeze my eyes shut. "It's just that—I was denied. There were apparently some problems with the information on the form. So I'm not eligible for aid or scholarships or, like, anything for tuition. I thought—"

"What are you accusing me of?"

And *here we go*. That's the thing with any interaction with Buck North—it becomes all about Buck North. But this isn't about my father's ego. It's about the tiny spark of hope I'm desperately trying to breathe life into—the thought that maybe, *maybe*, this is fixable.

"Nothing," I backpedal. "I just thought you might have accidentally made a mistake somewhere, and I was hoping we could try to figure it out. I know the deadline has passed, but maybe—"

"I filled out your form, Viveca. I didn't make any mistakes. You can ask Genevieve." Dad's voice is stern, a wall around whatever it is he's protecting. "You think I got all these promotions by making mistakes? You think I support us by making mistakes?"

I don't say anything, not that he wants me to. These are rhetorical questions. If I were to respond to them, it might start to unravel the threads he's cocooned himself within these past few years. At this point, he probably really believes the line he's told himself all along, that he was let go from his corporate job because they were all jealous of his brilliant ideas, and not because his blatant and unexplainable storytelling became a liability for the company. All his former coworkers distanced themselves and moved on, and now his ever-changing circle of new friends lap up his sob stories—I'm probably the only human on earth who has held on to the truth. I clutch it so it doesn't escape. I take it out and marvel at it every time I have to hand over my earnings to support the basic lifestyle we can no longer afford because of his lies.

Dad sighs. "Look, I can't stand here and chat with you all day, princess. I'm sorry that school you like didn't give you any money, all right? But there's nothing I can do about it."

"What about my college money?" I blurt out.

I can't believe I said it.

It's the thing I haven't said. The thing I've *never* said, that I never *would have* said. But I can't find a spark of hope left except for this one, small and sad and dangerous to touch.

Dad is quiet for a long time. "What are you talking about?"

I swallow. "I know Grandpa put some money aside for me. For college."

"Hell." There's another long silence. Then, "Well, it's gone."

And there. Just like that, the spark has been snuffed out. I knew it would be, in the deepest part of my heart. I knew nothing existed for me, that Dad would have burned through any money my grandfather had saved for my future long ago if he possibly could. At my core, I knew that if I tried to make it become real, it would be gone. Like the images in a dream you just can't hang on to once you wake up.

"How could you?" I murmur.

"What's that?"

My voice hardens. "How *could* you? If you were going to spend my college money from Grandpa—*my money*—the *least* you could have done would have been to fill out my stupid *financial aid forms* without screwing them up!"

"Viveca!" He sounds shocked. How can he possibly be shocked by this? "I don't have time—" he says.

"But you had to lie." I'm spitting venom now. "You always have to lie. Your made-up stories about your life are more important to you than the real people in it." I take a breath, and my venom is exhausted. All I can do is stare at a hairline crack that splits one of the tiles on our kitchen floor.

"I'll see you when I get home," Dad says. And he's gone.

I rest my phone in my lap. I'm already late for tutoring; I can kiss that session fee goodbye. Not that it matters. With my savings, I could barely afford to get *to* Everett College now, let alone be a student there.

All because of a lie. My blood froths. I've done *everything right*. I got the grades, took the exams, filled out the forms, wrote the essays. I'm well-rounded and trustworthy, and I would make Mom *so proud* in college if I only had the chance—and I've worked so, so hard to get that chance. Yet one stupid, egotistical lie is all it took to undo everything, years of sweat and anxiety and loneliness.

It's the liars of this world who deserve to see their dreams crashing down, not me.

It's the liars who should lose everything.

20

I'm still boiling two days later. It's my default state at this point, a breath away from bursting into scorching shards. I sit through my classes with a veneer of calm that hides the dangerous vibration underneath. What a waste my life has been, what a *waste*.

Wren asked me to come to a rehearsal after school for a one-act play the drama club is taking to a festival just before the holiday break. I haven't told them about the Everett financial aid disaster. They don't know about my dad's issue, and how do you even begin that conversation? Watching a rehearsal sounds like hell, to be honest, but it's as good a reason as any for me to linger here and not go home, where Dad and I force bland, fake interactions when we can't avoid each other.

I watch, glassy-eyed, as Tyson and Min emote under the bright lights. Kasey Wheelwright flits across the stage in a neon costume, and Dylan Boyle delivers a few stiff proclamations. Ms. Racine, who coaches drama, calls out encouragement from the front row.

As I sit in the auditorium, I notice my mind is surprisingly empty. I'm not even really following the play; the words are too fast and too far away. Somebody gets murdered, I think.

"You come here often?" A figure plops down into the seat next to me; Jade, covered with paint. The house lights have come up for a ten-minute break. I straighten in my seat a little.

"Only when I need an alibi," I say.

Jade laughs, and it feels as comfortable as it could, I guess. Wren barrels toward us from the stage, parkouring over rows of seats, leaping from arm to arm like a rabbit.

"Wren Beagle, do not break those armrests!" Ms. Racine yells.

"We are so close to being done with that backdrop," Wren says, skittering to a halt. "It'll probably even be dry by the time we have to roll it up and throw it in the bus." They lower themself into the seat behind me. "What do you think of *Death at the Disco* so far?"

I turn around, perching backward, and give a reassuring nod. "I thought Min was very—ebullient."

Wren kicks their feet out onto my seat back. "I have no idea what that word means, but neither do you, and it's clear you're trying to be complimentary, so—yay!"

"You're ebullient, too," Jade says, and I force myself to laugh with a lightness I don't feel. My spirit is all the way down under my seat, weighed down with rocks. At least my misery is making my brain too apathetic for social anxiety. So that's working out.

"Too bad we're still missing Detective Aubergine," Wren says.

"Oh, is that what those long, awkward silences were?" I ask.

Wren laughs. "No, those were just people forgetting their lines. I know you're not a super-discerning theatergoer, but you might remember Detective Aubergine as the nervous, stage-managery-looking guy onstage reading Jamison's part from the script."

I blink. "Jamison? Jamison Sharpe is in this play? Jeez, when does he sleep?"

"When does he *rehearse*?" Jade asks. "He's been out since Tuesday."

"Well, look at this," Wren says, their gaze stolen by something behind me. "Enter stage right."

I twist around. There's some kind of a commotion happening. A knot of students has formed at the foot of the stage, with more meandering over curiously. And at the center, hair disheveled and face grim, is Jamison.

"I guess he decided to show up after all," I say. And suddenly, I'm boiling over. I don't want to. But there's something about Jamison's dumb, handsome face, his magnetism, the fact that he just assumes everything is going to go his way—I *know* he thinks there's no chance he's going to face consequences for missing our calc midterm. And that mindset alone makes me practically erupt. I'm sitting here grasping at the few wispy strands of my college prospects that Dad hasn't destroyed, and here's Jamison breezing in like nothing's different after ditching school and doing whatever stupid crap he wanted for the entire week. I get to my feet.

"Where are you going?" Wren puts a hand on my elbow.

My anger comes out as a laugh. "I want to know what sob story he's concocted. This is going to be amazing."

"Dude." Wren is trotting beside me as I stride down the aisle. "Is this about your math midterm?"

Jamison has hands laid all over him. People are bowing their heads. It looks like some kind of religious ceremony.

"I just don't know what I'm going to tell everyone," Jamison is saying, eyes shimmering. He hands his phone to a kid with black-rimmed glasses, who looks at it somberly and then passes it on. "I missed two midterms. I'm so late for dress rehearsal. I'm sure Ms. Racine won't let me do the festival now. I can't believe it."

My wires are all flickering and zapping. I cross my arms. So Jamison is throwing himself a little pity party. Let's see how far he takes it.

"Teachers understand about pets. I missed a track meet when my cat was sick, and I didn't get penalized," Kasey says, rubbing Jamison's shoulder. That's as close to Jamison Sharpe action as she's ever going to get and she knows it, so she's really getting in there, deep tissue.

Oh, this is precious. Home with a sick pet for three days? *That's* his excuse? I suppress a smirk.

Wait a sec. I look at the solemn faces, the slow blinks, the rubby hands . . . do people actually believe this?

"There's no way we're doing the festival without you," Glasses

Boy says, "and I'm sure the teachers will let you make up the exams." Everyone nods enthusiastically except Jamison's understudy, who looks a little annoyed.

"No," I blurt. "Mr. Howard said Jamison's getting a zero on the AP Calc midterm." I might as well have sounded an air horn. Everyone stares at me.

"Oh," Jamison says in a small voice.

"What are you *doing*, Viveca?" Kasey says.

Wren looks at me, frowning. "Viveca?"

I'm holding my breath for a second, frozen. It was like the words I spoke shut my body down. Thoughts that were supposed to be inside somehow escaped to the outside. But I'm also frothing. There's a sloshing sensation in my chest. Then I electrify. "He *did* say that," I double down. "You heard him, Kasey. He said it in front of the whole class."

Jamison pales. "He did? That's . . . embarrassing. And kind of unprofessional, honestly."

Jade steps toward Jamison. "Don't worry, man," she says—the traitor. "Things happen. Teachers get it."

Jamison raises his sparkling blue eyes. "Well, I did speak to Mr. Howard a few minutes ago, and he seemed to think it would be okay if I took the exam after the break."

"That is such BS," I mutter. I don't really mean to say it out loud. Everyone is staring at me again.

Wren nudges me. "Hey, pal, you're at like an eight right now, and I'm gonna need you at about a three."

"I don't care," I say. Jamison doesn't utter a word, just looks at me placidly. But I've got his number. "It's *obvious* what happened. You skipped out because you weren't prepared. You wanted to be able to sneak off into the library with your phone and whatever else. Well, guess what? We *all* would have liked that. But we had to suck it up and do the freaking exam using our own brains."

I look around for support. Obviously Kasey is too absorbed in Jamison's pheromones. And the rest of the drama kids have no clue what I'm talking about. Jade rolls her eyes. Tyson uncomfortably slides his fingers into his fauxhawk.

But my pulse is through the roof, and I keep going at Jamison. "You blow in here every day like you're the center of the freaking world, and people *fall* for it. You waltz in with all these supposed accomplishments from your old school—baseball star, national academic awards, *cover model* for Taiwanese *Teen Vibe*." I raise my eyebrows, gesture to the ceiling. "Did you guys know that? Did you know Jamison says he was a *cover model* for Taiwanese *Teen Vibe*?" I give a cold laugh.

Nobody laughs with me. What is wrong with them? Am I losing my mind?

Kasey huffs. "Who are you to say he wasn't?"

"I know it seems far-fetched," Jamison says, "especially since I'm not, you know, that handsome."

Come on.

"That's why I don't talk about it that much," he goes on. "I wanted a fresh start here. This school—everyone here—has been so amazing. Especially you, Viveca. You're brilliant and generous and you challenge me. It's exciting."

COME ON.

"All she does is pick on you, Jamison," Kasey spits.

I scoff. "You're delusional."

"No, *you're* delusional," Dylan Boyle says, and my skin flushes cold. *Don't you dare bring seventh grade into this*, I think. He looks right at me, but before he says anything else, Wren puts a hand on his arm and he shuts his mouth.

Jamison lowers his eyes. "I think I need to be alone right now. I'll . . . I'll double-check with Mr. Howard about the test. I wouldn't want anyone to think it was unfair."

Now everyone is looking daggers at me. And theater kids can look daggers better than anyone. Can't they *see* it's all an act? Am I in Crazytown?

Someone passes me a phone—Jamison's. I look down. There's a photo pulled up of a flop-eared black dog with one white paw. A burgundy collar around its neck says *Checkers*. "Jamison, this is yours." I hold out my hand. "I'm assuming this is your sick dog or whatever."

He reaches for it, then pauses. He fixes me with a deep gaze. "I don't want you, of all people, to think ill of me, Viveca," he says. "Go into my contacts, *V* for *vet*. Call up Dr. Salcowicz and . . . and ask him to verify—" He breaks off in a sob. Three girls and a guy instantly embrace him.

"I'm not calling your stupid vet," I say.

Kasey gives me the most venomous look I've ever gotten; I can practically see her cobra hood flaring. "Then call the police," she says. "I'm sure they can verify the accident."

I twitch. "Accident?"

Jamison is now a quivering mass of restrained sobs. Kasey narrows her eyes. "Yeah. His dog, Checkers, got hit by a car Tuesday morning. The day of the midterm. Jamison spent all week keeping vigil at the vet's."

"Oh." My electricity is petering out. "I don't know what to say."

"You *could* say you're sorry," Kasey spits. "Sorry that Checkers *died* in Jamison's arms two hours ago."

I could. Except I can't. I'm frozen again. Jamison just keeps apologizing as his fan club escorts him out of the auditorium toward the vending machines. His fan club apparently being everyone at Elton Prep except Wren and me, and I'm not even sure about Wren at this point.

The double doors click shut, and we're alone. Wren doesn't say anything, which is unlike them.

My mind is oatmeal. I open my mouth. "You don't believe him, do you?"

They raise an eyebrow. "Why wouldn't I?"

"Because it's just too convenient!" I splutter. "You have to see what a fake he is."

Wren hoists themself up onto the end of the stage like they're getting out of a pool. They dangle their legs and tilt their head. "I see a guy who missed three days of school, for reasons unknown, and who comes back to rehearsal only to be met with vitriol from someone who barely knows him and has no stake in his life or his choices."

My face prickles. Dammit, am I going to cry? In front of Wren? "Fine," I say. "I'm a terrible person."

"That's not what I said."

I don't know what I'm feeling right now. If something happened to Ruckus . . . I can't even think about it. Of course I would miss school; I'd be camped out in that vet's office like a barnacle.

"But Jamison sucks at math," I say. "Then his dog—it's all so . . ." I trail off. Do I sound like a lunatic?

Wren closes their eyes. "It's . . . You're just so bitter, Viveca."

Bitter. It's an ugly word, and Wren said it ugly. I don't know what to say. They're not wrong.

21

Mr. G drops me off at dusk. I can barely register my own footsteps.
I'm in a sickly haze, flashbacks to junior high. I just publicly ridi-
culed someone over the death of their beloved dog. How did I get
here?

The curving driveway is framed by strange shapes, trees and
underbrush lit by the dying day or the rising night, light that
seems at once brilliant and murky. It's the in-between moment
when you can't tell if you can see or not. By the time I get to the
top of the hill, the shadows have won out. Our house looks like a
ghost.

I'm surprised to see Genevieve's car in the driveway, especially
since Dad's not home yet. Ruckus isn't on his run, either.

"Hello?" I push open the door and toss my bag in the kitchen.

"Viveca." Genevieve's voice comes from the living room. She
sounds different, flatter.

I go in. "Hey."

She's on the couch, her legs tucked underneath her. Ruckus is squished up against her in a giant orange ball. Genevieve is sitting up now, but I can tell from the creases on her flushed cheeks that she's been curled over with her face in Ruckus's fur for a while.

"I, uh, let myself in," she says hoarsely.

I slide onto the arm of the couch. "That's fine." When she doesn't say anything, I ask, "Can I get you a drink or something?"

She laughs at this. It's a bursting laugh, staccato and wretched. Then she starts crying. "You're so kind, Viveca."

I look down. "I'm not so sure about that," I say. I take a deep breath. "So, hey . . . what's wrong?"

Genevieve's weeping intensifies. Ruckus raises his head in concern and starts licking her face, and this makes her laugh again. I'm in stasis, observing, wanting to take some kind of action but unable to move. I'm not used to all this rawness. Dad shows emotion, but you never know what his real feelings are; they're far away and not for you. He's like a person projected onto a screen. But here, now, it's like Genevieve's insides are outside. It's a tidal wave of authenticity, and it's frying my circuits.

She wipes her eyes on her sleeve and rubs Ruckus's jowls. "Good baby," she says. "Good boy, Ruck." Now she inhales wetly and blinks at me a couple times. "Viveca. I thought I'd see your dad first, but . . ." She shrugs. "I guess I don't know why I thought that. Who even knows where he is?"

I glance at the cheap grandmother clock in the corner. "He's probably still at work. I think they're restocking or something."

"Is that right." It's sour and definitely not a question.

"I mean—yeah?" I'm not sure what she's getting at. Then I realize—Genevieve has had the moment of realization with my father. *Oh, Dad, what did you tell her?*

She stops petting Ruckus and folds her hands together like she's going to deliver bad news. "Viveca, I'm not sure what to say, but . . ."

She doesn't finish, so I ask, "Did Dad lie to you about something?"

Genevieve's eyes widen. "Don't you *know*?"

I almost laugh. The list of lies I could possibly know about could fill Mr. Reinhardt's file cabinet. But I widen my eyes back at her. "I guess not?"

She points to the coffee table, and I notice a small stack of papers. I pick up the top one—my acceptance letter.

"This is my packet from Everett," I say. "I got in." I give her a weak smile.

Genevieve takes a couple gaspy breaths. "But, Viveca, your financial aid!"

Oh. "Yeah." I nod slowly. "That kind of sucks." *Hugely. Hugely sucks.*

"So you knew?"

And I'm deflating again. All I can do is nod.

Her lips get very thin. Then she says, "How long have you known about *her*?"

My head does a little bob in surprise. "Her? Who?"

She looks down at Ruckus, then up. "Viveca, your dad has betrayed us both. I think he's—seeing someone else." Now she's crying again.

This bizarre line of thought jolts me up from my funk a little. I slide down from the arm onto the couch cushion. "Hey, I don't know what you found out, but I don't think he's, you know, cheating on you. He's not really like that." *I don't think. Who knows?*

She leans forward. "But your financial aid application! The discrepancies!"

"I— Yeah?"

Genevieve throws up her hands. "Where does all that money go? If it's not in his accounts, not on his taxes—where does it go? I know his manager's salary is quite generous. He must have a double life. Otherwise, where's the money?"

"Oh," I breathe. "Oh, Genevieve." I instinctively bite my bottom lip, chewing my words over before they escape my mouth. I scroll through a dozen softening blows, but the last thing she needs is more lies. So I just pat her hand. "There is no money."

Her eyebrows draw together. "What?"

"He doesn't make that much at the store. I'm sure he was just trying to impress you." Even though Dad's on my list right now, I throw that one soft sentiment out there, because it's probably true.

She's quiet for a moment. Ruckus lets out a snore and flaps his feathery tail. "But your future, Viveca. What are you going to do?"

I swallow. "I don't know." In the back of my mind, I'm still holding on to the idea of the Pinniped County Futurists' essay contest and its impossibly large prize. But it feels like pinning your hopes on the lottery.

We hear Dad's truck crunch to a stop. I inhale and look at Genevieve. "Do you want me to stay?"

She smiles and shakes her head. "No. I think we need to talk alone. Thanks, Viveca."

I retreat to my room, relieved I don't have to deal with Dad right now. Ruckus opts to stay with Genevieve. I splay out on my bed, listening but not wanting to listen. The front door. Dad calling out for her, confused. Her muffled response.

I'm used to the people in Dad's life coming and going. I've learned not to get too attached to ladyfriends, work buddies, game night groups. But I messed up and let Genevieve get to me. She's not even exciting or that interesting. It's just that she fit. She felt like she belonged here, to me, anyway. I didn't realize that until this moment. But all things are impermanent—especially houses of cards left open to the wind.

22

That night, Wren summons me to Fort Kearsarge. It's a welcome escape, if anything can be "welcome" at this point, from the somber murmurings of what is probably Dad and Genevieve's relationship imploding. I'm still wounded by what Wren said to me after school, but if they want to pretend nothing happened, that's fine by me.

Wren blinks the flashlight on their phone on and off. Old graffiti, vines, darkness, flaking paint, darkness. "The internet sibyls have declared that you'll be in the right place at the right time today," they say. "So, obviously, your anti-horoscope compels me to lead you to what must be the wrong place." They glance at their phone. "And it's definitely the wrong time."

"No argument here." I sit back against the grimy concrete, sweeping empty beer bottles out of my personal space with my legs, and breathe in the staleness. The corpse of Fort Kearsarge was exciting when we were kids, like a horror movie. A forbidden, half-buried monster made of stone, iron, and chain link. Dark, narrow spaces filled with the old ghosts of war and recent traces of rebel teenagers who would always be cooler than us.

Now, as I sit surrounded by garbage at eleven o'clock on a cold Thursday, with other crap pressing on my frontal lobe, Fort Kearsarge just seems gross.

Wren pulls out a juice box. "Surf Berry?"

I shake my head.

"I feel bad about Jamison's dog." I say it because it feels like the right thing to say, but as the words come out, the awfulness of what I've done rushes over me again, knotting my innards.

"Checkers," Wren says. "He of the One White Paw." They squeeze my knee.

I exhale and lean back, closing my eyes. Be in the moment. Hear, touch, smell.

There's that heavy silence again. Finally, Wren says, "You're so smart, Viveca. You see all these connections. You should really get into astrology. But sometimes, you know, things are just a coincidence."

I know. My cross-wired, connection-hungry brain has betrayed me plenty of times—like with poor Checkers. But sometimes things *aren't* coincidences, and it feels like nobody sees that except me. Still, all I can say is "I don't want to talk about it."

"Right." Wren's face is striped with moonlight through the room's iron bars. "I guess I do, though, Viveca. Want to talk about it."

My stomach does that tiny wobble-wobble, like Jell-O, like the ground is spongy. "What do you mean?"

Wren gets this look on their face. It might be distorted by the moon or the intermittent flashlight, but my lizard brain recognizes it instantly. It's the look that precedes a Difficult Conversation involving Gentle Suggestions About Therapy.

I *was* wrong about Checkers. The thought tightens my throat. Jamison didn't deserve what I said to him today. Nobody deserves that. If anything happened to Ruckus, I'd crumble to dust.

Wren is still looking at me. "It was just . . . I don't know. Do you really think Jamison did all that stuff? Called in a bomb threat for no reason?"

I roll a bottle with my shoe. It glides away across the cement into the darkness.

"The reason was that he needed more time to study. With me. I have the highest average in that class, and he knows it."

Wren looks down, contemplating their plastic straw. "Do you see how this is all about you, Viveca?"

"Okay, what does that mean?"

They do this slow blink like they're about to have to explain that the sky is blue, but in that moment, we hear a car pull into the sandy parking area at the bottom of the hill. Wren peeks through the bars.

"Cops," Wren says. "Since when do they patrol here during the week?"

By rights, Fort Kearsarge should be one of those mythical

places left to decay in the woods, its triangulation towers blending with trees and its sunken circles of fairy mushrooms sprouting where artillery used to sit. But the fort sits on the hill that overlooks Elton, in a scrap of wilderness that fringes golf courses and HOA neighborhoods. The cops here don't have much to do, but the duties they do have they must perform to the satisfaction of Elton's elite. That includes nabbing teenagers who jump the NO TRESPASSING fence, get wasted in the munitions storage, and tag the walls. "It's just a juice box" isn't going to fly.

"Do you think they saw my light?" Wren asks.

"Maybe." I peek out the barred window. Blue lights flash farther down the hill on the other side of the locked gate. The beam of a flashlight moves through the darkness, painting pale patches onto slender tree trunks, underbrush, and cement walls. "Someone probably reported your crappy sedan."

"Ugh, all I need is another ticket," Wren whispers. "Busybodies."

I duck as the beam gets closer. "Yeah, well, parking on the street's not illegal."

"Trespassing is." Wren's voice is carefully controlled, but they're freaked out.

"I know," I say. I also know the worst part won't be the cops, but afterward, when they bring Wren home.

"Yeah, so, I'm making a run for it," they say in that calm-not-calm voice.

"You can't run. He'll see you."

"Well, I sure can't stay here. I've already got enough strikes for a no-hitter."

All of a sudden, this *glorp* of guilt bubbles up from my stomach. Wren is afraid, and they're *never* afraid. And they're in this situation because of me. Even after I embarrassed them in front of the whole drama club, they only brought me here because according to my anti-horoscope they thought it would help. Crap, it *is* all about me, isn't it?

I swallow. "Okay. Look, I'm going to throw a bottle across the yard to that other wall and get his attention. Then you run." I grab a grimy beer bottle from the floor. The light is getting closer.

Wren shakes their head. "We both run. You'll get caught in here."

"I'm not throwing it until you're in danger. Go now and maybe I won't have to."

I see them cross their arms in the moonlight. "How are you going to hide—*crap*, Viveca, you're going down the passage, aren't you? Because *no*, you're *not*."

"Just get going!" I hiss. Wren gives me an exasperated look before making up their mind and creeping out around the iron door.

I grip the beer bottle; it's covered with filmy dust and grit. A tiny amount of liquid sloshes at the bottom. The cop is approaching faster than I expected, making a beeline for the munitions storage where I'm crouched. He's done this before. Wren can't be more than halfway along the wall by now.

I step into the doorway, close my eyes, and wing the bottle at the cement wall of the next building over. It's a long throw, but it hits, and the glittering sound of exploding glass draws the light beam in an instant.

Wren runs; I hear it. They'll be up and away, through the thin trees and over the chain-link fence in no time. I run, too, but not out the door. There isn't enough time. And if I'm caught, Wren will be, too, eventually. Wren may have a ton of friends, but I only have one, and it wouldn't take long for some Elton gossip to figure out who it is.

It's just trespassing, I tell myself as I make for the passage. But it's not—especially not for Wren. Another strike would mean bad stuff waiting for them at home. And with the empty beer bottles and graffiti around, it would probably be several strikes.

There are passages all over Fort Kearsarge—narrow spaces between the interior and exterior walls. I hop into one of them through a crumbled section of wall opposite the door of the munitions storage and start to ease my way along, behind the back wall of the room, my feet crunching debris. It reeks in here, like rot and dust and death. Every once in a while, my sneakers *squish* instead of *crunch*. The squishes are the worst. I can't see anything, but I don't dare shine my phone.

Clink. Someone in hard soles steps into the room.

I keep edging, sliding, holding my breath. I'm careful with my feet. My right arm feels the way forward—sideways—over the cool, rough surface of the wall, until at last I feel the corner. If I tuck around there, I'll be safe, even if the cop shines that flashlight all the way down the passage from the hole in the wall.

I hold my breath for a moment in the darkness. I've been around the corner before on dares, but not since middle school. And I've had a couple of growth spurts since then. Will I even fit?

There's a dull *crack* as I put my weight on some old glass. Footsteps quicken in the room on the other side of the concrete wall.

I have to turn the corner.

With a deep inhale, I slither around. I *do* fit, barely. My shoulder is still poking out, so I wriggle and squash until I'm sure I'm completely out of sight.

I keep absolutely still. After only a moment, there is a bright sweep of light, like an explosion, which illuminates the pitted gray walls. Then it's gone. The footsteps recede. *He's not coming any farther.*

My muscles unclench in the blackness. I count to five hundred to give the cop time to give up. I don't hear the cruiser leaving, but I'm certain I'm safe. Alone. I exhale. With a jerk of my spine, I heave back toward the corner.

But my body doesn't move.

"Okay," I say aloud. Grunting, I wrench my torso sideways. The walls press me tightly between them.

No. No, no, no. I kick out my foot, scrabble against the gritty floor. I scratch my nails against rough concrete. I suck in my stomach, exhale every molecule of air until I'm nothing but ribs and flesh. But I can't budge.

Not even a little.

23

Is this how I die, stuck between the bones of Fort Kearsarge? *Viveca, don't be dramatic.*

My phone is wedged in the right front pocket of my jeans. With a strain, I manage to grasp it between my fingers and pull it out. But as soon as it's free of my pocket, it slips to the floor. *Of course.*

I exhale. Okay. I try to bend sideways, inching, dropping my right hand straight down. My head is turned to the left, but it doesn't matter because I can't see anything, anyway. I wiggle my fingers, stretch my shoulder. Nothing. I can't reach the floor. I try to *twist*, but my hips are stuck. My phone might as well be on the moon.

"Command: Call Wren," I say. It feels weird, almost jolting, to speak.

The phone chimes. "You must unlock your phone to use voice commands. Please enter the passcode."

Freaking delightful. "Command: Enter passcode."

Beep. "Please use the touch screen to enter your passcode."

"Command: Enter passcode with voice command."

Beep. "You must unlock your phone to use voice commands. Please enter the passcode."

I laugh in the dark. It hurts, since there's concrete crushing my body, front to back and back to front. But the absurdity is getting to me. And if I don't laugh, things are going to start to get spongy. I can't tell if my head is spinning. In this utter blackness, I can barely tell which end is up. What happens if you pass out somewhere where you can't breathe?

There's a way to call 911 without unlocking the phone, right? I could probably figure it out. But then what's the point, if I'm just summoning the cops back to my location? Wren is safe, and I *have* to keep them that way.

I laugh again. Apparently my brain thinks this situation is *hilarious*. I'm laughing so hard I can't breathe. Or maybe it's something else. Maybe it's not a laugh, but that rapid *huh-uh-huh-uh-huh-uh* that means my body has started rebelling, preparing to shut down.

Will Wren put two and two together when I'm not in school tomorrow? How long will it take for Dad to notice I'm gone? Tomorrow's his late day, so he'll sleep in; he won't expect to see me in the morning. Then he won't be home until after eight. Will he even notice I'm not there?

I tip my head back the couple of inches it's able to move, a vampire in my upright coffin, listening to the sounds of the inaccessible living—the movement of air as it investigates the spaces around me, little scratches from tiny feet scampering, grit dislodging from the walls.

Then—a soft *thud*. It could be that a larger piece of masonry has let go and bonked off the floor. Or it could have been a footstep. I tense up. Do I call out? Maybe it's Wren, circled back to check on me. But what if it's that cop again? Or an escaped murderer? Or, worst case scenario, Jamison Sharpe? *Oh, hey, Viveca, what's up? Stuck in a wall? See, these are the kinds of experiences that matter, you know? Being valedictorian, modeling for* Teen Vibe, *getting stuck in a wall. I see how hard you work, trying to get unstuck from inside this wall. You have a lot of passion, Viveca. So do those rats.*

"Viveca?" comes a voice.

"Holy crap," I say.

There's a honk-laugh.

"Yep, that's definitely you."

I cough. "Wren, I'm stuck in the passage. I think I'm dying of fumes, and I'm pretty sure the rats are planning something."

The sounds of feet clopping across the munitions storage room reach me through the cement. "You are a *nut*, Viveca."

I snort.

"I can't believe I'm creeping through here again like I'm freaking twelve." Wren's voice is closer now. Now I see the light from their phone. They're slipping down the passage in record time.

I reach around the corner, and a bony hand grabs my arm. "Pull me out!" I say.

Wren tugs. "Sheesh, Viveca, you're a sardine. How did you even get that wedged?"

"I was in the wrong place at the wrong time," I say. "Just like you said."

They laugh. "No arguments here." They manage to get both hands gripping my arm.

"Pull like one of those Clydesdales," I say.

Wren gives a whinny, which cracks us up. It's an awkward setup—me, flattened, staring in profile like a pharaoh, and Wren's long arms gripping whatever solid parts of me they can reach around the corner.

On the count of three, we both *heave*.

And I budge. Not all the way, but a bit. On the second *heave*, I fall sideways. My lungs expand. I feel a little scraped up, but otherwise okay.

Wren stops pulling and wraps me in a warm corner hug. "You've popped free!" they say with a squeeze. "Like a zit!"

I squeeze them back. "Thanks for saving my life."

I grab my phone, and we sidle back down the passage and out through the crumbling wall. Wren peeks through the bars. "No sign of Officer Nosy. Guess he went home."

That *glorp* of guilt bubbles in my stomach again. "You didn't have to come back for me," I say. "That was risky."

They raise an eyebrow. "I obviously *did* have to come back for you."

I blurt a laugh. It's louder than I expect; maybe some other feelings and stuff are yelping out of me at the same time. "Yeah, well, let's start to phase out the criminal activity. My heart can't take it."

We leave the munitions storage and pad down the moonlit hill toward the entrance gate. Wren's car is a little ways down the road in a turnoff. There's no one in sight, just trees and gravel and brush. "Well," I say. "That was almost an adventure."

Wren leans against the metal fencing. "Was tonight at least better than midterms? I mean, the whole claustrophobic nightmare thing aside."

I give a dry laugh. "I guess."

Now their face gets serious, and I tense up. I want to break away and run before they can speak, because all of a sudden, I'm afraid of what's going to come out of their mouth. Maybe I am a little psychic after all.

"Viveca," Wren says, then stops, weaving their slender fingers through the fence wires. I don't say anything, just stand there holding my breath. They close their eyes, then open them. "Viveca, I promised myself I'd have this conversation. So here goes. You've got to stop this . . . whatever this is. With Jamison."

Okay, wait. *Wait*. Yeah, I made a mistake today—a horrible mistake that I shouldn't have made—but can Wren really not see what Jamison is? The mind games he's playing with me?

"What's that supposed to mean?" I snap.

Their face softens. "Viveca, I love you more than coconut custard; you know that. Almost as much as mocha truffles. I mean, it's *this* close." They hold up a thumb and forefinger an inch apart.

I give a cheerless laugh. Deflection is Wren's default, but sometimes it can be awfully close to gaslighting. I mean, *they're* the one throwing out insulting insinuations here.

"Look," they say, "and I mean this in the gentlest, kindest, kiss-your-beautiful-foreheadiest possible way . . ." They inhale. "You need to stop obsessing over Jamison. I know being valedictorian is important to you, but you're taking it too far. You need to stop it with these *theories*, these *ideas*. It's getting scary, frankly."

My heart balls like a fist in my chest. "But what if they're true?"

Now Wren purses their lips, looking at me for a long moment as though they're keeping something inside. "Do you hear yourself, Viveca? You sound . . ."

"Crazy?" I spit, giving way to something ugly that I want fiercely to protect.

"I didn't say that." Wren's voice is hard now.

I turn away, facing the dark hill. "Look, I was wrong about Jamison's dog. I feel terrible about it, okay? But are you seriously taking his side?"

"His *side*?" The voice behind me is one I've never heard before. It's Wren, but with their lightness stripped away. It's a dark, thin core of anger and angst.

I spin around. "Wren, I—"

"I can't do this with you," they say. "It's not fun anymore. This is destroying you, and that hurts *me*, all right? I've got my own future to worry about, and my own father to contend with, and I just don't have room in my life for your perceived, pointless war with Jamison Sharpe."

Perceived. They don't believe me. Wren, of all people, doesn't believe me. That's the long and short of it. Even Wren is against me.

They sigh. "The only sides here are Jamison's and mine, Viveca," they say, eyes bright with moonlight or emotion. "You have to choose. Who gets your energy? Please, pick me. Pick me over him."

I breathe in. The air is an icicle down my throat. Then Wren puts their hands on my shoulders, and I exhale my tension. It's Pavlovian. And I see the fear in their face, the exhaustion. God, when did Wren start looking so tired? I haven't even asked them about their father in—weeks? I don't even know if he's home. I don't know how Poppy's doing. I've been so wrapped up in *me*, I've pushed them away entirely. I've been a terrible friend. The cosmos spins itself into a moment of clarity, and I realize that, despite everything, Wren is just as uncertain about this world as I am.

This, right now, is the closest I've ever come to losing them. And I never, ever want to come any closer.

"Of course I pick you," I say, shaking. "Of course. I'm sorry. I'm sorry."

Wren takes a breath. "Promise me."

"I promise."

"*Promise me* you will let Jamison go," they say. "I can't watch you keep doing this to yourself. If you let this vendetta take you over again . . . I'm out." A tear glints at the corner of their left eye. "I'm gone."

Let Jamison go. How can I, when he dogs my steps? But I have to try, for Wren.

"I promise," I say, hoping desperately, with my whole heart, that I mean it.

24

Midterms are finally over, and the holiday break is almost here. This isn't the only year I've been less than enthusiastic about it, but it is the first time I've dreaded all the family togetherness. The acid I spewed at Dad over my financial aid forms seems to have eaten away some of his veneer. He's not as quick to tell me fake stories about work anymore, which is refreshing, but he's also not as quick to tell me anything else, either. We're both haunting the house and only occasionally manifesting together.

I also have guilt along with the dread, a special bonus feature, because I know Wren is dreading the break way more. They have a big family that deploys various battalions to visit them at different times throughout December, and I know *exhausting* is the most positive adjective Wren could use to describe them. Plus Wren's dad is a bastard. In ways that are a lot worse than mine, if we're having some kind of terrible parent competition. Fa, la, la.

Alone in my room on the last Saturday before break, I start sketching. Let's see what kind of trouble Lola the Gorgeous Minotaur gets into today. I hold my pencil over the paper, make a few lines. But my head is a boundless gray plain, not even rumbling faintly with creativity. My thoughts just keep coming back to Everett College. What good is a college acceptance letter if you can't actually go there? What was the point of all my hard work?

What would Mom say?

Still, I can sense cogs turning underneath the mire, in my subconscious. Then, like a distant cowboy riding in from the horizon, a thought takes shape.

There's still the Pinniped County Futurists essay. If—*if*—I could manage to win, the money could get me to Everett, get me settled, get me through an entire year. I could be saving more as I work. I could reapply for financial aid as a freshly minted, adult eighteen-year-old. It's a long shot, but it's a shot.

I set my sketchbook down and pull out the hard copy of the essay I printed out at school. Sometimes I like to edit with pencil, especially when staring at screens all day has turned my eyeballs to applesauce. On the corkboard behind my desk, two cranky lions cradling a stalk of wheat glare at each other. Right there is the difference between the Pinniped County Futurists' essay contest and everything else I've ever written. The members of this club may like to think about the future, but in reality, this essay *is* my future.

I read over my essay, cutting or adding a word here and there, nabbing a couple of typos. I only get one shot at this. I find myself nodding as I read; the words flow, the vocabulary is spot-on, the structure is good. Then I open my laptop and make the changes.

Still, I realize, there's something whispering at the back of my brain. There's an artificiality to this essay, a thousand excellent words about me that, if I'm being honest, aren't really about me at all. But I'm being ridiculous. Am I shooting for *more* than perfection now? This essay is flawless. I wish I could just hand it to Ms. Racine right now. I wish I could send it off to the Futurists myself. But I have to wait until the January deadline. Sometimes it feels like all I do is wait.

My phone buzzes. It's Wren. "I'm on my way," they bark. "Get dressed."

Oh, right. It's the day of the one-act festival. The Elton Prep drama club is taking *Death at the Disco* on the road, and Wren wants me there for moral support even though I'm the worst possible pick for the job.

"I don't want to."

"We are done talking about this," Wren says, not having it. "Getting dressed is your choice. Getting into my car is not. I'll see you in ten minutes."

So Wren picks me up, and we get on the drama bus at school. People are acting a little more human toward me than I thought they might, so that's good. A few dirty looks, but mostly indifference, the most human of all emotions. Best of all, Jamison Sharpe isn't with us. I remember Jade complaining about how he missed so much rehearsal—could he actually be facing the consequences of his actions?

The festival performances are taking place in a big auditorium at a university in the next county over, and the college atmosphere is giving me a bunch of feelings I'm not sure how to sort out. As the Elton Prep students get set up in a sparse classroom near the bathrooms, I take a field trip to the vending machines in the lobby. Just as I pull my mini donuts from the trough, I'm disappointed to see Jamison arrive. Late, as usual. Nobody will care, as usual. As he parks his SUV, another car pulls up next to him.

I'm not a car person, but I know what it means when a sports car is that low, that red, and that fast-looking when it's standing still. And I know what it means when you see a logo featuring a black horse on a yellow field.

Jamison goes over and opens the driver side door for a tall blond woman in a tight suit as fiery red as the Ferrari.

Mrs. Sharpe, I think. She doesn't look particularly sick. But that's not fair—she might have an invisible illness. Or it might be a good day. Who knows? *Not you, Viveca.*

Jamison's mom gives the building a critical eye, hands on hips, as Jamison pops the hood and pulls out a garment bag. I can't hear what they're saying, but after a minute, Mrs. Sharpe gets back into the car and drives off.

I hurry back to the Elton club's classroom before I get stuck meeting Jamison in the lobby. There are a lot of drama kids here, a lot of costumes, a lot of snacks, and a lot of noise. Wren is helping some people run lines, so I scrunch up in a vacant corner and pull out my sketchbook.

A prickling on the back of my neck makes me raise my eyes to the busy room. And there Jamison is, a dozen feet away, staring. We lock eyes for just a moment; then he turns back to a cheap full-length mirror and proceeds to tie a bow tie.

Creep.

───────

The play goes well. I think. It seems to go well from where I'm sitting. Afterward, Wren, Jade, Tyson, and Min join me in the audience—or maybe Jade, Tyson, and Min just join Wren, who has joined me—and we watch a few of the other entries.

"Do you think we have a shot at winning?" Jade whispers.

Min shakes her head. "Nah. But we did all right."

"I agree," Tyson booms, prompting a couple of people to turn around and shush him.

"Jamison might get the Best Actor prize, though," Min murmurs.

I'm glad it's dark, because I'm rolling my eyes so hard right now. "*Of course* he's up for the Best Actor prize," I hiss to Wren. "He wasn't even the main character!"

They turn their hands over, flashing their palms to the ceiling. "What can you do? He convinced Ms. Racine to nominate him. Anyway, he won't win. He wasn't that good."

At the break, the judges mingle with hopeful theater students in the lobby. Wren seems to know who they all are—a local leading lady who made the leap to off-Broadway, a minor TV game show host, a news anchor from the city. As we twine through the crowd on a quest for the less-busy bathrooms, we pass a couple of judges in deep conversation with a charming Best Actor nominee.

"She really wanted to be here today," Jamison is saying. "She's my biggest fan, my mom. And she's so much more than her diagnosis, you know? She's really the strongest person I know. But when her condition flares up—sorry." He chokes up a little. "When it flares up, that means she just has to build up those amazing strength reserves again."

I pause behind Jamison, my back to him. Wren gives me a look, but I wave them on, pretending to dig a pebble out of my sneaker. I'm resolved to keep my promise to Wren: no more *ideas* about Jamison. I have to be good, and I will. But there's no harm in a little eavesdropping. I'm just curious.

"I'm so sorry your mom can't be here," says a voice I'm assuming belongs to the heavily made-up judge in the stilettos.

"I'm not ruling it out yet," Jamison says. "She was very determined this morning, especially when I told her Ms. Racine had nominated me for Best Actor. She said if she could get her O_2 levels under control, she'd be here with bells on."

So now it's *Mom* who's on oxygen. Are both his parents on oxygen? Is Jamison a registered nurse?

Sounds of sympathy wheeze from Jamison's admirers. *That lying basket of cat turds.* I wonder what the judges would think of him if they knew Mrs. Sharpe was not only *not* dragging her oxygen tank around with her today, but that she was at this moment speeding around the city in a sports car, looking like a million bucks?

I could just spit on the ground. I should step in and say something. But I stop myself, close my eyes, and breathe. *No, Viveca. Let him go.* A chime rings, signaling the end of the break. I still haven't even gotten to the bathroom as everyone heads back to the auditorium for the presentation of awards.

And after that bit of schmoozing in the lobby, Jamison Sharpe, who wasn't even that good, has an edge in the Best Actor category.

———

"You missed a bunch of stuff," Wren says as I clamber back into my seat. "We did not win Best Set Construction."

"Sorry."

"Well, we weren't nominated, so it wasn't too much of a letdown."

Most of the Elton Prep students are sitting in our area now. Their enthusiasm keeps sparkling as the awards part of the festival drags on. Lights, props, costumes, stage managing, directing. Plus all the acting awards.

I just *know* Jamison is going to win Best Actor. And I shouldn't even care! I'm not a drama student! But seeing his manipulation tactics at work—using his mother's *illness* to get the judges to feel sorry for him!—is so gross I might barf all over the seats if he wins. I should go out into the hallway.

A man in a suit that seems too formal for the occasion steps to the lectern set up on the stage. The audience murmurs; I'm not sure if it's because the man is some kind of celebrity, or because we're getting into the final awards.

He looks at an index card and leans in to the microphone. "Nominees for Best Actor." After each name, a different section of the house sends up wild cheers. Is it my imagination, or does Jamison's name seem to get hoots from all over the auditorium, not just from Elton? Figures.

"And the winner is . . ." the man says, opening an envelope. "Elton Preparatory—Jamison Sharpe!"

Figures.

The audience loses it. Has Jamison made friends with every theater kid in the state during one festival?

I *hate* his stupid *face.*

———

The end of the festival is a flurry of packing up, giddy shouts, tears, and melodramatic hugs. I lose Wren in the hubbub but saunter in to the Elton Prep classroom to help cart stuff out to the bus. It's swirling with activity, voices jutting and weaving in the air. I look around for—

Wren. In the far corner. Hugging Jamison.

My arms go rigid. *These are theater kids. They hug.* I try to convince myself. I shout it inside my head. But I know Wren, and I know Wren's hugs. This is a full-on, face-snuggled-against-neck bear hug. I watch in horror. Jamison's hands are running up and down their back, squeezing. It's borderline *romantic.*

Okay, *what* is going on? And how long has it been going on?

I locate my muscles again and turn away. I zip out of that classroom like it's on fire, coming to a stop in the lobby, where all I can do is lean against the wall.

Is this the real reason Wren asked me to leave Jamison alone? Not because they were worried about me, but because they're interested in him?

But the delegation from Elton Prep comes spilling out after me, still chittering. I can't get away from them. A whole group of them stops in the center of the lobby, and I realize it's Jamison himself, lapping up his accolades.

"Thank you so much," he's saying. "You are all the best." And I get squishy. The room prickles. It's the one-act festival, but in my head it's also graduation. Jamison is up there collecting his awards, absorbing his cheers, while I'm here in the dark with nothing. In the end, nobody believes me about his lies. The teachers don't care. The students don't care. Even Wren only pretended to listen to my evidence. What will it take to make people see?

Then, as Jamison blathers on to his rapt fan club, I glance out the window—and my irate gaze falls on a pair of shoulders just outside the door to the lobby. A crisp red suit. Perfect blond hair. And not a single oxygen tank in tow.

She's here.

Now I focus on Jamison. I'm tuned in. What is he saying? "Yeah, Mom missed the performance . . . I know, it sucks."

I take a couple steps toward the Elton contingent. Jamison is actually talking about his poor, sick mom as she's waiting outside the door. It's astonishing.

"Sorry your mom couldn't make it, Jamison," I say. His head pops up. A few people turn to me with suspicious expressions. Wren, still at Jamison's side, gives me a weird look. "What's wrong with her again?" I ask.

Jamison seems a bit taken aback, and so does everyone else, but there's no way he can slither his way out of this. "She's very sick," he says, sort of to me, but mostly to the others. "Over the last few years, she went from running marathons to barely being able to do the grocery shopping. But you know what? I think she's getting stronger, not weaker. I think her strength is flourishing." He pauses for the coos of sympathy. Then, "All I want is to make my mom proud. I want to thank her for always believing in me, you know?"

"Why don't you do it now?" I yell. I sort of don't mean to yell it. I also sort of thought there was going to be another round of sympathetic noises happening right now that would have covered up a tiny yell from several feet away, but there's apparently more of a respectful silence going on instead. Oops.

Jamison looks across the lobby. "Hey, Viveca. I'm so glad you came to support us."

Now everyone in the lobby is looking at me. That's Jamison's thing, isn't it? Just like at the party. All eyes were on *me*. Like he wanted everybody to know who to be mad at. He wanted there to be no mistake.

But I haven't been caught with his phone in my pocket this time. I've caught *him*.

"What were you saying?" Jamison calls out.

I should just leave. Wren's looking absolute knives at me. And maybe they'd have a right to, if they hadn't been hiding their true feelings for Jamison from me like a weasel. But I just keep thinking about those red tailored shoulders just outside the door. This is my chance to show Wren that I was right. I clear my throat. "I said, 'Why don't you thank your mom now?'"

"Viveca, what are you doing?" Wren mutters.

I step forward. "I mean, your mom is *here*, isn't she?"

Jamison looks confused. "Uh," he stammers.

"And oh my god, she's made a miraculous recovery!" I spread my arms wide. The drama club is staring. They don't know what to make of all this yet.

"Viveca!" Jamison snaps. He's losing his cool.

I put a hand on the door handle. "Congratulations, Jamison. In a matter of hours, your mom went from an oxygen tank and a walker to perfect posture and high heels. All thanks to the magic of Jamison Sharpe's acting skills!"

I pull open the door, keeping my eyes fixed on Jamison's face.

"Viveca!" Jamison turns beet red. Everyone turns their attention to him. I stand, waiting, holding the door. Jamison composes himself, then speaks calmly. "That's not my mom."

"I— What?" I freeze. My heart stops like it's been plunged into a bucket of ice. I spin around. The woman in the red suit on the front steps has turned around and is scowling at me. She's definitely not the woman I saw driving the Ferrari this morning. She's not even wearing a red suit, just a red jacket.

You see what you want to, Viveca.

"Excuse me," she says, and strides away down the steps and into the parking lot.

"I . . ." I start.

Jamison is back to his cucumber-cool self. "I actually would like to thank my mom in person. She missed the performance but texted me that she just arrived a few minutes ago. Come on, everybody, I'd love for you to meet her."

And as I stare in disbelief, Jamison ushers the Elton Prep drama students out the lobby doors and down the steps to where his SUV is parked. Next to it stands a frail woman I've never seen before, bent over a walker. She seems older than the woman in the Ferrari, but it's hard to tell her age; after all, sickness ages people. As the bois- terous group approaches, the woman makes her way slowly toward them. Pulling a little oxygen tank on wheels behind her.

But Jamison isn't focused on her. He's focused on *me*. And he's angry. He's angry at me again, because I've been forcing myself into his life again. Because he caught me looking at his private files, because I drew a mean picture of him that everyone saw, because I'm nosy about his piano skills, because I accused him of making up his dog's death, because I just embarrassed him and insulted his mother in front of the entire drama club.

And for the first time, I realize he has a right to be.

25

"What's the matter, princess?"

Dad is in my room. I'm not sure this has ever happened before. It's not quite shocking enough to draw me out from under the covers, but it's definitely noteworthy. He must have heard me crying last night. Or this morning. Or, you know, constantly since I got home from the drama festival. It's embarrassing, but there's not much I can do about it.

He sits on the bed. "It's Sunday afternoon."

I don't answer, but I give him a courtesy groan so he knows I'm alive.

"Are you sick?" he asks.

"No."

He pats the comforter where my shoulder is. "Did something happen?"

I wouldn't even know how to answer that, if I were to answer that, which I'm not. I'm staying under this comforter until I turn into a smooth, warm worm. There's nothing for me outside of this bed.

Dad sighs. "I think you should eat something." I hear the crinkle of thin plastic.

Oreos. My weakness.

I uncover one eyeball. "Are those Double Stuf?"

He smirks and hides the package behind his back. "You won't know unless you come out."

"I'm not coming out."

He gets up. "I'll leave them here, then. You have some when you're ready."

And suddenly, I don't want him to leave. I don't know why. I stick my head out from the covers and blink in the sunlight. "Wait," I say. It's quiet, but he hears.

"You don't have to tell me." He sits back down on the bed and holds out the package of cookies.

I take one. Maybe I should tell him about the drama festival. But it's too much. Instead, I say, "Everyone's mad at me."

"Oh." He takes a cookie, too, and twists off the top. "You know, once I— Well, never mind. Why's everyone mad at you?"

I emerge a little bit more. "Because I broke a promise."

"Uh-huh," he says. Then, in an astonishing display of knowing more about me than I thought, he asks, "A promise to Wren?"

I study the black top of my Oreo. "Yeah. How did you know that?"

He shrugs. "Wren's your BFF."

"Oh god, don't say *BFF*."

He laughs. "Well, whatever. I know all about broken promises." He says it in the way he does when he's bragging about something imaginary, but it's not a brag. It feels like an admission of something real, propped up by the habit of bravado.

Huh, he's acting halfway like a regular dad. My crying jags must have really freaked him out. Or maybe we're both ready to move on from the tundra we've been living in since my financial aid outburst.

"Yeah." I don't know what else to say, so I take another cookie. They'd be better with milk, but I haven't eaten in twenty-four hours, so they still taste amazing.

Dad leans back, looking around my room as though he's never seen any of these objects before. "Do you think you should apologize?"

Apologize. I never apologized to Jackie Boynton, not really. That day in the principal's office, I read my prepared paragraph aloud in a monotone, but it wasn't out of empathy. It was pure guilt and shame and a desperation for all of it to be over with.

"What's wrong with me?" I ask my dad. "Do I have, like, no empathy? No brains? Am I delusional?"

Dad pats the comforter. "You're not delusional, Viveca. You made a mistake. We all do. We get caught up and out of control."

It's weird sitting here telling the truth to my dad and having him tell it back to me. I think about Jamison, taking care of his sick parents, burying his sweet dog. Why *wouldn't* he fixate on his accomplishments, the positive things in his life—even if they're embellished? How different are we, really? Didn't I lie to the Everett admissions department?

And maybe it's the same with Dad.

"How's Genevieve?" I ask. I'm not sure why. Maybe it's because we're on a roll with all this authenticity.

He looks at me, and his face is so sad and haggard. It makes me heartbroken and happy at the same time, getting a glimpse of the real him but seeing him so miserable. "I don't know. Why?"

It's an opening. So I take it. "I like her," I say.

He gives me a weak but genuine smile. "Really?"

"Yeah. And I think . . . we—owe her the truth." I'm not even sure what I really mean by that. It's a feeling too big for the words I'm using to carry it, but they're all I have right now.

He nods. "Okay, princess. I'll try."

I sit up. The air on my arms feels harsh after my weekend of soft darkness, but it's invigorating. *I'll try*, he said. If my dad can come within ten feet of apologizing, of owning up to his mistakes, I think I can do the same. Even if it's the last thing I want to do. Even if it's Jamison Sharpe.

"Dad," I ask, "how do I see the world?"

"You, Viveca?" He gets this bemused expression. "You make sense of this world, Viveca, in your own way. And you make this world make sense for me."

"Thanks, Dad," I say.

I'd know one of my dad's lies anywhere. And right now, I believe him.

26

Flap . . . flap . . . flap. The Elton sidewalk is smooth under my sneakers. I could run it if I wanted to, no rogue chunks of asphalt waiting to twist my ankles. I could fly.

But I don't. I plod. The slower those bright, uniform slabs of concrete scroll past my feet, the better. Maybe all of us—Wren and Mr. Howard and Danny Park and the Everett dean of admissions and Jamison and me—maybe we'll all age and shrivel and desiccate into crumbles before I ever reach 162 Apple Tree Lane. Jamison's house.

No such luck. The sidewalk is gently interrupted by clean, sloping pavement that curves away to the right, where the entrance to a sunny cul-de-sac is framed by old snow apple trees. The trees' elegant forms are echoed in the wrought-iron gate that stands open and welcoming.

Bitter, that's the word Wren used, but I think they meant *jealous.*

At least, I hope so. *Bitter* implies finality, that the thing is over and done with and there's nothing to do but look back and smolder. Jealousy leaves room for change.

My stomach twists. I don't want to be jealous of Jamison Sharpe. It's brought me nothing but anxiety and isolation and a slithery boil in my blood and . . . and delusion.

It's lost me my only friend.

School today might as well have been another in-school suspension for the amount of human contact I had. I was a ghost, a malevolent presence to be warded off by dirty looks and scoffs. I haven't felt more alone and more visible at the same time since the weeks after Jackie moved away. Wren isn't speaking to me. *Nobody* is speaking to me. Not even Ms. Racine. And you know what? They shouldn't. I've been a *monster* to Jamison. If I were them, I'd never speak to me again.

Number 162 is buffered from the sleepy road by a hedge I can just about see over. The house is three stories, with wide garage doors and crisp white bay windows that jut out over the slumbering flower beds. No visible tar paper. Classy.

As my sneakers slide onward, dingy against the power-washed cream of the poured driveway, I inhale. I'm not used to apologizing. Certain conditions have to be met in order for apologies to happen; for one thing, someone has to care enough about something you've done, about you, to get angry about it, and then *you* have to care enough about that person to want to make it right again.

Only that's not quite right, is it? You also have to care enough about yourself. Maybe you only have to care enough about yourself. As I approach the door to Jamison's house, stretching my shoulders back and adjusting the hem of my thermal undershirt, I want to make myself right with the universe. It's a strangely terrifying feeling. Exposure. Like tearing off your clothes, or your skin. I don't want this pent-up thickness of breath, this miasma, between Jamison and me anymore. Whatever happens. Even if it doesn't change how people see me at school, even if it's too late to convince my teachers I'm not a psychopath. *I was wrong.* Just thinking it is a weight lifting.

I knock. Immediately, barking starts up inside the house. The sound is gruff and roly-poly; I picture the dog the same way. Like Ruckus, who's probably wondering where his dinner is right now. My heart gives a little shudder as I think of the flop-eared retriever Jamison must still be mourning.

I didn't know he had another dog at home. I don't know much about Jamison, really, not about his actual home life.

The friendly barking continues, but no other sound comes from the house. I knock again and risk a peek through the etched glass that frames the door. There's the barker, butt wiggling, nails scratching the shiny wood floor as he scoots this way and that. *Like an electric eel*, Jamison said. I almost laugh. Only I remember he said it about Checkers, the dog who was hit the day of the calc midterm. At the time, I didn't know that was why Jamison missed school; it didn't seem to matter. All I cared about was that stupid *Race to the Top!* list. *I was such a jerk.*

I watch the barking dog, sick in my guts as I imagine trying to take a midterm after dragging my suffering dog from the road, sitting with him at the emergency vet's, only for everything to fall apart, to have been for nothing. My smile dissolves. Then—

Through the glass—and, okay, there are designs etched into the glass, and it's kind of multifaceted in places—this dog looks . . . a lot like Checkers. I mean, in that one picture of Jamison's I saw, the one everybody saw. The lolling tongue, the flop ear.

The one white paw.

I don't . . . I . . .

I squint through the narrow window. The dog has a collar with a tag. I press my fingers to the window frame and peer, squeezing my eyeballs just about out of my skull. The little tag glints in the sunlight, impossible to make out through the decorative glass even if the dog weren't bouncing around. But then a paw appears against the window and the dog jumps up, his nose inches from mine, his pink tongue ready for a sloppy greeting if I would hurry up and open the door already. The collar is blurry through the translucence, but it's so close, I can see the burgundy leather is adorned with wide gold letters. The collar isn't hanging straight, so the word is twisted around the side of the dog's neck and partially peeking out from fluffy fur, but I can make out the beginning: *C-H-E-*

My breath catches. ". . . Checkers?"

The barking and wiggling continue. There's no sign the dog on the other side of the door recognizes the name, although chances are slim he even heard me.

I straighten up and turn away. *No.* I shake my head; I physically shake it. This is what got me into trouble in the first place.

I don't know what to do other than escape, like if I get out of here fast enough, I was never here in the first place. I run back down Jamison Sharpe's driveway and scoot around the hedge onto Apple Tree Lane. *Sometimes it's just a coincidence, Viveca. Sometimes it's really, actually, not what you think.*

The dog in that house can't be Checkers. Checkers is dead. Everyone at school knows Checkers is dead. The teachers know it. If they're wrong, if that's Checkers in that house right now, barking and wiggling . . .

When I reach the wrought-iron gate, I stop. I let my shoulders fall against an apple tree. I blink, like in a movie when a shlocky actor is going for "confused" and they blink way too much, but it's true, I'm actually blinking like crazy; I can't stop.

That was Checkers. I don't want to think it, but my brain says the words so loudly they vibrate my vocal cords and shoot out my mouth. "That was Checkers."

What the *hell*? I mean, who would do that? Who would *lie* about something like that?

Just to get out of a math test?

27

I run all the way back to school, cream-colored pavement and dingy concrete sidewalks and sand-sprinkled tar by the marina.

My lungs heave and my teeth grind as I race. I knew it. Everyone thinks I'm crazy, while Jamison cost me my top spot, Everett, even Wren.

A handful of people are still hanging around the student parking lot, laughing and making videos. I barely slow down as I push through the door by the main office and stride down the first-floor hallway. Mr. Howard's door is closed, but in response to my knock, a voice calls, "Come in."

He's at his desk, hunched over in a classic paper-grading position, but as I approach, I see he's actually cutting snowflakes out of construction paper. "Viveca," he says in that way teachers do that means I'm being too much but they're not quite willing to say it. Yeah, I'm here a lot. Put my head on a spike, okay? Besides,

Mr. Howard is half a year away from never seeing me again.

"Mr. Howard, I have to talk to you."

"I assumed that was why you were here." He folds his hands.

"It's about Jamison Sharpe," I say carefully.

Mr. Howard is quiet for a moment. I'm not sure if I should continue. Then he says, "No, it's not."

"What?"

He goes back to cutting his shapes. "It's *not* about Jamison Sharpe, because I do not talk about students' grades with other students."

I whip a chair over to his desk with a clang and sit heavily. "You don't have to tell me anything about his grades. I need to tell *you* something." I close my eyes, quickly envision how this will go. Probably not well. But I inhale, anyway. "Checkers isn't dead."

The scissors stop. Mr. Howard looks up. "Pardon my language, Viveca, but who the heck is Checkers? And what does this have to do with math?"

I shake out my arms. "Sorry. Back up. Checkers is Jamison's dog."

". . . Okay."

I wait, but he's not getting it. "The midterm?" I say. "Jamison missed the midterm because his dog got hit by a car and died. Then you let him make it up under—let's just say much looser scrutiny."

He eyes me suspiciously. "You're saying Jamison Sharpe lied about his dog dying in order to get out of the midterm? Why would he do that? And how would you know?"

I lean forward, elbows on his desk. "I know because I saw Checkers."

"Checkers." He crosses his arms. "The dead dog."

"Yes. I saw him at Jamison's house just now. Through the window."

Mr. Howard frowns. "So you were looking through Jamison's windows. And how do you know the dog you saw was the one that supposedly got hit by a car?"

"I recognized him from his picture," I say. "And I saw part of his collar. It definitely said *C-H-E*. Listen, Jamison is *obsessed* with being valedictorian. So he *has* to get a better grade than me in this class. He always has to be number one. It's a sickness. He'll do anything. Lie about anything. I *see* the *lies* in him."

Now Mr. Howard's expression changes, softens. And it's a punch to the gut, because I recognize it: It's the pitying-bordering-on-horrified face people make with my dad, when they have that moment of realization that he's out of his mind. No. *No.*

"Viveca," Mr. Howard says. "I think you should worry about your own work and let other people worry about theirs. Okay?"

I stand up, energy coursing. I could just explode, a balloon filled with fire. "You don't have to believe me," I spit. "Just know that in real life—out there, on his own—Jamison *sucks* at math. I've seen it. I tutored him! When he pulled ahead of me in this class, and when he passed me in the top ten, that's why. It's because he lied about the midterm. He lies and he cheats and he steals the answers from the teacher's editions. That's how he gets ahead. And honestly, he probably didn't even go to some fancy Paris school last year, because that letter was *faked* and I know it." I lean forward, sparking. "I know everyone hates me already. And for a second there, I thought they were right to. And maybe they still are. But it's different now. I don't care if you think I'm crazy, if everyone does. Because now, finally, I have proof that Jamison has been lying to this whole school the entire time, and that proof is at 162 Apple Tree Lane wiggling its butt *right now*."

This is supposed to be my big, angry moment, but when Mr. Howard sighs, it gives me pause.

"Listen," he says. "I'm going to break my own rule." He leans back. "Jamison Sharpe *is* doing better than you in this class. And it's not because of the midterm."

"I . . . What?"

He slides his desk drawer open and pulls out a folder. "Extra credit assignments," he says, tapping the folder. "Jamison is a good kid, and he's worked his rear end off in this class. You're right, Viveca. He does struggle with the material." He shakes his head. "Do you think I couldn't see that? I've been teaching for thirty years."

I'm stunned. I don't even know what to say. Extra credit? *That's* his secret? "But . . . but . . ." I stammer, "how did he do that? Get all that extra credit?"

Mr. Howard shrugs. "He asked."

I leave, reeling. The hallway is deserted. It's late; most of the teachers have gone home already, but the custodians are still cleaning. I pass Mr. Valdez's biology classroom and spontaneously decide to try the handle. It's unlocked.

The room smells like rubber and rotting leaves. Islands set with steel sinks fill the space instead of desks, except for the teacher's desk at the back of the room, which is overflowing with stray papers, clipboards, and half-full packages of latex gloves. Leaving the lights off, I pad to the desk and try one of the big file drawers. It takes me a minute, but among the manila folders, I find one labeled *Sharpe*. Inside are a couple of essays with *extra credit* written across the top in red ink, as well as the printout of an email addressed to Mr. Valdez. I can't help a quick scan—apparently Mr. Valdez had the nerve to give Jamison a B-plus on a lab assignment, and Jamison responded with questions, vows to try harder, bold compliments . . . and a seemingly offhand reference to Jamison's father's friendship with the president of Elton Prep's board of trustees. Talk about manipulative.

I can hear a janitor moving around in the next room, so I carefully replace the file and leave the biology classroom. But, morbidly curious, I make my way around the shadowy campus, slipping into the not-yet-locked rooms. I go through Jamison's schedule in my head. In each of his classrooms, I wriggle open the teacher's desk drawers and root around. In three of them, I find a similar file: Jamison Sharpe, extra credit, along with more notes and emails from Jamison dissecting everything from quizzes to hall passes, exquisitely tailored to elicit sympathy, admiration, or uneasiness, depending on the teacher.

Jamison hasn't been stealing test answers. He doesn't have to. He makes sure the world bends to his reality. If he doesn't feel like taking a test, if he wants to be valedictorian, if he wants to be Mr. Popular, he just points a finger at the universe, which shrugs and says, "Okay."

I leave through the front doors just as debate club is getting out. Debate club—I'd forgotten. That's why Jamison wasn't home this afternoon. And then there he is, the man himself, standing at the bottom of the stairs. I keep my expression neutral and try to get past without him noticing, but he steps into my path.

"We've got to stop meeting like this, Viveca," he says. "People will talk."

"What do you want, Jamison?"

He tilts his head, smiling. "I want to apologize. That whole thing with the drama festival got out of control. You clearly made an honest mistake. I think we both spoke without thinking."

I cross my arms. "I saw Checkers."

For a fraction of a second, his confident expression ripples. "What?"

"Your dog. The one who died. He's been resurrected. I saw him through the window of your front door."

Now the smile goes away. "Don't joke about that," he says, low and menacing. "And don't go near my house."

I lean in. "Don't pee on my shoes and tell me it's raining."

Now he smiles again, reptilian, keeping eye contact. I shoot that intensity right back at him. We stand there, testing wills.

Until I hear a tiny sound—crackling? No . . . *trickling*. I yelp and jump back, horrified.

Then I look down: Jamison has tipped his bottle, letting a little stream of water cascade down onto my feet.

He laughs, turns the bottle upright again. "What? It's just water, Viveca. What did you think it was? Did you let your imagination run away with you again?"

Heads turn toward us, questioning. Jamison laughs. And after a moment, so does everybody else.

28

It's Tuesday, before school. The lunchroom is mostly empty. Wren wasn't here yesterday morning, but as I shuffle into the room, I see the familiar shape of their sleek, dark hair and sharp shoulders facing away from me at one of the tables. The sight makes my heartbeat quicken. I try to convince myself it's because I'm nervous that I don't know where Wren and I stand right now, but the opposite is actually true. I know exactly where we stand. I made a promise to them, and I broke it, hard. I smashed it to pieces in front of everybody they care about at this school.

But everything has changed now. Yes, I was wrong about Jamison's mom, but I'm not totally delusional after all. Checkers is alive, and Jamison can't hide anymore. Maybe he can hide from everyone else, but he can't hide from *me*. Wren has to understand that.

They're reading a comic book and don't look up as I slide into the seat opposite them. I keep quiet for a moment, not sure what to say.

Finally, I croak out, "Hey."

Wren glances up, then goes back to their comic. "Hey, Viveca." Their voice is cold. Of course it's cold. I don't know what I expected.

I tap the table lightly like I'm playing a song in piano class. "Look, I'm—I'm sorry about what I said. At the drama festival, in front of everybody. It was . . . unkind. And stupid. And not even true."

"Yep." They flip a page and don't look up.

"I'm sorry I let you down." I drop my hands to my lap and weave my fingers together. "I just—I think it's important that I tell you, that I *warn* you, since . . ." *Since you and Jamison might be a lot closer than I thought, which turns my stomach.* I clear my throat, wondering how to go on. "It's possible for a person to have been mean to someone else, to have been wrong about them in a certain way, but for that someone else to *still* be a bad person, you know?"

They're still looking at their comic book. "No, Viveca, I don't. Are we done?"

I want so desperately to tell Wren that I've finally found proof of Jamison's lies, but I can't bring myself to do it, not yet. It's like his name is a magic spell that will sever this tenuous thread of connection, and I don't want to let Wren go.

"I've been having a hard time, I guess," I say, changing the subject for now. "I never told you, but I might not be going to Everett after all." They're silent, but I go on spilling my guts, anyway. "My dad fudged the financial aid application. He wanted Genevieve to be impressed or something. I don't know. So the school's not giving me any aid or scholarships or anything." I give a sardonic little laugh. "At this point, I don't even know how I could physically get to campus."

Now Wren looks up, and for a moment, I'm swelling with hope. But they just shrug and say, "So what?"

I feel my mouth open in surprise. "I— So what?"

They shrug again. "Why do you *care* about Everett, Viveca?"

"I . . ." I trail off. *Where it begins.* "There's so much possibility in college, you know? Life after Elton Prep. I . . . want to start over. Away from all this."

Their face is blank. "Do you care about psychology?"

I frown. "Psychology?"

They shake their head. "Your *major.*"

"Oh." I swallow. "It's my best class," I say. "I had over a one hundred average. And I took the college prep version, so I know it wasn't just a softball."

Wren's expression doesn't change. Neither does their flat voice. "Great. But you are not *interested* in it."

"I—guess. I'm not sure what you mean." I shift my weight on the seat, as though I can physically shift this conversation.

They turn their attention back to their comic book. "Exactly."

I look at my hands for a moment. Then I say, "There's this scholarship. The Pinniped County Futurists. Ms. Racine told me about it. It's a lot of money—enough to get me to Everett, to get me started."

Wren flips a page. "Good. Do that."

"I did. It's a perfect essay. But that's the thing." I lean forward. "I had to write about myself. And I don't think I really did that. It's like I have nothing to say."

I watch Wren as their eyes move over the brightly colored pages. *Who am I?* I think. I try. But when I look into myself, I don't see anything. There's a box there, where my heart is, that I can't open. What's inside? Muppets? Dogs?

. . . Nothing?

First bell rings, and Wren snaps their comic book closed and slips it into their bag.

I stand as they do. "Hey, do you want to—"

They hold up a hand. "No, Viveca, I don't."

I inhale sharply. "I—"

They fix me with a humorless gaze. "I told you what would happen if you chose your sick obsession with Jamison Sharpe over me." Their voice is ice. "And I'm done."

They start to leave, but I hurry after them. "But I didn't tell you— Checkers is alive! Jamison's dog that supposedly—"

Wren stops abruptly in the doorway to the cafeteria. People stream by us in the hallway. "And you're *still talking about him.*"

I gape. Don't they see? This is *real.* And the venom sprays. "Well, at least I'm not *hugging* him!"

As soon as I say it, I regret it. It was stupid. Wren's face hardens into granite.

"Viveca," they say flatly, "we're halfway through senior year, and there's a lot I still want to do with my friends and my art and my education. And all you want to do is run down the clock so you can finally be rid of it all. Of me. So fine. Do that. And leave me alone."

So you can finally be rid of me. Oh god. Is that what Wren thinks? I recoil. Why wouldn't they think that? Here I am, fixated on escaping West Bore and starting over—how could I not see that Wren thought I meant, well . . . without them? How do I make them understand that in all my hopes and envisionings of the future, I never *once* imagined a life without Wren? That I never could?

I touch their arm. "That's not—I don't even know anything anymore, Wren. I'm sorry. I don't even know how I see the world."

They pause. "How you see the world?" For a long moment, they look at me. Then they say, "I'm not sure you do."

29

Do you care about psychology?

As Ruckus and I run the Scruton Back loop, icy branches flashing by us, Wren's words keep coming back to me. Part of it is the fact
that I'm hanging on to that final conversation like a precious keep-
sake. But part of it is that I've realized what they know, what Ms.
Gagnon, the dean of admissions, knows—that beneath the bril-
liance of that Everett-shaped light in my future is nothing but
emptiness. *Where it begins.* Whatever Mom meant by *it* was hers and
hers alone. I can't borrow, or even decipher, her meaning. I have to
find my own.

It's the last Sunday of holiday break, and Dad has been called in
to work. I leave Ruckus at home and run to the convenience store at
the end of our street for a couple of prepackaged sandwiches so Dad
will have something ready to eat when he gets home. He was at the
store until late last night as well and was looking a bit rough around

the edges this morning. That's the life of a manager, I guess. At the last minute, I toss a mini package of Oreos onto the checkout counter, too.

Back in my room, I pull out my sketchbook. I flip a few blank pages past Lola the Gorgeous Minotaur's last adventure and start a new comic. *The Calculus Times* I write at the top in my best approximation of a 1980s futuristic digital font. I sketch in the first panel. A round-cheeked dragon with thick-rimmed glasses spills from the frame. *Hi!* he says with a toothy smile, waving. *I'm Digit!*

"Digit." I snort-laugh to myself.

"I would like extra credit."

Mr. Howard looks up as I toss a folder onto his desk. "Excuse me?"

"I would like extra credit in AP Calculus this quarter, Mr. Howard," I say. "Here is a project I've completed."

He furrows his brow like I'm speaking Martian. "What time is it?"

I glance at the clock behind him on the wall. "Seven forty-five a.m."

Now he looks at the folder on his desk, which I've helpfully labeled *Viveca North: AP Calculus Extra Credit Work*. "What is this?" He pushes his glasses up his nose with one finger and squints up at me. "Extra credit? Viveca, you've got an A in this class already."

"I don't care," I say. "I would like to do better." *Better.* It feels good to let go of "perfect." Perfect has never made me happy.

He pushes the folder back toward me. "I'll see you in class."

"Might I remind you," I say in my most neutral voice, "that you allowed Jamison Sharpe—currently the *top student in the senior class*—to do extra credit work."

Mr. Howard narrows his eyes at me. "Viveca . . ." But he doesn't finish the thought. Instead he heaves an exasperated sigh and puts a hand on my folder. "This isn't how extra credit works, you know," he says, flipping the folder open and scanning the contents. "Your teacher assigns *you* a project, you don't just . . . Heh . . ." He flips to the next page. After a moment, he mumbles, "Oh, Digit, that's not how you graph a function." He looks up at me, closing the folder. "Yes, well." He clears his throat. "I suppose I can accept *The Calculus Times* for a few extra credit points."

I can't help the grin that spreads across my face. "Thank you, Mr. Howard."

He raises an eyebrow. "But!"

I hold my breath.

"If you want as much extra credit as Jamison got," he says, "I'm going to need a few more issues."

———

If Jamison Sharpe can do it, so can I. *You don't need extra credit*, my teachers say. But when I point out that they allowed valedictorian Jamison to pad out *his* grades, suddenly the arguments disappear. Now I'm kicking up my GPA with book reports, original board games, and dioramas. Lola the Gorgeous Minotaur features heavily in some of my bonus work.

And I have to say—I actually enjoy it. My teachers start treating me a little differently, too. Mr. Howard doesn't even roll his eyes when I pop in at lunch anymore. It's not a substitute for friendship, or financial aid, or a clear path to a sunny future. Or Wren. But it's a lightness I haven't felt in a long time. On good days, I open the file *PinnipedCountyEssay* and imagine freshman year at Everett, maybe undeclared—it's still possible. Everything is possible. I find a school with rolling admissions that's accepting candidates and apply, just to give myself backup. I don't need my perfect college in order to have a future. I give myself options, just in case.

I can pass Jamison Sharpe in the halls now and just think *fraud* and move on with my life. Knowing he's just as shady as I always thought he was is a kind of power, and it turns out that's enough. I can finally let him go.

———

The night before the Pinniped County Futurists deadline, I sit at the kitchen table with my laptop open, listening to the nature documentary my dad's watching in the living room. Ms. Racine needs all the essays tomorrow morning so she can mail the Elton Prep entries on time. No more than a thousand words, pages paper-clipped with a single identifying cover sheet on top for the blind judging.

And that's what I have. Or what I will have after I print everything out tomorrow at school. But as I read over my perfect essay, that little wriggle of doubt I've tried to ignore for so long starts to jump and shimmy.

My essay is missing something. It's wrong, somehow.

Wren would know how to fix it, probably. Too bad they're still not speaking to me. It's not even an *active* "not speaking" at this point; it's like we just don't know each other at all. Like we're strangers.

I keep reading, but I'm thinking about the title. *Finding My Path*. How could I have written anything about finding my path all those weeks ago, when I had no idea where my path was? And I realize I still don't. I wrote a thousand words about having found a path that doesn't exist. I wrote past tense when I should have been writing present. Finding my path isn't a thing I've done. It's a thing I'm *doing* and probably always will be.

I go back into the essay, working on it as a voice in the other room talks about life in the Serengeti. I cut fields of words like tall grass under a scythe. I delete every single buzzword I took from the website. And I start to add *me*. At the same time, I'm thinking about Wren. I'm thinking a lot about Wren lately, and a little about Jade and Min and Tyson. A little about Danny Park. I'm thinking about how I realized all that stupid stuff about apologizing, and then I decided to apologize to the exact wrong person. I should have run to Wren's house that day, not Jamison's.

How do I see the world? I think about Kermit the Frog leaving his swamp with nothing more than a banjo, and Lola the Gorgeous Minotaur fending off hordes of nameless bandits. I think about Wren and my dad and the walls of Fort Kearsarge crumbling to dust in the golden autumn sunlight.

I lean back in my chair. *Your future depends on that essay*, I told myself before. But that's wrong. Nobody's future depends on one essay. Lives are not lived around one essay. My future has depended on so many different things for so long.

I write my Pinniped County Futurists essay again.

It's the best thing I've ever written.

———

"Miss North, I hope you have a Pinniped essay for me this morning," Ms. Racine calls out from her office as I pass by. I poke in, and she's looking up from the ancient photocopier behind her cluttered desk, which is spitting out what looks like copies of a scene from a play. Everywhere, books, scripts, and stacks of student work are interspersed with paper flowers, dirty coffee mugs, and sparkly figurines.

"I just have to print it," I say, gesturing toward the computer lab next door.

"Hop to it, ducky!" She points to the clock. "I'm popping out to the PO during first block."

"Will do!"

There are a few other students in the computer lab printing out work. Kasey Wheelwright and Gabe Ford are hunched over an ornery inkjet that's having some kind of issue. I scan the room for another free printer, but one of them has a fluorescent-orange *Out of Order* sign taped to it, two have multiple students hovering around them already, and Mr. Howard is monopolizing the last one with some kind of enormous project. I should have left more time. I didn't think I needed it. I'm only printing four pages! Too bad they might be the most important four pages this year.

"I've got to print something," I say to Kasey.

"Yeah, well, welcome to the club." She gestures to the sputtering inkjet. "Ol' Reliable is reliably freaking out."

"It needs magenta," Gabe says, rummaging through the cabinet underneath. "Hang on. Here we go."

Kasey beeps in the cartridge change commands, and Ol' Reliable makes some encouraging noises.

I look at the clock. Five minutes to first bell. "I need to get something to Ms. Racine before class."

"Yeah, your Pinniped Futurists essay," Kasey says flatly. "So do we."

"Oh," I say. "Right."

With its new bounty of magenta, Ol' Reliable quiets down, and Kasey sends it her file, then Gabe prints his. At one minute to the bell, the computer lab is as crowded as ever, but I'm finally clicking *print* on *PinnipedCountyEssay*. I slide on a paper clip and rush back to Ms. Racine's office.

"Printer issues, sorry." I place my essay on her desk. Seven hundred words, three pages plus the cover sheet with my identification. It looks like such a little nothing sitting there, but it's my whole heart. "I'm proud of it," I say.

She flashes a leading-lady grin. "I'm sure it's wonderful, Viveca, dear. I was telling Vice Principal Reinhardt, you know, I've looked at past winning entries, and I thought you could have a real shot if you applied yourself. I wish I could read it! But I've got to get these off this minute—you've just squeaked in!" She slides my essay into a large brown mailing envelope already bursting with paper. "So it's you, Kasey, Gabe, Jade, Miranda, and Robin. What a group!"

"Thank you, Ms. Racine," I say. "Thank you for the opportunity." Whatever happens now, at least I gave it a shot. I try not to hope too much, but I can't help hoping a little. Especially since I still see that Everett-shaped glimmer when I close my eyes.

I get all the way to the music room before I realize I left my laptop in the computer lab. Now I won't even be close to being on time. I hurry back for it, and as I pass by Ms. Racine's office, I almost collide with a tall figure striding out.

"Jamison!"

He gives me a cold smile. "Good morning, Viveca."

"Excuse me." I don't have time to wonder what he was doing in there. I sidestep him and keep going.

But I'm surprised to meet Ms. Racine coming the other way. She wasn't even in her office just now. So why was Jamison there? I stop as she passes.

"Oh, thank you, Jamison, dear," she's saying. "I'll take that."

Jamison hands her a large brown mailing envelope. Is it the envelope the Pinniped County Futurists essays are in?

My heart sinks a little. When Ms. Racine listed the students who were entering, I couldn't help but notice she didn't say his name. But now it looks like Jamison submitted an entry to the Pinniped County Futurists' contest after all, even more last-minute than me.

30

It's the day before the end of third quarter, which is when the vale-dictorian will be named, and I've pulled ahead of Jamison Sharpe. There's nothing he can do about it now. Finally earning my place won't fix everything, but it feels as though I'm drawing strands of shimmering galaxy around me in a cat's cradle, weaving a few tiny cracks back together.

This morning was the first time my name officially kicked Jamison's out of the top spot in the *Race for the Top!* list in the cafeteria. It's not about beating him anymore; I want to do my best just for me. But still—I can't *wait* to see his face when he breezes into Intro to Piano.

I set up at a keyboard and page through my lesson book until I get to the right song, "Alaskan Sunset." I practiced the crap out of "Alaskan Sunset" this week. I'm not sure why, but doing all these additional creative assignments almost makes me feel like I have more time, not less.

Ms. Pillay steps to the front of the class, and we quiet down. Then the door creaks open, and in slouches Mr. Second Place, Jamison Sharpe himself. He seems really bummed. A little too bummed maybe? But who cares.

He turns his sad eyes to the teacher. "I'm sorry I'm late, Ms. Pillay. I didn't mean to be disruptive."

"That's all right, Jamison," she says. "Take a seat."

He takes one step and continues. "I guess I'm a little spun up about this dumb thing that happened this morning. It's really no big deal, but sometimes the little stuff can get to you, you know?"

It's all I can do not to roll my eyes. As my classmates ooze equal parts sympathy and curiosity in Jamison's direction, I place my hands on the keys and silently make my way through the music, waiting for the other nonsense to end. When I come out the other side of the tricky part near the end, I notice the class has gone quiet. But when I look to the front of the room expecting Ms. Pillay to be starting the lesson, I see she's studying a creased sheet of paper. The other students pay wide-eyed attention. I glance at Jamison; his eyes are downcast, his shoulders slumped.

Ms. Pillay gives him a somber look. "Jamison, this is very concerning. You shouldn't brush it off. This needs to go to Principal Washington."

"I really don't want to make a big deal out of it," Jamison says. "It's just that it's happened before."

Ms. Pillay seems about to respond, then realizes the rest of the class is staring at her and the creased paper she's holding. She blinks. "Well. I'm sorry, class. This is obviously not something we should talk about right now. Jamison, we can discuss this after class, if you feel safe for the moment."

"Of course," Jamison says bravely. What's going on?

"Is Jamison in trouble?" Kasey stands up. "What's that paper?"

"It's none of your beeswax," Ms. Pillay says. "Here, Jamison." She goes to hand the paper to Jamison, but Kasey intercepts. To be honest, it looks like Jamison *lets* her intercept.

"Kasey!" Ms. Pillay snaps. I've never heard her raise her voice. Okay, now I'm curious about that paper, too. Is it a grumpy note? I remember the stupid message I put in Jamison's locker months ago. Is somebody else sick of his nonsense? Huh. Serves him right.

"It's really no big deal," Jamison says again, but he makes no move to take the paper back from Kasey.

She scans it as everyone watches. "This is a *threat*," she breathes. "How *awful*."

Intro to Piano explodes with questions and indignation.

"What kind of threat?"

"Who sent it?"

"What does it say?"

I lean back in my plastic chair. "Is it a bomb threat?" I don't say it loudly. I mean, I don't *think* I say it loudly, but it seems to bring the room to a halt. I turn my focus back to "Alaskan Sunset."

I can tell Jamison is watching me. "It's probably a joke," he says.

"'Dear Jamison,'" Kasey reads aloud. Ms. Pillay doesn't try to stop her. "'How dare you waltz in here like you're hot'"—she eyes the teacher—"*stuff* and think you can do whatever you want? You don't deserve to be valedictorian. You're a liar and a cheat and I'm going to cut that ravishing face of yours first chance I get. Watch your back.'"

A stunned silence follows.

"It's kind of funny, you know, because I'm not actually valedictorian anymore," Jamison says with a sad laugh.

"Didn't you get another one of these?" Kasey asks, handing the note back to Jamison.

"Yeah," Jamison says. "I guess I should have reported that first one."

"Seems they're escalating, whoever they are," Ms. Pillay says. "The threat of physical violence is particularly disturbing. Any idea who sent it?"

The class is fascinated, like we're in an Agatha Christie novel. Then Jamison looks right at me, the jerk. He doesn't say anything, but it's clear as glass to everyone in that room that he's accusing me. I cross my arms.

"I have no idea," he says. "But I did notice this." He turns the paper over and shows the teacher.

"This is one of our practice sheets," Ms. Pillay says. "I only use this version for this class."

"Really?" Jamison says innocently.

Excuse me, but *what is going on?* I set my jaw.

Kasey speaks up. "Doesn't that mean that whoever sent it is probably in this class?"

Yeah, I realize. *Because it's Jamison himself.* But why would he . . . *oh.* Oh no.

"I have to go to the bathroom," I say.

Ms. Pillay holds up a hand. "Hang on, Viveca." She holds up Jamison's threat letter. "Let's nip this in the bud right now. Elton Prep does not tolerate threats of violence. Everyone, empty your backpacks."

And people do.

And I realize that Jamison knows exactly what's in my backpack. He saw it in my room, and he saw where it lives inside my bag: the supremely banned jackknife I'm never without.

Can Ms. Pillay really make us empty our backpacks? Probably not. Definitely not. It has to be against about a million rules, right? I could just refuse. That wouldn't look suspicious *at all*. Crap.

"I really have to go," I say.

"I'm sure it's fine, Ms. Pillay," Jamison says. "Don't want Viveca having an accident. Besides, why would she have any reason to threaten me?"

Yeah. Record scratch. The logic clicks into everyone's brains. I'm seemingly the only person in this room who *does* have a reason to threaten Jamison. With a cut to the face. Presumably to be done with a knife. Like the one in my backpack.

"Viveca, before you go," Ms. Pillay says, "would you mind emptying your bag out? You can do it behind my desk if you don't want everyone to see."

Jamison's head is tilted, and his bright smile is in full force.

I think he's forgotten that he's supposed to be terrified of his unknown stalker. Right now, he's just consumed by triumph over me.

A knife in my bag doesn't prove anything, I think as I hoist my backpack and slog across the room. Except it proves that I *have a knife*. That's not going to go over well. Is it grounds for expulsion?

. . . Maybe?

Ms. Pillay is casting glances over the piles of books, papers, pens, wires, tissues, snacks, and headphones that litter the music room carpet. But she turns her complete attention to me as I step behind her desk. And so does Jamison.

My stomach is a block of ice. Maybe I can grasp the knife through the fabric of the bag somehow, hold on to it as everything else tumbles out. But Ms. Pillay takes my bag from me and unzips it herself.

Then she turns to Jamison. "You can give us a little privacy, please."

He looks surprised for a second, then annoyed.

"Yeah. I have girl stuff in there," I hiss.

He gives me a glare but turns away. That's one tiny victory for me, I guess. Yay.

Ms. Pillay turns my backpack out onto the floor. There's not a lot of stuff in there; I've developed a pretty efficient system over the years. Now I'm wishing I were a little more of a pack rat. Every item in that bag is going to be on full, obvious display.

I don't look down. I don't know what I'm going to do. My vibrating breaths are starting, the air in the room becoming dense, almost liquid. I close my eyes.

"Okay," Ms. Pillay says.

I open my eyes. "What?"

She gestures to the small pile of Viveca's Life on the floor. "You can go to the bathroom now. Pick your stuff up before you go."

I look down. My sketchbook, a zip pouch of pencils, my rented graphing calculator, a banana, a couple pocket folders . . . and that's it. My eyes must be as big as eggs.

"What?" Jamison says. It might be the first time I've heard him genuinely surprised.

I make eye contact with him. He's boiling. *WHAT?* he mouths in silent incredulity.

I shrug. *I'm just as surprised as you, Jamison.*

31

I don't know why my jackknife wasn't in my bag this morning, and if it's lost forever, I'll be very sad, but—I shiver. My body is still shaking over an hour later, at lunch, as I sit contemplating my banana peel at the empty end of the corner table.

Jamison is escalating. And I realize that it's not enough for me to let go of him if *he* refuses to let go of *me*. I must really have gotten to him. After all, he didn't lie about *everything*. He still has a hard life, even if he's a jerk. But what can I do? Valedictorian is locked in, even if I wanted to give it up—which I don't. Can't. And I'm not going to apologize to him or make a big spectacle in front of the school. I'm done with big spectacles.

My breathing is slightly ragged. Not gaspy like I'm going to keel over, but that exaggerated, audible in-and-out that happens when you're too aware of your own breath, trying to keep it quiet, like a little kid hiding from monsters under the covers. I've got to get out of here.

I stumble out the doors and across the brick walkway of a little outdoor seating area to clear my head.

I sit on the stone curb of the walkway and lower my face into my hands. I just can't wait to be gone from here. Except I'm not going to be gone, am I? I haven't heard back from that other school yet, so unless I win that essay contest, I'm going to be stuck right here, just like Mom was. Just like Dad is.

I'll take a gap year like Wren, I think. Thinking of Wren makes my insides ache. I've taken control of so much these past few weeks, let *myself* emerge for the first time, and it's felt so good. I'm alive and I have potential, and I'm more than my résumé. But at the same time, I've pushed a lot to the back of my brain. I miss Wren. I don't have a plan for next year.

A minibus pulls into the parking lot, and I look up. It's not a school bus. In fact, it's the same pale lavender bus I saw through the window the day of my in-school suspension—Haverwood Senior Center. The driver steps out and moves toward the school entrance, but then he sees me and changes course.

"Hello, miss?" he calls.

I sit up and give him a wave. How dangerous could someone who drives the senior bus be?

He shuffles quickly over to where I'm sitting. "Half day?"

I squint in the sunlight. "Huh?"

He points to the school. "Half day today, right?"

"Oh," I say. "No, that's tomorrow."

"Ah." He nods. "Okay. Thanks."

As he turns to go, I notice the door to the minibus behind him has opened, and someone is very slowly making their way down the two steps to the parking lot.

"Tomorrow!" The bus driver waves his hat at the slothlike descender. "My mistake, Mrs. Reed! He'll take you shopping at noon tomorrow, not today!"

Mrs. Reed. Why does that name ring a bell? Oh, right—the lady Jamison volunteers to run errands with. Isn't he just a peach? I cross my arms and take a look at Mrs. Reed, who doesn't seem convinced by the bus driver's frantic attempts to get her back onto the minibus. She looks familiar to me. Did I see her the day of my ISS? No, that's not it.

I look at her bewildered, slightly suspicious face. She doesn't even look like a senior; there's something ageless about her. And I remember Jamison talking about her to Mrs. Sherwood the day of my ISS—*Mrs. Reed is such a lovely woman. She'd do anything for me.*

Suddenly, I remember when it was that I saw her. And I can picture her as she was that day—smiling, shuffling, and dragging a little oxygen tank behind her.

Jamison's "mother."

So that *was* Mrs. Sharpe driving the Ferrari the morning of the drama festival. Jamison lied about his own mom's grave illness! I can feel my eyes practically bugging out of my head. How deep does this go?

The bell rings for the end of lunch, and I get to my feet, making my way hazily back inside. Students are scurrying to class, talking excitedly. More excitedly than usual, it seems. I hear Jamison's name.

"Oh, great," I say aloud.

One of the sophomores who's working on the superhero story in comics club barrels into me, head down as she's looking at her phone. "Sorry, Viveca! I was just reading about Jamison!"

I put my hands on my hips. "So what has the amazing Jamison Sharpe done now? Perfected nuclear fusion?"

She drops her jaw like I just asked if the sun were hot. "Jamison Sharpe!" she says. "From our school!"

"He sure is," I say. "What did he do, if you absolutely must tell me?"

She squeals. "He just won *twenty thousand dollars!*" She holds up her phone so I can see it.

It's the Pinniped County Futurists' website. They've announced the winner of their essay scholarship competition.

Jamison Sharpe, Elton Preparatory School

"Oh, *perfect*," I say. Then I keep reading. They've listed a few glowing details about Jamison, as well as the title of the winning essay.

"Viveca?" The sophomore grabs my arm. "Viveca, sit down. You're all— *Jeez*, Viveca, sit down! What's the matter?"

The room is swirling. So are my legs, my eyes. I jab an accusing finger at the phone screen. "'Finding My Path' . . . That is *my essay*."

32

I'm called to the principal's office halfway through seventh period. As I make my way down the empty hallway, past closed lockers and bright posters, my brain floods. A dozen, a hundred little things Jamison has done and said come piling back. A hundred unverifiable dishonesties, maybe-exaggerations, questionable stories, but nothing I could prove. Nothing anyone would listen to me about.

Until now. Until the concrete, not-just-in-my-head moment he stole my essay.

How did he even do it? I think back to the morning of the deadline. He must have switched our cover letters. So simple. He might not have even been planning on it, just seized the opportunity. What a slimeball.

I knock on Principal Washington's door.

"Come in."

Her office seems too small for someone with so much power. Sure, it's just high school, but when I step through the doorway, I have this immediate, cold realization that the tidy person wedged behind that heavy oak desk is clutching a larger-than-comfortable handful of my future. And present.

"Viveca, sit down." Sweeping gesture. I turn my head to the empty chair before the desk. It's right next to a non-empty chair— one that's overflowing with Jamison Sharpe.

My eyes widen before I can stop them, like a cartoon character. *Boi-oi-oing!* I grip the armrests and freeze, but just for a second. Then I sit, eyes forward, not a word to him, even though I can tell he's looking at me. It makes sense that he's here, I guess. Just ups the awkward factor by about a million, but there was nothing about this that was ever going to be easy.

There are two essays with cover sheets on Principal Washington's desk. She rests four manicured nails on each and looks from one to the other with a frown.

My fingers are a web of tingles. I don't know how Jamison will react to this. It's not much comfort that I'm the one who will finally take him down after all the damage it's done to me in the process, but at least he'll seem a little less *perfect* to everyone in the world from here on out. At least we can begin to fix this.

Principal Washington gathers the papers into a single neat pile. She weaves her fingers and looks at us. "Well written."

I want to say *thanks*, but it sticks in my throat. Jamison is silent as well.

The principal picks up the papers and taps them together on the surface of the desk so the edges line up. "And certainly very similar. Except for the cover sheets, these are identical."

Wait, what? I lean forward. "You're saying there are two of the *same* essay?"

Principal Washington purses her lips but doesn't answer me. "What should we do about this?" she asks.

My throat is still sticking, but there aren't any words in it right now. Was that a rhetorical question? I look down into my lap.

Jamison adjusts himself next to me. "I'm sorry for this terrible predicament, Principal Washington." His voice is velvet. But he's not the fairy-tale prince; he's the scheming usurper. "I wish things could have been different."

I snort. I can't help it. He's *still* trying to pull this act? Now I risk a glance at him; he has the audacity to be looking at *me* with this soppy concern. Like there's all this soppiness just behind his lips that he's waiting to release, wrapping me with words of comfort and support. I half expect him to reach out and tenderly take my hand.

He's so *good* at this.

"I'm sorry, Viveca," Jamison says. I roll my eyes.

"Jamison, please," Principal Washington says, and I notice she's looking at me the same way. Like I'm some charity case.

"I don't want your apology, Jamison." I find my voice at last. "I just want the scholarship that my essay won." And there's something about saying the words out loud that snaps a switch inside me—*off* to *on*. On with the shaking, on with the rapid breathing. On with the waterworks. *Ugh,* why am I crying in front of Jamison Sharpe?

"Enough of that, Viveca." Principal Washington's hard voice is the opposite of Jamison's. I swallow and wipe away the three tears that managed to escape my hot eyes.

There's a sniffle next to me. I turn my head.

Jamison Sharpe is crying, too. Full on, red-faced, yet not *ugly*, not messy the way my insides feel right now. He's weeping *stoically*, like a superhero or an angel or a pure-hearted king. I could just vomit.

"For god's sake, Jamison," I snap.

"Viveca!" Principal Washington is looking at me with unfiltered contempt.

I'm jolted. "Holy crap, you feel *sorry* for him." I spit the words before I can stop myself. "What about me?" I raise my voice. "Don't you feel sorry for *me*?"

The principal straightens her shoulders. "No, Viveca, to be perfectly honest, I do not."

My eyebrows jump up on their own. "Wha—"

"Please, Principal Washington," Jamison cuts in. "It's not her fault. I know what it's like to have your dreams shattered."

My voice is venom. "Shut up, Jamison."

"Viveca North!" The principal uses my full name like she's my freaking mother. As though she knows anything about me. I don't give her the shocked, obedient reaction she's looking for. It's not etched into my psyche since, obviously, my dead mother has never yelled at me in my life.

Instead, I lean forward, put my hands on the principal's desk, invade her bubble. "I don't care what his line is or how many crocodile tears he squeezes out. What are you going to *do* about this?"

Principal Washington gives me a hard stare. She blinks and looks over to Jamison, then back to me. She steeples her fingers. "What I'm going to do, Viveca, is recommend to Ms. Racine that you receive a zero for this quarter. You will be removed from consideration for valedictorian, or any class ranking, and then I'm going to seriously consider whether or not you should even be allowed to walk at graduation."

My body turns to ice. "I— What?"

Principal Washington tilts her head. "Viveca, what do you want me to do? You *know* this scholarship belongs to Jamison. We do not tolerate plagiarism here. That is a very firm line."

"*What?*" A million jagged bombs are going off in my brain. "You think *I* stole *his* essay? That I would plagiarize *Jamison Sharpe?*"

Principal Washington holds up a piece of paper. "This letter is from the Pinniped County Futurists, who were quite confused at receiving two identical essays. However, they decided not to penalize the school as a whole, especially since the essay in question won the judging. Instead, they awarded the prize to the student who submitted an original printout, not a photocopy."

Now Jamison turns to me with a look of such pity that it approaches heartbreak. "I'm so sorry, Viveca. I really didn't want to turn you in. If the scholarship hadn't been on the line . . ."

My mouth flops open. "You—*prick!*"

"Jamison, you may go back to class," Principal Washington says flatly. "Thank you for your integrity and composure during this ordeal."

And it hits me. *A photocopy.* Not only that, but a photocopy that is *obvious* it's a photocopy—like the ink-smudged ones put out by the ancient photocopier in Ms. Racine's office. And the morning of the deadline comes back to me. When I went back to the computer lab, Jamison was coming out of Ms. Racine's office, but she was coming down the hall. Which means Jamison had been all by himself in that office with a copier and the whole envelope of Pinniped essays, including mine.

"He photocopied my essay!" I say. "He was *alone* in Ms. Racine's office that morning." I do the math in my head. "All he needed was five minutes. It took me that long to walk to the music room and back. He had enough time."

"Viveca, don't be silly," Jamison says. "It was you who was alone in her office."

"Liar!" I point. I turn a pleading gaze to the principal. "Don't you see? Jamison photocopied my essay and switched the cover letters!" Then lightning strikes me. "The file," I say, unsnapping my laptop case. "I have the original file on my computer." I turn to Jamison. "Do *you?*"

He shrugs. "No, I deleted it. I don't hang on to assignments after they're turned in. I dislike clutter."

Now I've got him. "Well, we'll just see about that. You didn't delete it; it never existed on your computer. But it's on mine."

Principal Washington nods. "That would help your case."

I flip the laptop open and navigate to the folder. And—

"It's gone." I gasp, dig through other folders, search files, go through the trash, but . . . nothing. "It's not here."

"I'm sorry, Viveca," Principal Washington says.

"Jamison deleted it," I murmur. And I realize—the reason I had to come back to the computer lab that morning was because I forgot my laptop. And Jamison was there. He couldn't print the essay out—the lab was too crowded, and besides, he needed an obvious photocopy to prove which was the "real" one. But he knew exactly where the file was. It would have taken him ten seconds to erase it from existence.

I underestimated him. I underestimated him so much.

I can't think. I can't even move. I'm a paperweight in Principal Washington's office. I'm a doorstop, a file cabinet. Jamison Sharpe rises and gives my shoulder a tender squeeze before disappearing through the door, leaving only the scent of jasmine.

33

West Bore Coffee & Donuts is open late on Fridays. My choice of places where I can exist without complication right now is extremely limited—the school is closed for the night, Dad's at home, Wren's at the sub shop, who knows *who* is at Fort Kearsarge—so I'm set up at my corner table pretending to work on my laptop. But there are no files open. No websites. I'm not even farming parsnips in Stardew Valley. I'm just staring at the sunset beach on my desktop, one of the default images that came with the computer. It's probably pretty obvious that I was crying on the way over here, but that's the least of my problems right now.

"Top-up, hon?" The employee—*Fran*, her nametag says; I never noticed her name before—looks at me with concern.

"Sure," I rasp out. "Thank you. Thank you, Fran."

The corners of her eyes wrinkle with a smile as she pours. "Don't you mention it, sweetie." She scurries away.

I sip my coffee. It's starting to make my stomach hurt, but the bitter flavor is the closest thing to comfort I've been able to find since dragging myself out of Principal Washington's office.

No file. No proof.

. . . No money.

Jamison covered his tracks well. He thought of everything. I was too busy letting him go and gunning for stupid valedictorian to notice the quiet vendetta *he* was pursuing against *me*. Now I'm paying the price. I've paid the price. And it was everything.

I give a start as someone sits down across from me, setting his own extra-large dark roast onto the table. "Dad?"

"Here you are," he says, sounding strangely fragile.

"Oh. Were you worried about me?" I close my laptop.

He tilts his head, and I can see the relief on his face. "Of course I was." He checks his watch. "It's nine o'clock. I didn't know where you were, and you weren't answering your phone."

I feel the blood drain from my cheeks. "Oh god, I'm so sorry! I had no idea it was this late." I pull my phone from my pocket. It's dead. How long has it been dead? No clue. Then I start crying again, which is stupid because Dad probably thinks I'm actually crying about staying too long at the donut place.

"Hey," he says. "It's okay. I'm just glad you're safe." He clears his throat. "I, uh, got a call from your school."

My stomach plummets. "Oh." So he knows I've been accused of cheating. Lying. Stealing. I remember my angry outburst at Dad over the phone; he must think I'm such a hypocrite. And I don't even have the energy to argue about it.

Dad tosses a bag of donuts onto the table. "Had a bad day, huh? I know what that's like."

"Yeah."

We sit in silence for a moment. There are a couple times Dad looks like he's about to say something, but then he stops. Finally, he says, "I did you wrong, princess. I shouldn't have . . . I should have paid more attention to that form. It was important." He looks down. "It's because of me that you got so desperate, isn't it?"

The words hit me hard. Dad's face is a landscape of sadness right now—and it's because he thinks I'm turning out like him. He wants me to do better. And, somehow, my realizing that makes up, just a little, for all his lies.

"You didn't drive me to anything," I say. "I promise. I didn't even plagiarize. The school got it wrong."

He looks up, and his face lightens a little. He believes me. "Okay, Viveca." He nods. "But what are you going to do?"

"I'm not sure. Maybe nothing."

He frowns. "Well, it might not be a good time to talk about it, I guess." He gestures to the bag of donuts. "Aren't you hungry?"

And I am. I'm suddenly ravenous. "I'm sorry you had to come looking for me." I pull a Boston cream out of the bag. "But I'm impressed you knew where to look."

This makes him smirk. "It's West Bore, and you don't have a car," he says. "How many possibilities are there?"

I honk out a laugh at that. But it's short-lived and sticks in my throat. "It's hard to get out of West Bore," I murmur. I'm not even saying it to him, just letting the words slither out.

He gives a chuckle. "Yep. Well, I've certainly never done it. Flew to Vermont once for a maple syrup festival. That was exciting. But, of course, had to come back."

"Yeah," I say, staring at the bitten place on my donut where the pale cream is starting to goop out. "Mom never did, either."

Dad turns his coffee cup around like he's going to read it. "Mom never what?"

We don't talk about Mom that much. Or, like, ever. But I feel like if I don't say the thing I've been holding in for weeks—no, years— it's going to pop my seams from the inside. "Mom never got out of West Bore."

Dad frowns. "What do you mean, princess?"

I close my eyes. "Everett, Dad. She was supposed to go to Everett. And she got robbed of that chance. She came back here, and . . ." I stop. I don't want to say something hurtful.

He's quiet for a moment, but I can't bring myself to look at him. Then he says, "You have *nothing* to make up for, Viveca."

"That's not what this is about," I say. "That's not why I want to go to Everett." Although now I'm not so sure. Everything feels unstable, cloudy. "I want to have the choices that Mom never did. That . . . you never did."

"Princess." Dad takes a sip of coffee. "Mom made her choices. You go ahead and make your own, okay?"

"She chose to drop out of school? To get sucked back into West Bore forever?"

Dad looks tired, and I suddenly feel bad for poking his sore places. But they're my sore places, too, and I can't keep them inside any longer. Besides, pretending nothing is wrong has never helped Dad and me get to a better place. Not even a little.

"Yes," he says.

I scoff. "Sure."

He leans forward. "I'm serious, Viveca." That's usually a precursor to one of his lies, but my radar's not going off. It seems like he actually *is* serious. "Your mom chose to come back here and look after Grandpa," he says. "She wouldn't have missed the last two years of his life for anything in the world."

"I guess not," I murmur.

"And as hard as it might be to believe," he says, twinkling, "she also chose to marry me."

I nod. "I know. I'm sorry. I know that. It's just—"

"No, listen to me, Viveca," Dad interjects. "She *chose* it. She could have gone back to school anytime. Maybe she would have, eventually. Who knows? But if there's one thing I'm sure of, it's that Hannah never did anything she didn't want to. She lived her life in exactly the way that made her happiest. And that includes you."

The bursting feeling inside me dissipates. "She did?"

He nods. "I promise."

I reach into my backpack and pull out my Everett College folder.

I'm not even sure why it's still in there. But I slide off the photo clipped to the front and push it across the table. "Do you remember this?"

Dad picks it up and smiles. "That was her freshman year," he says. "Before we got together." He turns it over and reads.

"'Where it begins,'" I say.

He nods. "It sure did." He slides the photo back over to me. "Are you about ready to head home?"

"Yeah," I say, taking a final sip of coffee. "I'll walk, though. I'm going to make one more stop."

———

I walk down the main road and past the fire station, wrapping my coat around me as I pass small houses with peeling paint, the playground, the cemetery. Until I eventually come to Spike's Subs-N-Gas.

The florid-faced woman behind the counter looks up half-heartedly as I enter, but I veer off to the right and step up to the deli counter.

Wren doesn't say anything at first. It's hard for Wren to *ever* not say anything, so they're still really mad at me. They look small in their uniform, dwarfed by a starchy apron, except for their long arms hanging limply at their sides.

A man encroaches on my space. He wants a sub. Who gets a sub at ten o'clock at night? I step back as he orders, running my hands along the crinkly bags of chips. The man emphasizes "no hots" in an irritated voice and insists on picking out his own tomato slices.

He's talking to Wren, but he doesn't see them. They're not part of his world.

After the man leaves, I approach the counter again. Wren still doesn't say anything, but they haven't run to the back room, so maybe that's good.

"Hey," I say. "It's me, your terrible friend."

Wren raises one eyebrow.

"I, uh," I say, "I've been doing a lot of stuff lately. Drawing stuff and doing extra credit and practicing piano. And feeling bad. About being such a jerk."

Wren raises both eyebrows.

I sigh. "You were right. I was obsessed with—him. Even when I thought I wasn't anymore, I still was. But that's not the worst thing." I lean forward, wrapping my fingers around the edge of the counter. "The worst thing is that I was obsessed with myself. I thought perfect grades and the perfect school would give me the perfect life. But the only thing all that chasing did was make me spend time on stuff I didn't care about just because it looked good on a résumé. But that's not the stuff that matters. I know that doesn't make any sense."

Wren crosses their arms. "It makes a little bit of sense."

"I guess what I mean is I'm sorry. I failed you. I do care about you, so much, about what you're doing and your future and all of your—glittery stuff. I failed you and I love you and I'm sorry. And I'm doing better."

Wren is still for a moment. Then they come out from behind the deli counter. I don't say anything, just watch them with my breath held.

Finally, they say, "I'm so glad you care about my . . . glittery stuff?"

There's a terrible, awkward moment, and then we both burst out laughing.

"That's not what I meant to say," I say.

"It's what you *said*." Wren smirks. "You are a terrible friend sometimes. And I'm glad you're drawing stuff. And I love you, too."

I feel a spiderweb of cracks form all through the invisible cement that I've been encased in. It's like I took the walls of Fort Kearsarge with me and just wrapped up in them, becoming my own battering ram against the world. And now the pieces are falling away in chunks.

Wren's looking at me with this cheeky half smile, elf-like, and in this moment, I want to tell them everything and cry about most of it. But I just reach for them, and they automatically reach back for me, and we hug, and hug, and hug.

34

Ms. Gagnon, the dean of admissions at Everett College, was sympathetic when I told her I'd claimed the valedictorian title too early. She said that happens sometimes, especially with early admission candidates.

She was not sympathetic when she received a letter from the Elton Prep administration about my plagiarism.

"It's not true," I said fruitlessly into the phone.

"It's not my place to judge that," the dean said. "I'm sorry." I think she could hear me snuffling like a truffle-hunting pig on the other end of the line, because her voice softened and she said, "I remember your interview well, Viveca. I really hope you can clear this up. Please let me know if that happens, and I'll do everything I can to help you."

Well, I have no hope of "clearing this up." I mean, I feel like it would be clear to anybody who knows me *or* Jamison that that winning essay has "Viveca North" stamped all over it in bright red ink. There's a whole paragraph about the Muppet funk band, the Electric Mayhem, for god's sake.

But Jamison is set to ride off into the sunset, and I'm still figuring out where my sunset is. Still, I know one thing for certain.

I'm going to take down Jamison Sharpe.

No, I'm not backsliding into the old Viveca. I'm not going after him because he makes me feel inferior. Not because of jealousy, or obsession, or some impossible quest for perfection. Before, I was angry at Jamison because I felt like he didn't deserve what he had, like he was stealing from me. But now that he actually *has* stolen from me? It's not even about him anymore. No, I'm going to destroy Jamison Sharpe because it's the only way to take back *my life.*

Because it is my choice to do so. To stand up for myself.

As I crest the hill of our driveway, I'm surprised to see Genevieve's car. Dad's truck is there, too. My fingers do this tiny twitchy thing, and I realize I'm excited. Like maybe they're going to make up after all.

But this is *Dad* we're talking about, I remind myself. Even though he's seemed a little different lately, I don't get my hopes up.

When I come in, they're at the kitchen table peering at Genevieve's laptop with their shoulders touching.

Dad turns around. "Hey, princess."

Now Genevieve. "Hi, Viveca. How have you been?"

They seem . . . pretty relaxed. Normalish. What's going on? "Hi,"

I say, leaning over to look at the laptop screen. "Looking at—" I pause. "Real estate?"

Now they both get these big grins on their faces. They look at each other, then at me, like it's choreographed.

"What's, uh—what's going on?" I ask.

Dad clears his throat. "Well, we're—I guess you could say we're downsizing."

"Consolidating," Genevieve says.

I've got my grouper fish act going now. "Consolidating? Downsizing?" I blink. "*We?*"

"With you out of the house, your dad just can't afford to live here alone," Genevieve says. My eyes flick to my dad, ready for the torrent of protestations and lies surely to come spewing forth. But he doesn't say anything, just sits there looking—happy?

"I . . ." I start. "Well, a couple things. I'm not actually going to be out of the house, for one. Unless, you know, you're kicking me out."

Dad swivels his whole chair around. "Don't be ridiculous, Viveca. We'd never kick you out. But you're going to college next year."

My breath freezes. "But, Dad, no, Everett—"

"Everett is not the only college in the world, as much as you seem to think it is," Dad says. "Start somewhere small. Build up your reputation. Then maybe transfer." He looks at Genevieve. "I know it will be tight, but we think it's important. We know it's your dream. So we're going to help you however we can."

My ears start to get hot. Is this really happening?

"It's not all about your college," Genevieve says. "Together, your dad and I—and Ruckus—can live comfortably. In a smaller way. In a smaller house."

"We're thinking condo," Dad says. "Goodbye, snow shoveling!"

"That's great," I say. And I realize I mean it.

"We will be happy," Genevieve says, and I notice a breeziness to her I haven't seen before. There's truth there, at least. In both of their faces. They're both happy.

"We're starting over," Dad says.

"Yep." Genevieve takes his hand. "Fresh start."

———

Genevieve stays for dinner. It's awkward and fragile, but Dad is on his best behavior. I guess they really do like each other. But it's apparent that Genevieve isn't going to put up with Dad's crap anymore, which is a good thing. Maybe they'll start hiking for real.

"So, what are Wren's plans for next year?" Genevieve asks, pronging some asparagus from a gold-edged bowl we save for special occasions.

"They're taking a gap year," I say. "A city somewhere. Going to try to get some more professional theater experience."

"I was an actor when I was younger," Dad says, almost like a reflex. "Did quite a few feature films." I laugh internally. Okay, so he's not fully reformed just yet.

Genevieve rolls her eyes, but she's smiling as she cuts her asparagus into tiny pieces. "Are you excited for graduation, Viveca?"

I give an involuntary shudder. "Well, at least I don't have to give a speech. Speeches aren't really my thing."

"It's true," Dad says. "She got a zero on the only speech she ever did."

And we laugh. Because in that moment, for the first time, it's funny. And it's odd, but part of me feels kind of—good?—that Dad remembered my sixth-grade public-speaking failure. I mean, at least he noticed, even if he's reminiscing about my humiliations instead of my successes. *They're probably easier for him to process*, I realize with a pang of compassion. *He probably understands them more.*

"This asparagus is really good," I say, holding up a forkful. "I obviously can't comment on the chicken."

Dad looks up. "Genevieve made it." He gives her a smile. "Great job. I'm proud of you."

My throat closes up. Because even though he pretended that he was—he wasn't saying it to her.

Genevieve looks so happy it seems as though she might just balloon up with it and float away. "I'm sorry you're stuck with frozen pizza as a main course, Viveca."

I shake my head and give her a smile. We might never find the closeness she dreams of, but I'm glad she's sticking around. She belongs here. And I don't feel sad for her anymore. "You know, Genevieve, I love frozen pizza."

35

Wren and I are in comics club for the last time. I haven't told them about Dad and Genevieve's rekindled, downsized romance. I haven't even told them about getting booted from Everett before I had a chance to get there. It still doesn't seem real, any of it. And part of me is still terrified that I'll be letting Wren down again when I mention Jamison's name. But a bigger, brighter part of me knows that if I'm going to take him down, I'll need Wren in my corner.

"Warm-up!" Tek yells. "Where's the jar?" He glances around, then finds a glass jar filled with scraps of paper sitting on one of the tables. He steps to where Wren and I are sitting. "Viveca North, choose our destiny!"

I reach into the jar and pull out a slip. "'Dreams,'" I read.

Tek claps. "Wonderful! Ten minutes of dreams, everyone!"

I'm not sure how to draw dreams, so I start with a bed. It's a bit lopsided. After a minute, I look over at Wren's work.

"Is that a . . . donkey?" I ask.

They turn their paper toward me. "You bet your boots."

I snort. "Do you dream of donkeys?"

"Always," Wren says, "but that's not what this is about. See, it's the carrot and the stick. He's dreaming of the carrot."

"I see," I say, not seeing. I erase half of my bed and try to fix the perspective.

After a moment, Wren asks, "So what's your carrot, Viveca?"

"I'm sorry?" I say. "Is this an anti-tarot question?"

They point a marker at my nose. "Nope. It's a stick-versus-carrot question. Your problem is you spend all your time worrying about your sticks and not enough time looking for your carrots."

"Do you need to lie down?"

"It's very simple. You're the donkey, see?" They swivel their paper. "You're moving forward because West Bore is a stick hitting you in the derriere—see, it's right there. But what are you going toward? What's your carrot?"

"Oh, I get it now." I lay my pencil down and find myself thinking about the photograph clipped to the front of my folder. *Everett. Where it begins.* That was my carrot. *Was.* For a second, I feel like I could just turn into goo and seep down through the floor like the cream from a squashed donut. "Well, what's your carrot?" I ask.

Their expression flickers. "I've got too many sticks at the moment to think too much about carrots," they say. "But I'm trying. And so should you."

I look down at my half-finished sketch and pretend that *choice* is a thing I have right now. "I like things that make me laugh."

Wren grins. "Me too. And you like to draw."

"Okay. That's true, I guess." *It's something.* "So do you," I say.

"So let's be artists. Let's draw comics and be funny."

I let myself picture that sparkling future for a tiny while. It's exhilarating and sad. "You could be an artist," I say. "I'm not good enough."

Wren locks their fingers behind their head casually. "Yeah, you're not."

I almost choke on my own spit. "Thanks."

They lean toward me. "So what? So maybe you don't have this amazing innate superstar talent. Most people don't. They work hard. And that's what you're so amazingly good at. You have an *incredible* work ethic, and you are obsessed. You have been obsessed with drawing your whole life." They stand up, attracting the attention of the other members of the comics club. "You have love in your heart for drawing, Viveca!" they proclaim. "That has to count for something!"

"Hear, hear!" Tek says.

"Yeah, okay," I say, turning red. I want so badly to give Wren's words a fighting chance to penetrate my hard shell.

"Warm-up time is over," Tek announces. "To your masterpieces!"

Wren takes a seat. "Oh, and, by the way—" They discreetly drop something into my lap under the table.

I look down. "My jackknife!" Paranoid, I lower my voice. Now's probably not a good time to get caught with this, either.

"Ten points!" Wren says.

I look at them. *"You* took my jackknife?"

"Yeah, that was me," they say. "Sorry. Or—you're welcome? Either one. I heard about piano class."

I'm stunned, turning the knife over and over in my hands. "But why did you take it?" I ask. "And when? And how?"

"Don't forget *where*," they say.

"Exactly."

"Yeah, so I—owe you an apology," they say. "Also, we have to talk. And those two things are related."

I lean back in my chair and raise my eyebrows.

"I've always known you were—*intense*, Viveca," Wren says. "It's one of the things I like about you."

"Okay."

"But I never thought you were out of your mind."

"Thanks?"

Wren goes on, "So when Jamison was talking at drama club, and he sort of casually mentioned that you made him nervous—"

I snort. "Yeah. I'm sure I make him *so* nervous."

Wren nods. "Right? But even then I thought, okay, maybe I would be freaked out in his place, too. Like if I didn't know you and thought you were a bit too obsessed with the valedictorian thing, which you *were*, as we know. And also congratulations, since we weren't speaking when you officially knocked him out of the top spot."

". . . Thanks?"

"But then he was talking about how you had started carrying a knife to school and that you told him about it. He was wondering if he should let a teacher know."

My eyes bug. "What?"

Wren nods furiously. "I know! So that seemed really weird to me. You would never do that. I don't care how many calculus midterms someone cheats on or whatever. It just made me nervous." They shrug. "So the next morning before school, I swiped the knife from your bag." They pause. "The end."

"Wow." I realize that Wren has been making their own strange apology to me, now that they know Jamison is more dangerous than people think—and that I wasn't obsessed for no reason. And that realization makes a warmth spread through my core.

I hand the knife back under the table to Wren. "Why don't you hang on to this until school's out?" I say, trying to make it sound like a joke.

Wren understands. "Yeah. Okay, killer."

We draw in silence for a while. This whole year, I've been just itching to get out of Elton Prep, fly away. But now that it's actually ending, I'm grasping at these little moments. Sitting here with Wren, pitting an archenemy against Lola the Gorgeous Minotaur.

"He's very blond, isn't he?" Wren says, looking over. "And seems quite friendly. And—wow, what a lot of tentacles."

"He also sucks at piano," I say, shading a white tooth flying out of Lola's archenemy's mouth after a hoof to the face. "If only I were a gorgeous minotaur."

Wren is affronted. "Who told you you weren't?"

I laugh drily. Then I take a deep breath and go for it. "Look, hey, this hasn't gotten out, but you should know . . ." And I tell them. In hushed tones, I tell them about the Pinniped County Futurists essay, about the photocopy, the deleted file, the meeting with Principal Washington. The call with the dean of admissions. It's a risk, and my heart is going like a hummingbird the whole time, but it feels good to get it out there.

When I'm done, Wren looks at me. If I thought my grouper fish impression was good, Wren's is positively spectacular. Their eyes are two brown dots floating in pools of white; their mouth gapes.

They close their mouth, then open it again. "I'm sorry, *what*?"

The other members of the comics club look over at us with interest. I shush Wren. "Yeah," I murmur. "So that's why I'm no longer accepted at Everett."

Wren looks at me for another moment, then says even louder, "I'm sorry, *WHAT*?"

Tek looks up from his critique of Butt Man. "Something is blowing Wren's mind!"

"It's my new villain," I call out. "The, uh, Blond . . . Jerk."

Tek nods. "I dig it." He turns his attention back to the Butt Man sophomores.

Wren seems to veer back toward reality as the shock wears off, but they're still opening and closing their mouth. Finally, they say, "So what are you going to *do* about this, Viveca? How is Lola going to vanquish the Blond Jerk? Because if you need someone to hold his legs—"

"I'm forming a plan," I say. "But it requires some specialized skills."

They put a hand on my shoulder. "I have many specialized skills."

I grin. "I know."

36

You can have all the determination and pluck in the world; you can have truth on your side, but if you want to take down a liar as skilled as Jamison Sharpe, you also need a plan. That's what I don't have right now. But I'm working on it.

I'm in Reinhardt's office again, only this time, I'm not flying solo. I've got a copilot, and at this moment, they've got the vice principal cornered all the way on the other side of the school. Wren's promised me ten minutes minimum, and I have absolute faith that they can blather on for at least twice that long before Reinhardt can get away. With the enthusiasm Wren has demonstrated in executing Operation Blond Jerk, I can't believe I ever thought there might be something romantic between them. "It was a *hug*, Viveca," they said. "What, are you the Hug Police now?"

I take a page out of Wren's book and lock the door behind me so there won't be any surprises. Now it's only a matter of finding that alluring manila folder, the one with *Sharpe* written on the front.

It's in the big file cabinet. I flip the folder open on Reinhardt's desk, but I don't start reading. Instead, I leaf through every document, snapping pics. Transcripts, letters, forms. I know it's wrong, and forbidden, and I don't expect to find anything blatantly earth-shattering, but it will be worth it if I can just find *something*. Some tiny thing I can get Jamison on, some incriminating, embarrassing fact I can bring to Principal Washington. Or blast over the loudspeaker. I will plant the first seed of doubt and nurture it from there into a reputation-spoiling tree. Jamison can't be flawless—every liar screws up. This folder will be my treasure trove. I hope.

Plus, there's that other little idea I've had, which will involve a carefully crafted phone call or two if Wren can just find the right numbers in Jamison's phone.

After only six minutes, I slide the folder back into its place and slip into the hall. Wren's going to meet me outside the cafeteria when they've released the vice principal. As I pass the foyer by the front doors, whose voice do I hear but Jamison's. It's the tail end of the rush of school getting out, so I weave away behind some groups of students.

But then I hear something that makes me pause. Jamison says, "Yeah, I realized reality is sort of made of waves, you know? Waves and tides. You just have to read them."

The people around him make some impressed noises. I step

around the corner from the foyer and lean against the wall where Jamison and pals can't see me. Waves and tides—it reminds me of the language on the Pinniped County Futurists' website. I keep listening. Jamison isn't really explaining the metaphor correctly, but it's pretty obvious where he got it. He's bragging about the scholarship. He's actually got the nerve right now to be flaunting his victory.

"And I started thinking of myself as a tennis ball, floating, carried along on the currents of society," Jamison says. It gives me a jolt. Because *that* metaphor is 100 percent Viveca North.

Jamison goes on, "I think that's what the judges appreciated, maybe, that I recognized how much we're all influenced by what came before. How we're all tennis balls."

His entourage agrees with him, but I'm groaning inwardly. All that stuff about tennis balls and society was what I thought passed for intellectual when I first wrote my Pinniped essay. It wasn't until I really dug deep, until I started over, that I realized I'd been using a lot of buzzy words to say very little.

And then it hits me: Jamison read that first version of my essay, that day in my room when he came over to study, but he has no idea I rewrote it. And from the way he's talking, he has no idea that the essay he read isn't the one I submitted.

He photocopied my essay the morning of the deadline, but he didn't read it. He didn't have time, and he probably figured he didn't need to—after all, he'd read it already. Except he hadn't.

And now I have a plan.

37

I'm technically banned from graduation rehearsal, but Wren and I sneak into the auditorium, climb up to the audio-visual booth, and stretch out on the floor where we can peek down between the slats.

"Don't you have to, like, rehearse?" I ask them.

They shrug. "What's there to rehearse? I'm not giving a speech or singing a solo. I just go up when my name is called and get my diploma. Pretty sure you could train a chicken to do that."

"But won't they notice you're not there?"

"Probably."

Below in the auditorium, our class starts to file in. Principal Washington and Vice Principal Reinhardt are there with clipboards, checking people off a list and directing them to their places in the alphabetized seating arrangement. There's a gap in the Bs where Wren should be, and I watch the thirty seconds or so of confusion as Reinhardt notices their absence and asks a few students about it. After some shrugs and head shakes, and a frowny stare from the VP that inventories the whole room without success, the search appears to be over.

"See?" Wren whispers. "I'm not there. And the world spins on."

I snort. "Rebel."

Wren props their head up on their wrists. "So, this is all very touching and emotional, Viveca, but I'd much rather skip altogether and go get an ice-cream cone."

"I just want to check a couple of things," I say.

"You're so mysterious."

I brush some grit out from under my elbows. "Did you do the thing with Principal Washington?"

"That would be an affirmative," Wren says, jiggling their bag with a toe. "Effectively distracted. Black folder forgotten on her desk, then expertly pilfered by an attractive cat burglar."

"A-plus," I say. Graduation practice is gearing up now. Principal Washington is using her teacher voice to go over the intricacies of the proceedings. Reinhardt is stalking the rows of restless seniors, shushing chatterboxes and keeping eagle eyes out for verboten gum. There are a lot of questions about hats.

"Outside," the principal is saying in response to one question. "No tossing of caps indoors." She points to a raised hand and pauses, listening to a student whose voice doesn't reach us here in the audio-visual booth. "No, we went over this," Principal Washington says.

"Markers and paint are fine . . . yes, puffy paint is fine. Sequins if they're sewed on, not glued . . . No. No glitter."

"Too late," Wren whispers. "I've already covered my hat in glitter."

"Is there no end to your depravity?" I ask.

The rehearsal drags on. It didn't start until one o'clock, so it can't go more than two hours, but really—is it going to go *two hours*? Especially when nobody is doing any of the things; they're just talking about the timeline of when they'll do the things?

Wren starts snoring at one point, but I don't let myself get distracted. "Hey." I poke them. "Here's Jamison's reading." My pulse hurries up a little. "He's really going to do it. No shame at all."

"Is this where it's going to go?" Wren asks. "After the—what just happened? I may have drifted off."

"Remarks from the student council president," I say.

"Lord help us." Wren rolls over onto their back. "Please tell me someone will be waiting backstage with a giant hook to drag Kasey off after, oh, six hours or so."

I peer down as Jamison Sharpe strides over to the lectern that's set up in the center of the stage. "Testing, one-two," he says into the microphone. My classmates think this is hilarious for some reason. It is not hilarious.

"Yes," Principal Washington says, "after Kasey's remarks, we'll have you come up and read your scholarship-winning essay, Jamison."

"Thanks so much," he says into the mic. There are a few hoots from the audience. Suddenly, an earsplitting wail screeches out over the auditorium. Students cover their ears. Principal Washington glares up at where Wren and I are concealed.

I spin around; Wren has a long finger delicately placed on one of the sliders over at the complicated audio setup. They silently mouth, *Oops!* and push the slider down. The shrieking feedback disappears. We stifle our laughs.

"Who's running the mic?" the principal shouts. "Can we fix the sound problem?"

Wren cups their hands over their mouth. "Sorry about that!" they shout. "All fixed!"

Principal Washington stares suspiciously up at the booth for a moment longer, but then resumes the rehearsal. "So, Jamison, this is where you'll read your essay, all right?"

He flashes her a thumbs-up. "Do you mind if I do a practice run?" he asks. "I'm a bit nervous about speaking in public." The charm is dialed all the way up, and I have no doubt the principal would have made an exception for him today, despite the fact that nobody else is getting to practice their speeches. However—

"Oh!" Principal Washington says, shuffling through some papers sitting on the lip of the stage. "Oh dear, Jamison, I'm so sorry. I seem to have forgotten the folder. I'll bring it tomorrow night, I promise." She claps. "Now, who needs to get up here for show choir and where are you sitting? Please raise your hands."

I watch Jamison stalk off the stage and take his seat again. He's not happy. Poor Jamison.

"Well played," Wren says, lowering themself next to me again, cross-legged. "That's what's in Principal Washington's black folder, I assume. The scholarship essay."

I smirk. "Yep."

"Too bad Jamison didn't bring his own copy."

I sit up. "How could he? He never had the file in the first place, and he stealth-deleted it off my laptop. So the only copies that exist are the paper ones the Futurists returned to Principal Washington."

Wren's eyes light up. "You devil!"

"It's the little things." I lean back on my palms. "I still can't believe he managed to photocopy it and switch the cover letters so fast," I say. "What a mind he has. Seriously."

"Aw, he had plenty of time," Wren says. Voices float up from below, and the squeaks of seats flipping up. "Sounds like rehearsal is getting out. Mission accomplished for today?"

"Yes," I say. "Today has gone very well."

———

That night, Dad and Genevieve are asleep on the couch, and Wren and I are squished into Dad's chair under a quilt made for me by my grandfather. It's dark except for the flickering light of the television playing endless episodes of *The Simpsons.*

"I can't believe it'll all be over tomorrow," I say.

Wren's head vibrates against my shoulder as they talk. "That's a weird way of putting it. Nothing's going to be over. We'll just graduate, that's all."

"Yeah." I try to tamp down the shivery nausea that seems to

show up when I think about graduation. "It's so sweet of Principal Washington to let me walk with the class even though I'm banned from rehearsals."

"Maybe she wants us to throw stones at you in the middle of the stage." We snort. "Seriously, though," Wren says, "are you going to be okay with Jamison giving the valedictory speech?"

"Who cares?" I say. "It's not like I enjoy giving speeches."

"Yeah." They stare at the television, snaking their arm through mine, and we sit quietly. A tranquil, TV-watching, two-headed pretzel.

"You know what ticks me off the most, though?" I say. "That essay meant so much to me. And Jamison just took it, probably on the spur of the moment, because he knew Ms. Racine thought I would have the best shot at winning."

Wren squeezes my arm. "But here's the thing, Viveca. You have a million more essays in you. You have drawings and ideas and stories in you. And Jamison Sharpe has nothing."

As Wren and I sit there, warmed by my grandfather's quilt, entwined like trees, I think about the large house at 162 Apple Tree Lane, about the Ferrari, about Paris. I think about the confident, insubstantial creature I tutored in calculus that day in my room, an entire human being made of smoke and mirrors.

"You're right," I say. "He has nothing."

38

The Elton Prep auditorium is decked out in blue carnations and gold streamers. A stately cream-covered table center stage is piled with new diplomas ready to be handed out.

I'm sitting behind Miranda Nazarian, who's in the last row of seniors. Principal Washington has allowed me to perch in this no-man's-land, not quite with my class but not quite shoved out of the way, either. Graduation purgatory.

Dad and Genevieve, in their best outfits, watch from somewhere in the back. I feel bad that Dad won't be able to brag about me being valedictorian, but all that really matters is that I exit this building with my high school diploma in hand, right?

I crinkle and uncrinkle my program. The man next to me, forty-ish in a T-shirt and blazer, glances over. "Sorry," I say. "Nerves." He nods.

Graduation is not the nonstop wave of joy and tenderness

we've been led to believe it would be. I'm actually relieved when the choir does a sappy number about flying or dreaming or something, which breaks up the parade of sappy speeches. Jamison's valedictory address is the best. And by best, I mean worst. The audience is teary. My eyes are rolled so far back in my head I can see my brain.

Miranda catches me as she's looking around, and for a moment, I think she's going to give me a dirty look, but she actually stifles a laugh. I give her a secret smirk in return.

Finally it's time for the big event—the nadir of the evening, Jamison's shame read of my stolen essay.

"We have a very special presentation for you this evening," Principal Washington has the audacity to say. "For the first time ever, an Elton Prep student has won the prestigious Pinniped County Futurists' senior scholarship essay contest, worth a grand prize of twenty thousand dollars."

The audience *ohhhhs*. They can't believe it. I can't freaking believe it, either.

Principal Washington beams. "Here to read his winning essay is the senior-class valedictorian, Jamison Sharpe!"

Jamison takes the stage to warm applause. "Thank you, everyone. This is such an honor." He clears his throat. "I'd like to dedicate this to my mom and dad, whose illnesses prevent them from—"

Principal Washington leans in and says something to Jamison. Suddenly, he looks shocked. The principal points into the audience, and I follow Jamison's stunned gaze to a well-dressed couple in the fifth row. The woman's blond blowout is perfectly draped over an immaculate white suit, and the man's gray-streaked hair and red tie both shine under the auditorium lights. Neither of them look particularly ill, and both of them have their arms crossed in an attitude of displeasure.

I can hear the whispers starting around me and see their movement through the crowd. *Are those Jamison's parents?* I glance at the drama kids sprinkled throughout the senior section, giving each other surprised looks.

I wouldn't say Jamison's parents were *nice*, but they were certainly interested in what the president of the student council had to say when she contacted them to discuss setting up a volunteer meal delivery plan to ease Jamison's burdens at home, seemingly unaware that she was speaking to each of them as they were away on separate business trips. They went quiet when she offered her profound sympathies for their respective illnesses, as described by their angel of a son. They promised to attend graduation as a surprise for their son and to watch him read his twenty-thousand-dollar essay, which for some reason they didn't know anything about. And they didn't even ask the informative caller's name before hanging up.

Not that I would have told them I was Viveca North. I would definitely have said Kasey Wheelwright.

After a moment of stunned silence, Jamison seems to steady himself. He clears his throat, opens a black folder, and takes out some printed pages.

"'What does it mean to see the world?'" he reads. "'*Really* see it? What are the lenses we use to shape our own realities?'"

I cross my arms. Miranda's head is lolled back like she's dead. The man next to me is looking at his phone.

"'The circumstances of our births,'" Jamison goes on, "'the singular point on this vibrant, space-borne sphere where we enter existence, naked and fearful, all our ideas about *self* and *other* and *being* preformed and malleable—'"

Principal Washington is eyeing Jamison over her signature fake "public events" smile. It's almost as though she senses something is not quite right. I look at the man next to me, still looking at his phone screen. Every once in a while, he glances up at Jamison with a puzzled look on his face.

Jamison is back to his old self, really hamming it up now. His arms are involved, flying around, gesturing to the heavens or whatever. "'Our environment,'" he declares, "'whether it be an arid—'"

"Stop!" a voice rings over the auditorium. The man next to me has gotten to his feet.

Jamison pauses and looks up, bewildered. Principal Washington stands, searching for the source of the disruption.

The man holds up a hand. "I'm sorry, ladies and gentlemen, but I can't allow this reading to continue."

Jamison looks like he's been slapped. I try and fail to suppress a grin about this.

Principal Washington's eyes are two white beams of intensity, glaring at the man in the blazer. She bustles over to the lectern and edges Jamison aside, motioning to a teacher in the corner, who pulls out a walkie-talkie. "Excuse me, sir, but we will not tolerate disruptions. I'm going to have to ask you to leave."

The man shakes his head. "That's fine, but I was told we'd be hearing a winning scholarship essay this evening."

"Yes," the principal snaps. "And we *would* be hearing it if you weren't interrupting the proceedings!" She looks like she's going to explode. Literally. She looks like she's going to just *detonate* into a million tiny, irate shards. "Who *are* you?"

The man puts a hand in the pocket of his blazer like he's posing for a fashion magazine. "My name is Tim Valentine. I'm from the Pinniped County Futurists organization."

The audience, which had been murmuring to greater and lesser degrees, falls silent. Jamison goes pale. A security guard enters through the stage door, but Principal Washington waves him away. She leans into the mic, speaking softly. "The Pinniped County Futurists?"

Mr. Valentine nods, then gestures to me. "This young lady invited me. Apparently she wasn't satisfied with the outcome of the recent plagiarism investigation regarding this essay. So, of course, I was happy to oblige."

The eyes in the auditorium shift to me. I straighten my spine and wait for the familiar rush of blood to my cheeks, wait for my ears to heat up. But they don't. I'm sitting here with the whole Elton Prep community staring at me, and I'm as cool as a cucumber. What do you know.

Jamison, however, has gone from pale to beet red. "Why did you stop my reading?" He glares at me, boiling. "What the hell is going on, Viveca? What are you trying to do?" He looks over at his parents, whose faces are stony.

My heart jumps into overdrive, thudding in my chest, but when I speak, I keep my words strong and echoing. "I'm trying to show everyone, Jamison, that not only did you not *write* the winning essay, you can't even tell that you're not *reading it.*"

"What are you talking about?" Jamison spits.

Mr. Valentine holds up his phone. "It's true, Mr. Sharpe. I have the winning essay right here, and the text you've been reading up there doesn't resemble it in the least."

Principal Washington folds her arms. "What does this mean, Jamison?"

Jamison throws up his hands. "It means Viveca is crazy! She's been obsessed with me since my first day here!"

The principal doesn't say anything, but I can see gears clicking into place. Maybe she's starting to remember the essay itself, from that time she gave it a cursory read in her office, and realizing it's not the same essay Jamison's been reading up there. Maybe some other puzzle pieces are falling into place.

Eyes and more eyes and I'm still not heating up. I sit tall in my purgatory chair.

Jamison, however, has gone from Mr. Charming to Mr. Completely Unhinged in an astonishingly short span of time. He looks pleadingly into the audience. "*Mom*, you remember—I *told* you about her!" It comes out as a whine. I don't think anyone at Elton Prep will ever forget the childish way Jamison Sharpe just said, *"Mommm!"* Into the *microphone.* His attractiveness is peeling off him like giant curls of damp wallpaper. And his mother doesn't even react, just keeps sitting there like an unpleasant statue.

I wondered before if anyone had ever called Jamison out, and now I have my answer. This experience is totally new to him. His circuits are overloading, blowing his perfect veneer right off into the stratosphere.

He shakes his fistful of paper. "This is the winning essay! I *know* it is. I *wrote* it. You're out of your mind, Viveca. And you, Mr. Futurist, who's probably just Viveca's uncle or something!" Mr. Valentine raises an eyebrow, but Jamison rolls on. "Principal Washington gave me this copy herself!"

I nod. "Yes. But Wren and I had already switched the copies she had in that black folder she keeps in her office."

Wren, from the front row, shoots a hand into the air. They're holding a small stack of printed white paper.

I fold my arms. "What you've been reading, Jamison, is the first draft of *my* essay. It's the one you read on my computer, which is why you recognize it. Luckily, I *did* have a copy of that version, which I'd printed out. But it's not the essay I submitted—and it's not the essay that won."

Jamison opens his mouth, but no words come out. The audience's murmurs turn to mutters, then to full-blown conversations.

Principal Washington looks stunned but quickly composes herself. "Is this true, Mr. Valentine?"

Mr. Valentine nods. "I'm afraid so. It was a rather—spectacular way of proving a point, but clever, I must admit."

The principal nods. "I apologize, ladies and gentlemen," she says into the mic. "It seems Jamison, Viveca, and I have some things to discuss. Jamison, you may sit down."

The stairs are at the end of the stage, and the lectern is in the middle. Jamison Sharpe has to do a hunched, humiliated, angry walk of shame all the way there. When he reaches the floor, I watch Mr. and Mrs. Sharpe rise from their seats and walk silently out of the auditorium.

Miranda Nazarian turns around, wide-eyed. "I just filmed the *whole thing*," she whispers.

Principal Washington clears her throat. "Now, everyone, let's, uh, let's move on."

But Mr. Valentine speaks up again. "Principal Washington, if I may?"

She blinks at him a few times, but everything is so topsy-turvy at this point she doesn't seem to have the resources to do anything but call on him as though he were a student raising his hand. "Yes, Mr. Valentine?"

"Since it is on the program, I wonder if Viveca might be permitted to read her essay?"

The auditorium is silent for a moment, but then, somewhere near the back, someone starts clapping. Soon, applause ripples through the audience, swelling from tepid to warm.

I can't read the look Principal Washington is giving me right now, but she nods and says, "Certainly."

I shoot Mr. Valentine a hesitant glance—this was not part of the plan, and I'm terrible at giving speeches. My hands are shaking already.

But he hands me his phone and gives me a smile. "Go on, Viveca," he says.

So I do. I sidle out from Row No-Man's-Land and make my way to the stage. It feels so much higher up than it looks, and the crowd feels so much bigger. But I set Mr. Valentine's phone on the lectern and breathe.

"Thank you, Principal Washington," I say, and close my eyes for a moment. Then I open them and look out over the audience. There's Wren in the front row. That bright yellow in the very back is Genevieve's scarf, where she's sitting with Dad.

I look down at the phone on the lectern, at the familiar words across its screen. My words. "'Finding My Path,'" I read, "'by Viveca North . . .'"

39

"But how do they ride the bikes?" Jade asks from her perch on the arm of Wren's couch, pointing at the Muppets on the TV, a few hours into a low-key graduation party.

"Nobody knows," says Poppy, her fingers in a bowl of chocolate chips.

Wren pats their little sister's head. "That's right."

I haven't been to Wren's house in a long time, but the atmosphere is much more relaxed than I remember it. Maybe because their mom and Poppy have filled every corner with balloons and every table with snacks. Or maybe because their dad is out on a job and won't be home for six months. No matter what happens, I won't wait so long before my next visit. I'm never taking Wren for granted again.

"I don't know how to operate this," Tyson says, getting engulfed by an enormous beanbag chair.

"You can't fight it," Min says, her feet up on a tufted ottoman. "You have to let it take you. Like the tide."

"Okay," he says, a little muffled.

Min taps her phone. "Danny's on his way," she says, and my guts do a little flip-flop. "He's getting a bag of hard candy."

"Hard candy? Come *on*," Tyson complains.

"Tell him my grandma's not coming," Wren says.

"It still doesn't seem real, us graduating," I say, in that casual way people talk to their friends. But it doesn't feel like I'm playing a part anymore. I don't feel like I'm on the periphery of Wren's friend group. Thinking back, I realize all of them have never been anything but welcoming to me, just waiting for me to be ready to accept their friendship. Well, now I'm ready. "No more high school. Like, ever."

"Not for us," Jade says. "But I bet Jamison has to go to summer school."

I stretch out on the floor, rest one foot up high on a bookshelf, snuggle myself into my mom's Everett College sweatshirt. "I can't even imagine it." And I can't. I have so much to do this summer. Starting with some seriously official meetings with Principal Washington and the Everett dean of admissions. Not to mention important correspondence with the Pinniped County Futurists. They seem like a pretty interesting bunch. I wonder how much their annual dues are. Maybe I'll take a fraction of that sweet scholarship money and apply for membership.

"Speaking of Jamison," Wren says with that impish glint I love.

"I went through that treasure trove of pics you took of his secret documents and followed up on the information provided. I also took a few minutes after graduation to say one last farewell to Elton Prep. And by *farewell*, I mean I snuck into all the everywhere and did some completely illegal snooping."

"Oh, *now* you do." I twist my head. I used to think there was something flawed about the way I find connections everywhere. And yeah, sure, sometimes I'm wrong, but that doesn't mean there's something wrong with me. We all see the world differently, and I'm finally starting to see more of it. I think about Dad and how hard he's trying, how proud he is of me, even though we'll never be perfect. Perfect just isn't a thing I want anymore.

"So what about Jamison?" I ask Wren. "Anything I missed? Anything juicy?"

"You just scratched the surface, my friend," Wren says. "I started with Mr. and Mrs. Sharpe's driver's licenses, and—"

"You looked at their driver's licenses?" Poppy chucks a chocolate chip at Wren's ear. "Bad! Bad Wren!"

"Ow! Yes, I know, I'm sorry. I promise I won't steal their identities," Wren says, protecting their head with their arms. "But there were photocopies tucked away in this file cabinet of formalities that nobody ever looks at, and I just couldn't help myself. All I did was check up on them online. They're both high-powered executives. Lots of travel, including very recent travel. No health complications mentioned anywhere. I mean, Viveca had already figured a lot of that out. But did you know their last name isn't even Sharpe?"

I sit up on the rug. "What?"

Tyson gasps theatrically. "You mean . . ."

Min is wriggling with scandalous excitement. "Are you saying Jamison *faked* stuff?"

Wren's face gets serious, which is unusual for them. "Guys, Jamison faked—*everything.*"

"How sad for him," Jade says. Then she points at the television. "See? Bicycles! How do they do that?"

It is sad, I realize. But I don't *feel* sad, not for Jamison. As I look around Wren's living room, bright with balloons and treats and people I care about, there just isn't a single square inch of space in my heart for any thoughts about Jamison Sharpe.

ACKNOWLEDGMENTS

Thank you to Ammi-Joan Paquette, Maya Marlette, the team at Scholastic, K, my mom and dad, Wini Young, the Chesley Writers, the Saturday Scribes, and the Plague Bagels.

ABOUT THE AUTHOR

Adi Rule is the author of *Hearts of Ice, The Hidden Twin,* and *Strange Sweet Song.* She received her MFA in writing from the Vermont College of Fine Arts. She lives in New Hampshire with her two cats, a blue-and-gold macaw, a flock of chickens, and her husband. Visit her online at adirule.com.